CW00866775

Under A Dark Sky

Under A Dark Sky

Worldburner Book 1

Johan M. Dahlgren

Published 2016 by Creativia
Cover art by Johan M. Dahlgren

Contents

I am Alpha and Omega

All around me the angels are falling.
One by one they burst silently into flame as we fall to Earth.
Blinding pain, searing heat and I'm burning too.
I scream myself awake.

* * *

The wall of light is cold and wet against my cheek as I lean against it.

I blink and the world tilts, the wall becomes an ocean, and with the return of smell the ocean becomes a glittering pool of vomit reflecting the flickering streetlights overhead.

Nice work, Perez. Real classy.

An early morning rainstorm batters the city, black clouds under a dark sky. Badly animated holo-signs cast dancing shadows over the alley where I'm lying. Fuck. Someone should tell me I have a drinking problem.

But this time I have a good reason to get drunk. A damn good reason.

Most of us would drink to forget seeing a helpless man murdered in cold blood. The rest would reach screaming for the bottle when they saw what the victim did to his captors afterwards.

A man in a dark coat watches me from the mouth of the alley. I can't see his face, but the way his coat flaps in the wind like a shroud draping a corpse reminds me of someone. There's something familiar about him that makes the hairs on the back of my neck stand up, but I've seen too many shrouded corpses in my life to be intimidated.

"What? Never seen a guy pass out in the rain before?" I rasp, my throat raw from too much cheap whisky.

Never again, I promise myself, feeling the asphalt grind against my cheek. I swallow and then instantly regret the action when my stomach turns over and I heave up sour bile and what feels like the major part of my guts all over again. Then I have to smile at the self-delusion. Who am I kidding? This is not the first time I've passed out after a night of drinking with Wagner, and it won't be the last.

At least I had the decency to do it outside this time. I roll over on my back and let the warm rain wash the filth from my face. A raving appetite rumbles my insides. How long have I been out? I don't have the foggiest, but it can't be that long, or Wagner would have come looking for me. Come to think of it, I have no idea how we ended up at this place at all. There's a hole the size of a headshot exit wound in my recollection of the night and I've got a headache to match. Not a first either.

In the sky above, the bright band of the Ring slices the sky in two, glittering like a frosted scimitar in the light from our not-yet-risen twin suns. To the east, a peach tint above the skyline heralds the birth of yet another dreary morning. Fuck this. It's time to get back to work.

I roll back on my side and the guy on the corner is gone. Either satisfied I wasn't going to ruin his karma by choking to death on his watch, or he figured I was not worth robbing. Either way, I guess he decided I was someone else's problem.

O tempora o fucking *mores*, huh?

* * *

When I finally scrape my ass off the ground and stumble back into the thundering noise inside the bar, Wagner is sitting in a corner booth, nursing a bleeding fist and a full pint. He sees me come in and I give him a nod, quietly impressed that he has managed to get into a fight while I was gone. Perhaps I was out longer than I thought. My giant Norse friend just gives me the evil eye and downs his beer in one long swallow.

I head for the bar through the rowdy crowd. My usual cure for a hangover like this is a stiff whisky or two, but my stomach is not up for it. Too bad. I could really use a dram right now because my hands are shaking and there's a dull ache in my back. Week-old bullet holes tend to do that to you.

Working as head of security for the largest corporation in the system has its perks, but the downside is you tend to get shot a lot. Somewhere out there I know there is a bullet with my name on it, but so far I've had the fortune to only get shot with nameless ones. Getting old in this business is not an option and I know it's only a matter of time before I get painfully acquainted with that bullet. Unfortunately, this job is the only thing I know how to do, so quitting is not an option. Talk about a bum deal. With my luck I would probably get killed by a speeding bus on my first day as a civilian anyway. I'm such a bloody cliché.

I squeeze in next to a noisy teen threesome snogging against the counter and wave to the bartender. "Water. On the rocks. Make it a double." I have to shout and use sign language to make myself heard over the rumbling dysFunk basslines shaking the foundations of the building.

An unusual order, judging by the time it takes the barman to whip it up. That gives me time to think about some things I'd rather not think about. Like why we are here.

Not in the philosophical sense, but why Gray has sent for Wagner and had him meet me here in this illegal bar on the Rim of Southern Masada.

We're here because Gray wants us to find a guy and bring him in. At first it sounded like your average, easy-in, easy-out, smash-and-grab assignment, but then I saw the video.

* * *

The camera points dead ahead, showing a concrete wall hung with a grim-looking banner bearing the crossed swords and stylised supernova of a Redeemer battle flag. A man in an expensive-looking black silk shirt kneels on the floor in front of it. His dark hair falls almost to the floor and a well-trimmed beard adorns his chin. He's a handsome man, and the blood running down his forehead from the deep wounds beneath the spiked metal crown is almost too much. You couldn't have created a more perfect rendition of the suffering of Christ if you'd commissioned Michelangelo. His hands are tied behind his back.

Head bowed in submission, tilted slightly sideways, he gazes one-eyed into the camera from beneath dripping brows. Where the other eye should be is only a red, gaping hole. He breathes heavily through flaring nostrils and it's obvious he's struggling to keep his calm.

From stage left comes another man into the frame. He wears the long, loose dress and headgear of a holy warrior. The vicious knife in his hand and the dark beard on his chin complete the picture. He walks behind the kneeling man and is joined by two similarly dressed men, one on each side.

You know what's coming.

The stage is set, and the scene is no different from a thousand such plays from the bloody repertoire of religious terror. The speech is no different either. Neither is the final gasp of fear and denial as a rough hand grabs hair, pulling back and to the side, and neither is the cruel climax. The knife does its grisly work on his throat with the frightening precision of a skilled butcher. God is great.

The head flops forward and the body sags, one bent leg twitching, a dark glistening spot of bodily fluids spreading beneath the kneeling form.

Looking steadily into the camera, the executioner declares this to be the inevitable end facing all false prophets, and then he starts counting off the political prisoners they want released. There are always prisoners they want released.

A wet bubbling sound comes from the corpse as air escapes from collapsing lungs.

The list of prisoners goes on and on and this is usually the place where the major news feeds cut to the inevitable government press-conference. Outraged officials denounce all forms of extremism. Promises are made of increased persecution of innocent civilians. You know the drill. Everybody knows they will not catch the people responsible for the slaying, but they want to keep their jobs, so what else can they do?

But this video is not on any of the major feeds. Not yet. On the underground channels they don't cut, they don't fade. Instead the video rolls on, and this is where things start to get really interesting.

As the list is being read, a sudden movement in the lower part of the frame draws the eye. The head of the corpse is moving.

Slowly lifting from the bloody chest, the head pulls back, blood still running feebly from the wide gash. Even to my untrained layman's eye the amount of blood looks remarkably small and his long hair barely sticks to the gore. As I watch transfixed, the blood flow stops completely.

The three men notice the movement and stare in silent disbelief. Any self-respecting executioner with an ounce of pride in his work would now start to wonder if he's losing his touch. This guy certainly is, judging by the look on his face. One of the other would-be executioners is crying ecstatically. He has pissed himself.

The solitary eye of the murdered man is once again level with the camera, and he's smiling, but it's not a smile you'd expect to find on the face of Christ. This smile is ancient and dark and filthy. It's the smile of death and decay and the suffering of little children. It's the smile of all the atrocities committed in the name of religion and a promise of nothing but more of the same.

He flexes his arms and his hands are no longer bound behind his back and he preaches to the camera like a first-rate televangelist. His single eye locks on mine beneath the bloodied brow, the iris an almost unearthly light blue. "… I am the Lord resurrected, I am the word retold. I am Alpha and Omega. Mine is the kingdom of God, and mine is the vengeance. Bow down before me and worship, for the day of judgement is nigh and the time for repentance is over. To each his just end, to the righteous, as to those weighed and found wanting. Rejoice, and let this be a message of unity for the lambs of the true flock. The man-god has once more been slain, and once again he stands resurrected. The armies of the Goat are approaching but a new kingdom is rising to stand against them, and this time there will be no forgiveness for the enemies of God."

He gets up from the floor in a single fluid move, like a trained dancer or a martial artist and turns on his captors. The camera is knocked over, the lens cracks and the image freezes, but the sound plays on.

It's the stuff nightmares are made of.

* * *

Something tells me this is not going to be a rescue operation. Why the hell does Gray want this guy? And why do I get the feeling we might all be heading for a very exciting future?

The Scars to Show for it

When I rejoin Wagner in the booth by the bar, he's already halfway down another beer, now left neglected by his tattooed elbow along with the glass corpse of its predecessor. He doesn't look up as I slide into the seat across from him.

The table's weak sound-screen is doing its damnedest to filter out the ridiculously loud music and the noise of the punters in the club. It's failing miserably.

"Vere ze fuck haf you been, Perez?" he says in his thick Norse accent, hunched over the table. He's busy carving what looks like a wolf's head in the white laminate table-top with a knife as long as my forearm. Not a bad likeness, considering Wagner's complete lack of artistic skills. Not something you would pay money to have on your living-room wall perhaps, but then bas-relief carving is not the reason Nero Gray employs Wagner. Neither are my art-critic skills the reason I'm Gray Industries' head of security. Even though knife-work is featured prominently in both mine and Wagner's CVs, our talents lie in another direction altogether. But we do tend to get rather creative sometimes.

"I've been out," I reply as I look at the giant across the table, frowning slightly at the blood on his knuckles. He's all cut up. I think I can even see a couple of glass splinters in the blood. Maybe I was gone longer than I thought? Then again, it doesn't take long for Wagner to get into a fight. Some people just have to challenge the biggest guy on the block. On most blocks, that guy is Thorfinn the Skullfucker, son of Ragnvald of house Wagner, heir to the Throne of Shields and captain of the Einherjar. *'The Skullfucker?'* I hear you ask. Don't. I just call him Wagner.

I've known him for close to twelve years and still it never fails to amaze me how big a Goliath really is when you get up close and personal with one.

Standing two metres tall at the shoulder, wide as a barn door and weighing in at an impressive quarter tonne, Thorfinn Wagner is a monster and he's not even big among his kind. He's not only a monster, but a crazy one at that. He's also the closest thing to a friend I've got. I really need to get out more.

"Just getting some air and enjoying the scenery. The usual." I shrug, looking around the place at the rowdy Friday-night crowd. "Look at all these assholes. Young, rich, pretty and spoilt, and nothing better to do than drink their parents' money away." I shake my head at the spectacle. Places like these make me lose faith in humanity. I'm not at all envious of their carefree lives.

"Is good place." Wagner shrugs, his grammar impeccable as always.

He's right though. The proximity to the Rim – four hundred metres of vertical rock to the jungle far below the city – means people can easily go missing out here. People tend to be very careful of who they mingle with in this part of town, making it the perfect place for famous people like Wagner to get away from both fans and authorities. Life in a militant theocracy is no fun at all, but if you keep a low profile, chances are the authorities will leave you alone. Besides, with Wagner being as big as a house, and me no dwarf either, and more than forty years of combat experience between us and the scars to show for it, they would think twice before trying anything.

"You were gone a long time. Did you puke your guts out in the rain again?" Wagner asks. He's not quite as stupid as he looks, which in his case is a very good thing. My soaked clothes, coupled with the smell of sour vomit is a dead give-away, though. I must not give the man too much credit.

I fake searching for the barman. "You got me there, buddy." A quick drum-roll of my fingers on the edge of the table and I turn back to my giant friend. Only now do I notice his beard is slowly dripping water onto the NoClean tabletop. The drops roll away over the no-stick surface like diamond marbles with a life of their own and fall to the sticky floor. It's hot in here but not hot enough for him to sweat like that. He smells like a wet dog.

"Did you go looking for me?" I can't hide the tone of surprise in my voice.

"Perhaps."

His long, blond hair lies plastered against his skull, tracing his swirling facial tattoos. He won't meet my eyes and continues to stare down at his carving, obviously engrossed in his work. His knife scratches another deep groove in the supposedly indestructible NoClean surface.

"Oi, da Vinci, stop that before the barman calls the cops." I try to make myself heard over the pounding music breaking through the sound-suppression. I grab his great, bloodied knife-hand across the table but it's only a ploy to get his attention and he knows it. His knuckles are still wet and sticky with blood and I can feel the prick of a glass splinter against my palm. He doesn't move a muscle to betray if he feels any pain.

"Jake knows I work for Gray," Wagner says with a dangerous glare at the barman.

"He wouldn't dare." He sounds almost disappointed.

The barman eyes us while he talks to one of the clients at the bar. I guess he's uncomfortable having someone of Wagner's kind in here, and no wonder. A Goliath with clearance to the inner planets is invariably here to do violence. Having someone like Thorfinn Wagner performing violence in your bar is potentially lethal to everyone in the building.

Wagner finally looks up, a dangerous glint in his deep-set eyes. "I wish he'd call them. I need the kills."

"Still on about that Breeder crap, Finn? Drop it. It's not your thing, you know that."

"Is great honour for my people. Honour lives forever."

"Come on. You're not even interested in women."

"It is the work of Frey. It pleases the gods."

He only needs ten more kills and he will be a Breeder, spending the rest of his days under the fur covers with the Valkyries on Nifelheim. I really need to keep an eye on him or he will run off on some high-score killing-spree.

"Anyways, we're the good guys now, Finn. We don't kill cops." I lean back against the hard sofa, sliding my arm out along the top of the seat to take the weight off my bullet-riddled back. "Fuck, that feels weird." And the bastard got away too.

Still, it's not as bad as it was when I woke up in the rain. There's a strange tingling in my back, and I hope it's not getting infected.

Wagner rolls up his lips into something resembling a smile. "Still sore, huh?" He doesn't even pretend to empathize. Getting shot in the back outside my own apartment by a simple robber is not the way to impress anybody. Especially not a Goliath.

"Like a whore in a cheap brothel." Had I been Nero Praetorius Gray, I would just have fired my sorry ass and most definitely not paid for the expensive patch-up job in that fancy clinic. In his own way, I guess Gray is an OK guy – for a capitalist oligarch bastard.

Wagner just laughs. I give him the finger.

"Thanks for the empathy, brother. Relax, Finn. I just had a couple of whiskies too many, that's all. I'm starving. Let's bring up a menu and forget about this crap, OK? Gray doesn't have to know. If you don't tell him, you will save him a spot of high blood pressure and everybody wins. He is an old man. Leave him alone and he might live a few years yet. Come on Finn, cheer up. I'm buying."

Wagner looks far from convinced, but when I tap the table's menu section and display the gastronomic treasures on offer in cheap, flickering holo, he grumpily orders a one-kilo steak. As always, he ticks the box for 'Bloody as Hell'. There must be a wolf somewhere not too far down Wagner's family tree. He's far too fond of garlic to be a vampire.

Feeding has never failed to put my big friend in a better mood, and if the food tastes half as good as it looks on the menu, this should have him purring like a kitten in no time. When our order finally arrives, we realize the pictures were probably stolen from some fancy uptown joint.

The food that gets dumped on our table by a busty waitress – aged past the point where make-up and push-up can hide the influence of even Elysium's weak gravity – looks like shit. After the recent crackdowns by the health department, most places have shaped up their hygiene standards and you will probably not die from a meal in a licensed restaurant in the city state of Masada any more.

In a place like this though, I'm not so sure, but my stomach is running on vapours and grumbling like crazy.

Hoka Hey. We take the leap of faith and dig in.

* * *

"So, what's the plan?" Wagner asks after crushing a cleaned steak bone between his teeth and noisily sucking marrow from the inside. Leave no food behind, that's the Norse for you. Living on that frigid ice world of theirs probably does that to a man.

He licks the bloody juices from his fingers and wipes his hands on his old army jacket. Me, I finished ages ago. The food actually didn't taste half bad. I'm still hungry, but I'm feeling better than I have in a long time. Are they putting something in the water again?

Behind Wagner, TV screens show flickering images from a news report of army forces moving off into the jungle on some major surprise exercise. It looks like the whole damn army, and I can understand them. You need some serious firepower to survive in the Elysian jungle.

"First of all, we need to get our hands on some new toys." I drain my third large glass of water and wave for a waitress to refill it. I'm thirsty as hell. That whisky must have been unusually bad, even for a joint like this. Oh, what sad times we live in. "That limpet bunker is one tough nut and we won't crack it without some serious hardware."

It was pretty obvious from the Redeemer banner in the video who was responsible for the failed execution. When the world lost contact with one of their limpet bunker hideouts a couple of days later, our suspicions were confirmed and we had our target. Now all we need to do is get in there, and that could turn out to be a bit tricky.

"Remember, these guys are the seriously inbred grandchildren of the people who broke the back of the Terran invasion back in the '50s. I have a feeling they will not be in Kumbaya mode when we get there. I think we need to go see Winger."

A short pause from Wagner. "Whatever."

He turns to practicalities. Things he can understand. "Air assault or stealth op?" He uses a finger-long splinter from the steak-bone as a toothpick as he looms over the table. On the table between us is a heavy-duty com-pad showing the rudimentary bunker schematics Gray's techs managed to dredge up for us. The woods are littered with such abandoned relics from the war, and it seems every one of them now houses a renegade sect. All of them worshipping their own marginally differentiated version of the Almighty, praying for the destruction of the Infidel – that's you, me and everybody else outside their circle elect – and the coming of their particular flavour of saviour.

I don't care about the battle for the souls of Elysium, and as long as they don't bother me, I don't bother them, but now that our paths are about to cross, I intend to take every opportunity I get to kick some fanatic behind. I never could stand those bloody Christian fundamentalists.

"Going in guns blazing would be a sure way to write ourselves into the hall of fame of Grandly Stupid Suicide Charges. I want my fifteen minutes of fame as much as the next guy, but I believe the pick-up factor of being on that particular list is pretty close to zero, so I think we'll go for door number two."

Wagner leers at me.

"Oh, for fuck's sake, *focus,* Finn."

For privacy, I've turned off the holo and we have to make do with a stylish but very boring, old-fashioned and two-dimensional display. I zoom out from the blueprints, trying to get a feel for the place. The bunker sits like a giant fossilised crustacean in the middle of the four hundred metres of ancient vertical rock isolating the southern of the twin cities of Masada from the jungle below. It's no more than a kilometre to the south of where we're sitting now. Practically spitting distance.

"How are your climbing skills these days, Finn?"

One of her Many Endearing Qualities

I press the call button on the ancient intercom beside the corroded metal door of Winger's place. It's raining again, only this time we're deep underground.

It takes a couple of hours for the rain to filter down through the cultural layers and detritus of the sky-scraping needle that is the megacity of Southern Masada. The humidity down in the Bottoms is not so very different from the rain forest climate uptown. The only difference is that down here, the sun never shines and the rain is blood-red with rust.

After a short while a tinny, metallic voice answers from the rusty grille, heavy with static.

"Who the fuck is it, and what the hell do you want?"

Winger is an unfriendly bastard at the best of times, and lucky for us, this seems to be one of them. With the surveillance camera above the door smashed since who knows when and the reputation of this neighbourhood I can understand if Winger is a bit touchy.

"Asher Perez," I reply. "I called earlier." A short pause and the locks disengage, motors struggle and the reek of burnt electronics tastes like nosebleed in the air. The huge door rumbles inward on creaking hinges, revealing a red-lit tunnel, sloping down into the underworld. Cue spooky music and you've got yourself a textbook entrance to hell. Like most places down here in the Bottoms, the smell is more septic tank than sepulchre though.

Wagner stoops low to enter the doorway ahead of me. Like all abnormally tall people he goes through life hunched over like a boxer, ready to take one in the face from life, but he needs to really bend over to get through the doorway.

As we walk down the damp concrete tunnel, randomly lit by weak light-panels behind rusty metal cages, the air grows noticeably colder and less breathable. Written on the wall in graffiti two metres tall is the age-old admonition that "Here be Dragons". The inference is clear; Abandon hope all ye who enter this shit hole.

Winger has always been a sucker for theatrics, but I'm too old in this business to be creeped out by a creative arms dealer. Even one as well equipped in the arms department as Winger.

* * *

We reach the end of the tunnel where another massive door bars our way. This time there's working surveillance gear tracking us as we approach. We stop in plain view of the cameras, allowing the scanners to read us. The door slides open, this time without a sound; a sure sign of expensive tech. Like I said, Winger is the best.

Despite its decrepit appearance, the outer door would probably shrug off a direct hit from a cruise missile and this bulkhead would keep you safe for the rest of the war. It's always good to know someone as paranoid as Winger when The War comes. In my experience, it's the paranoids who get the last laugh.

As we step through the door and into the state-of-the-art airlock behind it, the door behind us slides closed again. Our ears pop from a sudden change in air-pressure and we are hosed down with some kind of sharp-smelling disinfectant.

Winger is chronically suspicious of germs and viruses. For good reasons.

The airlock completes its cycle, and a door opens up in front of us, this time on a huge, dimly lit hangar filled with crates. In places they're stacked to the high ceiling, packed with the coolest kit you've ever seen. Men fall in love with the place at first sight. Women just shrug and wonder what all the fuss is about.

In the centre of the room, four banks of spotlights hang from aluminium trusswork bridges suspended from the ceiling on chains.

A massive industrial fan, stylishly backlit in morphine yellow, rotates slowly in the far wall. The rest of the room is unlit, the occasional twinkle reflecting off well-oiled technology the only indication there is anything out there in the darkness at all.

We walk down a canyon between the wooden crates and our footfalls echo around the large chamber. I run my fingers over the rough surface of the wood. Not a single speck of dust. There are no obvious security systems, but I know they are out there. We wouldn't get far if we were here to rob the place. We reach the central work area and there is Winger, bent over a work-table, her back to us.

She's wearing an oil-stained sleeveless top displaying her slenderly muscled arms and shoulders to great effect. The short top also reveals her dimpled lower back over the black leather pants which are not doing a very good job of hiding her long shapely legs.

The legs are the first thing you notice about Winger.

She straightens at the sound of our footsteps and turns to face us, stretching her back and showing off her ample assets in the harsh light. The cynic in me knows it's all a show to get better prices for her gear, but the romantic in me wants it to be all for me.

The second thing you notice about Winger is her strong but stunningly beautiful face, framed by a swell of curly dark hair. She's the kind of woman wars are fought over and poems written about.

The third thing you notice about Winger is Christine.

The small parasitic Siamese twin growing out of the side of her abdomen never fails to get people's attention.

At the moment Christine's asleep, and Winger has covered her in a soft blanket. If I didn't know better, I'd say she had a baby propped on her hip. Had they been born a decade later to a wealthy family, they could easily have been separated at birth and new organs grown for Christine, but they were not. When the price of the procedure had finally come within reach of ordinary people like Winger's folks, she and Christine had grown inseparable, if you'll pardon the pun.

They say a guy once fell in love with Winger and convinced her that her sister was not going to be a problem. Everything went alright for a while, and then the guy stabbed Christine in the face with a knife when Winger was asleep, hoping to force her to have Christine removed. The guy was never seen again, but ever since then, Winger wears a necklace of gold-plated teeth around her neck. They are much too big to be her milk teeth.

"Hey, Finn," she greets the giant. "Back so soon? Did you get to fight the Sumerian yet?"

"No, not yet." Wagner is unusually uncomfortable around Winger, and he keeps fidgeting with his belt buckle. He has never been very good with women.

Me, I've had a crush on Winger since I first met her a couple of years ago, and coming here always gets me in a good mood. I'm not one of her regular customers, but I try to find excuses to come see her every now and then. It's just too bad she's already taken. Her lover is a very lucky girl.

Her lover is also a psycho biker dyke, and I don't much fancy being the subject of her male-hating rage, so I keep my hands off. For now.

"And who the hell are you?" Her question smacks me in the face like a gutted cod and brings me out of my reverie. She's looking at me like she half remembers my face but can't decide if I'm a celebrity, unrecognisable out of makeup, or if I'm the guy from the sushi stand, unrecognisable out of context.

"Cut the crap, Winger. I called an hour ago." That doesn't seem to ring any bells, so I try again. "Hello? Perez, remember?" Still nothing. "What have you been smoking, girl?" I ask her, my good mood starting to evaporate.

She frowns, and then what I take to be recognition trickles in like cold water down a spine. She always was a bit absent-minded. That's just one of her many endearing qualities.

"Right. Sorry, man. No need to get grumpy. You're just not the Perez I was expecting, but since you're here let's see what I can do for you." A quick smile that could melt the ices of Nifelheim and she walks over to another desk, the light glinting off her leather pants, highlighting her smoothly rounded curves.

She picks up her com-pad and Wagner lets out a long breath I never knew he held. Funny that such a big man can be scared of a woman a fraction of his weight. He could lift her with one hand, easy. The image of it in my mind's eye brings a crooked smile to my face.

"There you go." Winger smiles back. "You're not half bad looking when you smile. You should try it more often. Might stop people from trying to kill you just to put you out of your misery."

I know it's all show and a calculated greasing of a customer, but her words still make me feel all fuzzy inside. Is it just me, or did it get hot in here?

"Cute, Winger, cute. Now, cut the crap and let's get down to business."

She leans back against the worktable, cradling Christine with one arm, balancing the pad on her hip with the other. "Aw, come on." She pouts at me. Damn, she's hot.

What's the matter with me today? I feel like a bloody teenager at the prom. I really need to get myself laid, and soon.

Then she's back in sales mode.

"OK, so, what do you need, mister?"

What I really need would probably make even her blush, so instead I count our shopping-list off my fingers.

"We need climbing gear. Four hundred metres of carbon line, spikes, hooks, the lot, and some chameleo-suits. Binoculars, and a good momo-blade."

"Mountaineering, huh?"

I shrug.

"Not my business, got it. Anything else?"

"Grenades, SMGs, handguns and a few cans of VX if you have it."

She just looks at me, her lips drawn back in a skeptical sneer and one eyebrow raised incredulously in a 'come on, are you for real?' look.

I spread my arms. "What?"

"Nothing." She puts the pad down on the desk so she can type in my order. "So, grenades check. Rifles check. Guns check," She ticks them off with a slender but dirty finger on the pad, then looks up. "No can do on the VX, I'm afraid. Nerve-gas was banned a couple of hundred years ago, you know. Crimes against humanity and all that."

"Always worth a shot. OK, lose the VX. Give us a lot of bullets instead. Same result, just more job for us." I play the macho card. She doesn't even pretend to know how to play that particular game.

"Lots... of... bullets." She reads the words out loud as she types them, slow and clear as if to a child or a total idiot. I really like this girl. "Is that all?"

"Yes. No, there's one other thing. Parachutes. And a chopper pickup."

Winger whistles through her teeth, reluctantly impressed. "Jumping into the jungle are you? With that hardware, I'd say you were raiding one of the limpets. Grave robbing, huh?"

"I hope not."

"Not my business, I know," she holds up a placating hand, "but you certainly know how to tickle a girl's interest." A pretty smile flashes across her face before Winger the hard-ass saleswoman comes back. "I hope you've got a load of cash secreted somewhere around your body because this shit is going to cost you."

"Not a problem. Send the bill to this address." I beam her the invoice address of a clean, twice-removed Gray Industries subsidiary from my wrist-pad. "They're good for it."

"I normally deal in cash, Mr, but if your credit is as good as you say I might make an exception. I need the money."

"The credit's good. Trust me. Can we take the stuff with us now?"

"The knife and the handguns you can have right away." She throws me a folded momo from the desk. I catch it and flick open the short blade with its mono-molecular edge. The sharpest thing in the universe. I like the weight of it. "The chopper will be there when you call. You got a ride?"

"Parked around the corner." I wave a thumb over my shoulder as I fold the knife back up.

She closes her eyes and inhales slowly, then sighs. "What kind of dream-world do you live in, man? If you're fucking lucky and it's still there and still in something even remotely resembling working condition when you get out, you can take it round the back and we'll load the gear. If not, you will have to carry that shit out of here, and don't even think about leaving it here for later. Good thing you brought Wagner along to carry it for you." She nods in the giant's direction. "You run with anybody these days, don't you, big guy? I hope the pay is good."

Wagner just shrugs.

"The car will be there." I have faith in no god, but I do have faith in the hardware of Gray Industries. No one will touch that car.

I hope.

Winger shrugs. "It's your money." At that moment her pad chimes. I'm guessing her trace of the decoy company completed with satisfactory results. Impressively fast. She really is the best.

She doesn't even look at her pad, probably able to tell from the tone of the chime that the company is good for the credit. I hoped she would do a trace, which is why I chose that particular company to front the deal. Hard to trace to the real owner, but not impossible. Childish, I know, but I wanted to impress her. I've never told her who I work for, and I don't know why I decided to share now, but there it is.

"Come see me again sometime." She smiles at me. "If you need anything else." She adds it casually as she puts the pad down on the desk again, and I'm not sure if the implied invitation is there or if it's only in my head. I linger a little longer than necessary to catch the look on her face when she sees the result of the trace. I'm not disappointed.

She looks up from her pad and just blinks at me, for once speechless.

As I turn my back on her, Christine pushes the blanket from her face and looks at me with a strange glitter in her shrunken eyes.

We go to get the car.

The General

The general steps down onto the ramp as it lowers from the back of his troop carrier. The scent of the jungle is strong in his nostrils, contrasted by the electric smell of smoking steel from the still scorching hull of the dropship. These are the smells of victory.

An insect the size of his hand buzzes too close to the red-hot surface of the ship and is singed to a crisp in the shimmering heat. General Caspar Batista Meridian smiles at its sad demise. He is no stranger to death. The rays of the setting sun paint the inside of the ship blood-red.

Taking a deep breath, he strides down the ramp in his powered armour, helmet under his arm, and steps onto the surface of the jungle-moon. In the clear evening sky above, Arcadia burns.

It is done, and tonight he will celebrate with his troops. They deserve the best. They've earned it.

Far overhead a few straggling Arcadian fighters streak through the moon's atmosphere chased by the Elysian air force. The Terrans have nowhere to run anymore, and they know it. Peace will come.

Major Amon Solana, his second in command, jumps down next to him, the servos of his armoured suit whirring to soften the impact. Solana removes his helmet and draws a deep breath of the rich atmosphere, so very different from the recycled air they've been breathing for so long. Space is their second home, but nothing compares to the full experience of filling your lungs with the smells of life and death of a natural habitat.

There's a smile on the major's handsome face, and he salutes his general.

"The men are ready to move on your command, sir."

The general smiles back. He sees himself in the major's face. Maybe a little younger and a lot more idealistic, but he sees himself there. In fact, he sees himself in all his men. That is why they work so well together.

"Excellent, Major. Dress uniform and side arms only. This is a triumph, not a strike op. We're celebrating."

"Yes sir." Solana lifts the helmet to his face and barks a few quick orders into the command module.

The war is won and Gray will pay his general handsomely for it. The Terran Commonwealth is beaten, already accelerating their remaining starships back to Earth. This is an hour of celebration for the free people of the Hope system, unburdened at long last of the yoke of Earth.

Even at close to light speed it will be forty years before the Terrans return for the next round, and finally the general can relax. There is no one left to fight and he is tired. The day of reckoning has come and gone and now a new world is rising. He does not yet know if there is a place for him in that world. He has no skills in demand in a world of peace, but with his special talents there must be something he can do. He is not worried. Those who serve will be rewarded.

Besides, if there is anything he has learnt over the years, it is that humanity will always need someone to do their violence, even in peacetime.

"Come Major. Let's lose the armour and bring the boys out."

"Sir."

He takes a final breath of fresh air before striding up the ramp again. At last he is content.

* * *

His men march down the ramp, splendid in the evening light in their white dress uniforms, the rays of the dying sun reflecting off the golden decorations on their chests. The least recognised man in his company carries more medals than the war heroes flaunted on the feeds by the church government. His men will never appear in those feeds. They operate too far from the eyes of the sensitive general public. If their missions became public knowledge, the government would lose face and heads would have to roll. Theirs is not a public part. They are the knife in the dark, carrying out the less noble but ever so important work that the leaders of the rebellion can never acknowledge. Without them the war would still be raging. The enemy has been destroyed and the children of Hope need die in the trenches no longer. General Meridian and his precious Cherubim played the game one final time, and this time they played for keeps.

The men stand at parade rest, smiles on hard faces, as proud as their general of what they have done. They are the peacemakers, and they know it.

Meridian gives a quick nod to Solana. The major calls the men to attention and Meridian addresses his men. "You know what to do, and I expect you to do it well. I know you are tired, but shape up and put on a good show, and tonight we will celebrate. You have earned it."

It fills him with a pride stronger than love to be the leader of such men. He has no children of his own and he never will. Gray saw to that. But he has his men, and they are dearer to him than mere biological offspring could ever be. That is why they work so well together. They have fought and bled side by side, many of them have lost their lives along the road. Every death has pounded and forged the survivors closer together until now they are as perfectly balanced and deadly as a samurai's sword. An unbending force, powerful as a ramstrike, with the precision of a mono-molecular scalpel in the hands of an expert surgeon. Never in the history of mankind has there been a finer strike force. They know it and they take immense pride in it. It saddens his heart that they will never be recognised for it, but that is a sacrifice they are all willing to make. In the battle for the future of humanity, theirs is a small burden to bear.

"Major?"

"Then men are yours, General. I'll lock up and join you in a little while."

"Very well, Major." He salutes his second in command who returns the salute, crisp and faithful as always.

Meridian gives the marching order and they all set out along the jungle trail.

* * *

As they emerge from the jungle Meridian spots the welcoming party at the other end of the field. Gray is there, standing in his white linen suit in the centre of a half-circle of security operatives. The mercenaries look cold and hostile in their dark Gray Industries coveralls, heavy weapons at parade rest. Behind them the fliers they arrived in, dark, powerful birds of prey, stand with their jet engines idly turning, aimed at the ground. It looks like the meeting will be brief.

The sun is setting behind the mountains on the opposite side of the wide valley. Its last rays catch the spray from the waterfall plunging from the plateau to the valley floor a hundred metres below. All around them, colourful, birdlike creatures wheel and dive, chasing insects in the golden mist. Their eerie calls provide a haunting soundtrack to the scene. It's a spectacular sight.

As Meridian and his men approach, Gray's guards start to look uneasy. Being in the presence of soldiers who take lives for a living tends to do that to lesser men. That's the difference between hired muscle and professional soldiers, Meridian muses. Men tempered in combat have a natural ease about them. They have learnt to live with the inevitability of death and it no longer holds any fear for them, and that makes them relaxed and ready for any eventuality. These mercenaries have probably seen their fair share of death, but never on the scale of true soldiers as Meridian's men have done. These mercenaries don't trust each other like brothers and therefore they are frightened in the presence of such men. It's only to be expected.

Meridian walks up to Gray, who stands relaxed and immaculate. The linen suit hangs off him like an old jacket on a scarecrow, but the old man never looked better. This is his victory too, and he can sleep well tonight.

Maybe today Meridian will get to shake the hand of the man he has been serving all these years. Gray has never given him that honour. It would be nice.

"Welcome, General. Congratulations on a job well done." Gray extends a hand and Meridian takes it, proudly. It's warm and dry. "We're all very grateful for what you have done."

"Thank you, sir." Meridian shakes Gray's hand. "The mission was a total success. The victory was absolute."

Gray shakes his hand back, not letting go. Gray's hand is unusually warm. Not the usual corpse temperature of ordinary humans. "As always, General, your results far exceed my expectations…"

"You are far too kind, sir."

"… which is why, in this case, we have a problem," Gray continues.

"A problem sir? How so?" A shiver of unease runs down the general's spine. Something is not right. Gray's hand is almost burning hot in his own. It's almost as hot as the general's own skin.

The pieces fall into place.

Gray is like him. He is no more human than the general is. That's why Gray never shook his hand before. If he does it now that can only mean one thing.

"I know your orders were to win the war at any cost, General, so semantically you have done nothing wrong, but I'm afraid that this time you have overstepped your authority, general."

"I won you the war as I promised. How could that displease you?" The general takes in the twitching fingers of Gray's men and now their anxiety makes a chilling kind of sense.

"Yes, you won the war, and you did it most spectacularly." Gray looks to the burning disc above them that is Arcadia, a smile on his thin lips. "But you realise I could never afford to have this mission connected to myself." His gaze returns to the general. "That just would not do."

Meridian untangles from Gray's hot grasp and clenches his calloused hand into a fist over his heart, swearing wordless, unending loyalty to Gray and the cause.

"I can assure you that my men will never say a word about this, Gray. They are not stupid. They understand their complicity in this. We are all aware of the Beijing Convention."

"I have no doubt whatsoever in your sincerity or that of your men, General, but I'm afraid I would not trust my life on either of them. I didn't get where I am today – and I have come a very long way," a small smile at the corner of his mouth, " – by trusting people."

Meridian looks deep into Gray's eyes. How did it come to this? Was this the way Gray planned it from the beginning? There is no light in the old man's eyes. None at all.

As Meridian lowers his fist from his chest he quickly opens and clenches it again, signalling to his captain, instructing him to alert the crew back at the ship and have them bring in the dropship to provide fire support. This is going to get messy. Fast. A quick nod from the captain informs him the order has been relayed.

Gray continues. "You see, I consider myself something of a surgeon, General, working to keep a dear patient alive. When a cancer runs rampant and threatens the patient's life, or maybe even has the potential to infect the physician himself, it is the physician's duty to weed out that cancer. If the physician dies, there's no one to take care of the patient any more, and this patient must live. You see, I consider this whole system my child, and a father must always see to the good of his children. I know you see the reason in this, General."

"What the hell are you talking about, Gray?" Meridian is stalling to win time for the ship to warm up and come to their aid. "We are all on the same side here, fighting the same enemy. We always have. Always will."

"Yes, we are, and we have. But you see, the difference between you and me is that I see the bigger picture. You have never been anything but a pawn, General. A useful pawn, I'll be the first to admit that, but a pawn nevertheless. After what you did to Arcadia, the threat of being associated with you now far outweighs your usefulness. Oh, how you have fallen from grace, General." A sad shake of Gray's head.

So that's it. The carte blanche is revoked, their actions denounced. The general looks out across the valley, nodding slowly. There are worse places to die. But the ship is on its way and there is still a chance. The cannons on the dropship will turn Gray and his men into pink mist from two kilometres away.

Gray must have seen the flicker of hope in his eyes.

"Oh, are you waiting for the cavalry to come charging over the hill to your rescue?" The old man nods towards the ragged outcrops behind which the dropship is just rising on twin plumes of fire and destruction as the plasma drives push it into the sky. The pilot angles the engines and the troop carrier comes speeding across the jungle, weapons bristling, training on Gray and his men as the ship closes in fast.

"Impressive. You always were a resourceful man, General," Gray says and smiles, not unkindly. "Too bad I can't stay and play your games."

A blinding spear of light flashes from the clouds like a falling star. It lances through the ship and pounds into the earth, sending a massive shock-wave through their feet, instantly destroying the general's fledgling hope along with his ship and its crew. The carrier bursts into a blistering ball of fire hurtling towards them.

"Hmm," is all Gray says as the wreckage hits the ground five hundred metres away. It bounces across the landscape and tears terrible holes in the beautiful surroundings before coming to rest mere metres from them, setting the jungle on fire. Gray turns to the commander of his men. "Kill them. No need to make it look like an accident, I believe, Decapitate them and burn the heads. And bring me Meridian's head on a plate. I really mean that. I want his head."

"Gray, you motherfucker," Meridian shouts after Gray as the old man turns and walks away through the ranks of his mercenaries, their lines quickly closing behind him again as they take aim. "I'll come for you, Gray. Do you hear me? I'll come for you and I will fucking destroy you and your fucking company."

Gray just waves goodbye without looking back. The rest of the General's words are drowned in the roar of fifty large-calibre assault rifles opening fire on his celebration parade. Instantly, they're turned from a group of brave but tired men in dress uniform into so much tearing flesh, ripping cloth and splintering bones. Even as they die his men flock to their general, shielding him with their bodies. His brave, faithful brothers. His precious Cherubim. He reaches out to them, consoling them with his hands as they die. The copper taste of blood fills his mouth and he has no way of knowing if it's his own or that of one of his brothers.

The last thing he sees before going down under the press of shredded meat is Nero Praetorius Gray walking away toward his flier, not even bothering to watch them die.

A Perfect Time for Blood Sacrifice

The afternoon rainstorm is pounding our high-tech camouflage tarp as we scope out the limpet bunker of the Church of Christ the Redeemer. The Redeemers were founded right after the war with the key selling point of intending to be the instigators and sole survivors of Armageddon. Hardly original, but these outfits seldom are.

The smart plastic of the tarp keeps the rain away, but it does nothing for the moisture and the noise. Wagner never says very much anyway, but talking is almost impossible over the drumming of massive raindrops on the tarp. The weak gravity of Elysium has some peculiar effects. The long time it took us to parachute down from the city into the jungle is one. The size of plants and animals is another. This is a world of giants and that, unfortunately, includes all the bugs. They are not only gigantic. They also seem to be blood-suckers, every single one of them, and since we're not originally from this place, they are all highly toxic.

Still, it's nice to be out of the city.

Elysium is not a very good name for this beautiful but deadly backwater of a world, but then we were never very good at naming our planets. We called our old home Earth when it should have been called Water, and by the same logic we named our new world Paradise. It's not the hostile wildlife, the poisonous plants, or the deadly diseases that pose the greatest threat to human life. It's the people themselves. The inhabitants of this system are the degenerate descendants of the original pilgrims who came in on the *Gormenghast* three hundred years ago. When mankind immigrates to a new world, the people who ride in on the first wave are always the outcasts, the religious renegades, the wonderful weirdos and the mischievous misfits. I bet there were not only tears back on

Earth when the *Galahad* disappeared during the Exodus, wasting ten thousand souls in deep space. Two out of three colony ships reaching their destinations is not a bad score for a human race on the brink of extinction.

From every major opening of the bunker hangs a huge banner with the Redeemers' precious cross, moving majestically in the wind. Down here in the marshy forest the air is fetid and hot like a sauna and I can't wait to start climbing. I know I will regret that thought when we are up there, clinging to the rock with our bare hands. The gravity of Elysium may be weak, but a two-hundred-metre fall will still kill you as surely as the sting of the arm-long centipede that comes crawling over my leg.

I pretend I'm a rock and hope the bug doesn't have the brains to call my bluff. I'm ever so happy I tucked my pants into my boots and pulled all the strings on my jacket tight enough to staunch blood. I definitely don't want one of those things crawling up my leg and mistaking my pride and joy for a mating partner. I slowly extend the blade on my momo-knife, getting ready to stab the thing. Lucky for both of us, it crawls away into the moss and disappears. It leaves behind a sickly sweet smell all over my trousers, no doubt secreted to attract a mate. Fucking A.

Wagner's huge jaws grind as he chews on a piece of dried meat from his pack. He looks at me but doesn't say anything.

I lift the binoculars to my eyes again.

Most of the gun turrets on the bunker seem to have rusted shut in the forty-odd years since the war, but a few are still moving, probably on automatic. That means the reactor is still functional, meaning the ventilation should still be working. Apart from the obvious upside of entering an air conditioned interior, it's always good to have the hum of great fans to disguise our little surprise visit. It also means the ventilation shafts need to be serviced on a regular basis, hopefully providing us with a means of access.

"What do you think, Finn?" I have to shout to be heard over the roar of the rain.

"Think about what?" he asks around the dried meat in his mouth. Manners have never been his strong side.

"The fucking bunker."

He keeps chewing and considers my question for a long while. Then he nods his great shaggy head. "I say we go in and kill them."

The Skullfucker has spoken.

"Easier said than done, my friend."

As the Limpet classification implies, the bunker itself looks like an enormous, gunmetal-grey crustacean, clinging to the forbidding cliff. The limpets were originally designed to prevent the Terrans from using the valleys to reach our major cities during the war. Short of a nuclear detonation or a ramstrike there's nothing that will crack its shell. No wonder the Terrans came from the air when they attacked.

"Alright, come on." I tap Wagner on the arm and we slip out into the rain and down one of the dark ravines that make the Elysian jungle such a deadly maze and head for the base of the cliff.

* * *

An hour later we have made our way through the jungle to the foot of the cliff. The rain is pouring off the bunker high above, thundering down around us in dark sheets. We take cover under the overhang and survey our planned approach.

The plants of this jungle are every bit as resourceful as its bloodsuckers, and the lower slopes of the rock are covered in foliage. The thick roots intertwine and form a slippery but stable ladder up the steep cliff. Thank you, Mother Nature for not being a bitch all the time.

The plants will keep us concealed for the first part of the climb, but then we'll have to trust in the camouflage suits and the approaching darkness to conceal us. We need to be careful, and we're going to need every bit of luck we have. Had I been a religious man, this would have been a perfect time for blood sacrifice.

"Tall as the walls of Asgard," Wagner nods to himself.

I have no idea how tall the walls of Asgard are, but this is one formidable cliff, and I stand watching it for a while, trying to memorise a way through all the overhangs and crevices. There's no use. We'll just have to make it up as we go. I turn to Wagner and give him a shrug. He shrugs back.

"OK then. Let's do this."

We set out. Initially the going is easy. We climb from moss-covered root to moss-covered root, and there are plenty of them to provide hand and foot holds. As we get higher, the branches grow fewer and further apart. After an hour of hard climbing we are out of the forest proper and stop for a well-deserved rest under the last umbrella-sized leaves before the cliff goes rock only.

I look out over the jungle and the rocky maze we've left behind, and I can't help but marvel at the beauty of this place. Hope-A is setting and its twin sun is not far behind, giving us the first true night in a week. Who says I'm not good at timing these little operations? Far away to the south, the roar of a mega-predator echoes across the jungle. A flock of avian lizard creatures are startled out of their preparations for the night and go screaming into the sky, soaring high into the dying light. They circle the tower of an overgrown and crumbling Centaur pyramid before returning to their roosts, the great beast silent once more.

The Centaurs were a race of highly intelligent carnivores with a society entirely based on violence and proving your worth in battle. Their brutal nature was their greatest asset and allowed them to conquer the planet in a relatively short time span. It was also the ultimate cause of their downfall. They were simply too violent to function as a civilized society and destroyed themselves in a bitter war. I believe there's a lesson in there somewhere.

I break out our rations and hand a couple of power bars to Wagner. He rips the covers off and pop them both in his mouth. Hell, Goliaths are even more expensive to feed than teenagers. The giant looks exhausted. He really needs to cut down on the beer and chips. I'm feeling pretty good. The climb wasn't half as bad as I feared. I stretch my aching back and realise hard exercise must be good for old gunshot wounds in the back, because I can't feel them at all. But then we're only getting started.

I'm still ravenous after passing out in the gutter last night and I cram down a couple of bars myself. They taste of artificial chocolate and sawdust, but they provide us with all the nutrients and energy we'll need for the rest of the climb. At this rate we are going to run out of rations fast, and it's a good thing this operation is only supposed to be a one-day affair. Go in, get the guy, call the choppers, and be home in time for supper tomorrow. No sweat, no hassle. What could possibly go horribly wrong with this simple job?

We stuff the crinkly covers back into our packs, careful not to leave anything behind to advertise our visit. Not that I think any Redeemers will go climbing around the branches down here anytime soon, but you never know. There is no such thing as too careful on an operation like this, and leaving a single wrapper behind can be even more informative to an experienced tracker than a pile of them. A single wrapper tells them their enemy is careful, smart enough to try to hide his presence and that tells them they are not dealing with amateurs. That knowledge can tip the scales in their favour when it comes to gunplay. Since we are already outnumbered and outgunned as it is, we don't want to give them that edge. We rope together, sling our packs back on, and start on the long, unprotected final leg of the climb to the bunker far, far above.

* * *

After three hours of arduous climbing, gasping and sweating, we finally reach the belly of the beast and huddle in the darkness where the ceramic fortress meets the rock. By now, both suns are long gone below the horizon and the rain has stopped. The night is full of the sounds and smells of a new shift going to work in the forest and even up here the noise is loud. If the jungle is lethal by day, it's positively murderous by night. Trust me. You don't want to spend a night outdoors on Elysium. You are safe in a limpet bunker, but that's about the only place you can sleep safe from the horrors that live out there. That very safety is going to be our next challenge, since we now have to make our way into this thing. I have the blueprints of the place on my com-pad and I scan them quickly before giving Wagner the sign. He pulls out the small grappling hook we brought along and makes sure he is safely secured to the wall. It would look very silly if he fell now. Meanwhile I search the underside of the bunker through my night-vision goggles. It's still almost bright enough to see without them, but they make my job so much easier.

There.

I spot the drain-pipe extending from what – according to the plans – is the kitchen sink. It's a good ten metres away, but for Wagner that's no big deal. I point it out to him and he nods silently in the green haze of the low-light optics. We dare not speak as we are hanging below the doorstep of an enemy whose strength and readiness we have zero intel on. After the events in the video, anything might have happened in there.

I secure my climbing harness to the underside of the bunker and Wagner starts spinning the grappling hook. He takes his time and I don't blame him. If he hits the bunker the noise will alert the inhabitants to our presence and they will be on us like leeches on a haemophiliac. Knowing the Redeemers, they would probably go medieval on our ass and bring out the boiling oil.

I hold my breath.

The first throw goes low, and the padded hook sails silently away into the night. Wagner curses under his breath in his native tongue and after a few seconds I hear the padded hook thump softly against the rock far below us. The sound is barely loud enough to register above the noise of the jungle, but we freeze nonetheless. We hold our breath for what feels like an eternity, but can't be more than ten seconds. When nothing happens, I exhale and motion for Wagner to give it another go. He reels the hook back in and tries again. This time his aim is flawless and the grappling-hook loops around the pipe and secures itself. He tests the line by pulling on it with all his strength. Apparently satisfied, he secures his end to the piton he's hanging from and gives me a thumb- up. I give him a mock salute and push away from the wall, swinging on my rope. I grab the line and swing my legs up and around it. I could easily climb it hanging by my arms alone, but this is the real world and not the movies. In the real world, shit goes wrong and the hero often dies. Besides, there is no-one to see me showing off except Wagner, and when it comes to shows of strength Wagner is rarely impressed.

I inch my way out along the line, being careful not to swing too much. Even though the hook feels secure I know from experience that enough jangling and jerking will eventually pull it loose, and that is something I am hoping to avoid.

Eventually I reach the pipe and secure my harness to it before giving Wagner another thumbs-up. Then I crane my neck around, looking for the service hatch. The people who design things like these must all go to the same crappy architecture school. There is always a service hatch or a reactor outlet conveniently placed to allow easy access to the interior. Perhaps they do it as an architect's inside joke?

Whatever the reason, the hatch is exactly where it's supposed to be. I pull the powered screwdriver from my utility belt and set about unscrewing the bolts attaching it to the hull of the bunker. As I remove the last one I hold the hatch in place with my other hand to prevent it from falling away into the night. Then I carefully lower it and peer inside, searching for any contact sensors or other devices that might set off an alarm. Even if these systems are forty years old the Redeemers might have maintained them and they could still be highly operational.

We seem to be in luck. No obvious trigger mechanisms, and I secure the hatch with one of the carabiners from my pack and leave it dangling beside the opening.

Then it's time for some acrobatics.

I unhook from the relative safety of the pipe and grab the lowest rung of the ladder inside the access hatch. It's rough and flaky and I can feel a sharp edge slice my skin but I ignore it and let go with my other hand. For a moment I'm suspended one-handed, two hundred metres above the forest floor. I'm staying alive by nothing more than my own strength and the simple fact that the ladder has not rusted to scrap over the decades. Perhaps I should have made sure of that before I let go, but hell, you can't go around checking everything in life. Taking calculated risks is part of my job, but every once in a while it feels so bloody good to just gamble a little. A few quick moves and I'm inside and I wave for Wagner to join me.

Damn, I like these jobs.

When We Start Finding Them

Inside the bunker, it's cool and dry and there's not a soul in sight. This is going way too easily. Did they see us climb and are waiting for us around the corner? It shouldn't be this simple to infiltrate a maximum-security bunker full of religious zealots. The Church of Christ the Redeemer is notoriously hard-assed and they have been responsible for more religious murders than any other cult on the planet. On a world as notorious for extremist violence as this, that is something.

When I saw the redeemer banner in the video, I knew what was in store for its main character, and he probably knew it too. I can't even begin to imagine what went through his mind in the hours before he unwillingly starred in his very own snuff movie. Nothing cheerful, I bet.

I really hope I will get to kick some redeemer ass this time. Previously they have shown the uncommon sense to stay the hell away from Gray Industries and thus kept themselves out of my jurisdiction and from the lack of a welcoming committee I'd say they are still avoiding me. Too fucking bad. Ever since Samarkand I've wanted a shot at paying the bastards back.

I haven't got the foggiest idea what their special branch of Christianity is about, and for all I know they could be having a full scale Roman orgy on the altar right now. I was prepared for something like that. The one thing I didn't expect them to do was go to bed and leave the corridors empty. From what we managed to gather before going in, this bunker is home to at least two hundred and fifty people, some of them women and children. It should be full of life. People eating, drinking, fucking. Something is seriously wrong with this place and it's starting to give me the creeps.

I motion for Wagner to move down the corridor and check another door. He moves very fast for a big man, Wagner does, and he doesn't make much noise. The Norse sure know how to breed 'em. He sidles up to the closed door while I cover him with my PDW.

The handle disappears in his big hand. On my command he tests it and finds it unlocked. I signal for him to go ahead and he throws the door open. He pokes his head in and gives me the all clear. It's empty.

I step up to the door, the Aitchenkai PDW held ready against my shoulder and pointed slightly downward as I scan the room. The space really is empty. It looks like some sort of storage facility for foodstuff, which seems logical since we just left the kitchen. I let the door fall closed again. All the doors in a limpet bunker are designed to fall closed of their own accord. Gas and fire are the only two things the inhabitants of a limpet bunker have to worry about. A nuke or a ram-strike is not something you really need to think about, since you will never notice when it hits.

We move down the corridor, checking doors and finding them all locked. More storage space, from the looks of it. That's probably where they keep all the good stuff reserved for the high priest and his cronies. From the smell, I'd say something is going stale somewhere. On the floor are a few abandoned toy cars. It looks like these people left in a hurry.

As we near the end of the corridor, I hear a faint whirring sound. Something is moving up ahead. It doesn't sound like a cultist, but you never know. It could be a slavering fanatic in an electric wheelchair. We're not taking any chances.

I motion for Wagner to stay back as I slide along the wall, slowly inching closer to the T-junction. As I approach the intersection, the sound grows louder. Something mechanical is definitely moving around the corner. I slowly pull back the slide on my PDW and check there is a round in the chamber. Like an old lady making sure she has turned off the stove before going to bed. I never do that. This creepy place must be getting to me.

I get down on my knees, trying to make as little noise as I can. A guard posted to look out for approaching enemies unconsciously looks for people at head-height. It's basic human psychology. If there is a guard there and I peer around the corner at ground level, I should have the precious tenths of a second I need to pull my head back in time to avoid a bullet in the face.

It's a great plan in theory. The only flaw in my reasoning is that robot-sentries don't give a shit about human psychology. The ceiling-mounted, twin-barrel machine-gun turret spots me, swivels in my direction, and opens fire in less time than it takes to blink. When the bullets come flying I am already pulling back, decades of training giving me an edge, but I'm not nearly fast enough. I feel my face exploding into pain as concrete shrapnel tears into my forehead before I'm safe behind the wall again. Mesmerized, I watch the corner disintegrate in slow motion under the storm of bullets. The opposite wall explodes into flying concrete and ricocheting metal as I fall on my ass and use my legs and elbows to scramble backwards to safety. Blood gushes down my face but I feel the adrenaline pumping into my bloodstream, shielding me from shock. I need to use the short respite before the pain comes crashing in to do something creative about that turret.

"Wagner," I shout and reach back.

"Coming up," the giant replies and I feel a heavy fragmentation-grenade slapped into my palm. It's a testament to the many years we've spent together that he knows my every move as soon as I know them myself. I pull the pin with my teeth and throw it into the junction. I hear the bullets from the sentry track the bouncing grenade and hope they don't deflect it. Then I cover my ears with my hands, curl up into a ball, and open my mouth in preparation for the detonation. In a confined space like this the shock wave will be as lethal as the shrapnel and if you're not ready for it, the pressure will rupture your inner organs.

One moment there is just the noise from the guns on the sentry, the next the explosion is the brightest light I've ever seen, the loudest noise I've ever heard, and the hardest fall I've ever had, rolled into one. The corridor fills with concrete dust, cordite and black smoke, boiling around us. I lower my hands and even through the ringing in my ears I can hear the gunfire has stopped. Pieces of concrete fall from the ceiling like calcified rain.

Got you, you bastard.

There is blood in my eyes and I can hardly see, but the pain is held at bay by the chemical cocktail pumped into my bloodstream by my brain. A marvellous machine, the human body. I collapse against the wall.

"A little help here, big guy," I call, probably way too loudly since my ears are still ringing from the explosion. I fumble the first-aid kit from the leg pocket on my combat trousers with one hand while I try to wipe the blood from my face with the other. My mouth is full of the taste of blood and I hawk and spit on the floor. The concrete is red and wet beneath me as is my t-shirt, and I probably look like hell. The upside is, I feel pretty good. It must have been a glancing hit. A cracked eyebrow will bleed like crazy, but once you get the bleeding stopped you realise you're not going to die. Wagner helps me bind the wound with gauze from the med-pack and I wipe the crusting blood from my face.

Wagner turns my head this way and that. "Close shave," he says with the first hint of concern I've heard from him since I woke up in the rain last night. He can hold a grudge for ever, and I've seen for myself the results of ending up on his blacklist. I'm grateful that he's at least talking to me again.

"I've had worse. Have you got a mirror, big guy? Am I still pretty?"

"No time, Cinderella."

I smile despite the pain and the blood. True that. Then a troubling thought bubbles up from my subconscious.

"Why the hell do they have an active robot sentry outside the bloody kitchens?" I turn to Wagner. "There are kids in this place. Something is seriously fucked up here."

"Whatever you say, boss." Maybe he's not entirely over that episode at the bar after all, but I can see his brain is processing the implications, and I take a moment to enjoy the miracle. Goliaths are not noted for their abundance of brain power, and Wagner is as thick as they come, but even he understands that you don't activate an automated sentry outside your kitchen door unless something has gone severely sideways.

It couldn't be our doing. If they had spotted us climbing in it would have been simpler to just have a sniper shoot us off the cliff. There's no need to arm the wartime defences just for us. Nope, something has happened here, and I have a feeling that whatever happened is the answer to the mystery of the missing zealots. Whatever it is, I hope it's long gone.

"On your feet soldier," I punch Wagner on the shoulder and get to my feet. Damn, I feel pretty good. I guess there's some truth to the old saying that only after courting death can we truly appreciate life.

I crouch and pick up the dusty PDW from where I dropped it and brush it off. Then I grab a handful of debris from the ground and toss it into the junction.

Nothing.

I wave the barrel of my gun around the corner. Still nothing. I take a deep breath and peer around the corner and there is the sentry. It hangs from the ceiling like a dead metal octopus. A red light glows like a baleful eye in the middle of the twisted metal, indicating it's still online. I can't help a cold shiver of satisfaction knowing the machine is aware of me when I step out into the corridor. It knows I'm there, and there's not a damn thing it can do about it. Fuck you, Mr Machine Intelligence. Maybe you will not inherit the earth after all.

As we move past the thing Wagner does the sign against evil when he thinks I'm not looking. The Norse have never been at ease around AIs, even low-level ones like this. I read the explanation somewhere, but I can't remember it now. It was probably very psychological and full of archetypes, racial guilt and repression and stuff.

We move down the down the corridor and the smell of something rotting grows stronger until it finally overrides the acrid smell of cordite. Perhaps someone's pet has starved to death in the absence of Redeemers to feed it? I try to tell myself that. It's not working very well.

Keeping a keen lookout for more sentries, we reach a huge chamber with a big double door marked by a wooden cross. Want to give me more than even money that's their church, and that's where everybody is hiding? No? No one?

"Wagner, crack it," I order as I cover the hallway. Wagner brings out his break-in kit and plugs it into the access hatch. He may not be the smartest man around, but he has some mean skills when it comes to picking locks and killing people.

He's got a connection up and running in no time.

"That's strange." Wagner looks puzzled. I risk a quick glance at the readout of his console. Strange indeed. And a major pain in the ass.

It looks like the door was locked from the outside using an override code, meaning there's no way we're getting through. They might as well have welded it shut. Whoever used that override didn't want anyone getting in there. Adding to the mystery, the log says the door was opened only twenty minutes prior to that, using the same override. So, someone broke in, did something, and locked up again after they were done. The question is who, and why? Did they steal something? Or did they leave something behind? And do we really want to look inside?

"OK, we're not getting through here. Come on." I nod down the corridor. "We'll have to find another way in."

We move on down the passage and that's when we start finding them.

Dead People's Remains

We move slowly down the corridor until we reach what is very clearly a corpse next to a steep flight of metal stairs going up. The body is reasonably fresh, as indicated by the fact that putrefaction has not yet set in, meaning he's been dead a few days, tops. The smell is still pretty horrible.

I flip him over with the toe of my boot, and my hopes of finding people alive in this place takes a torpedo in the side, burns, and sinks. A vision straight out of some deranged painter's very personal nightmare of hell should teach me to leave these things alone. His throat has been ripped out and the pipework hangs all over the place. The face is distorted into a silent rictus of terror. No matter how hard I try not to, my mind wanders in a direction insinuating he must have been alive when it happened.

The realisation that your breathing system has been torn away from you and you are about to die without a bloody thing you or anyone else can do about it must be a truly horrible thing to have going through your mind in your final moments. Judging by the bloody trail leading down the stairs, he was making for the church. What was he hoping to find there? Whatever it was, it inspired him to stumble quite some way before he collapsed and expired. You have to admire the sheer tenacity of the human mind. I close his dry eyes and my fingers leave rotting grooves in his dead flesh.

When I get to my feet Wagner is waiting for me by the stairs. "Up or on, boss?" he asks, indicating our choices with nods of his great shaggy head.

"Up," I reply, nodding at the bloody trail coming down the stairs.

Wagner hawks and spits on the floor. "After you."

His knuckles are white around the grip of his assault rifle.

* * *

The upper floor is dark. Some light must still be filtering through from somewhere because it's not pitch black and I can make out the shapes of more bodies on the floor. I can also make out the insane amount of blood. These poor souls have been torn to pieces, and it looks like the guy downstairs got away lightly. Gore and pieces of flesh are splattered thickly on every surface of the room and blood has been dripping from the ceiling, creating miniature stalactites. The smell is pretty horrible.

The damage to the bodies is horrifying. I've seen similar damage on the victims of car-bombs, but there are none of the tell-tale marks of shrapnel or burns consistent with explosives. It looks like a carnosaur went through them. As we move through the mess, I make out pieces of body armour, hyper-carbon helmets, and more than one assault rifle. These were heavily armed men and something went through them like a whirlwind.

Normally I don't have a problem with dead people, but these men are so very, very dead, and that gets to me. The pile of dead flesh reminds me of something, but I can't remember what. Whatever it is, it's not good. Piles of bodies seldom are.

Who, or whatever did this to them certainly has a knack for mayhem. Murder is an acquired taste, and killing on this scale takes a gourmand. Hell, even Wagner is spooked. I can see it in the way he steps over the bodies. He doesn't like this one bit, and neither do I. Getting into that church suddenly lost some of its appeal. There were children living here.

* * *

When we finally find a way into the church through a side door on the upper floor, it's painfully clear that we will find no survivors. The smell is a physical blow of nausea and I have to fight hard to keep my professional attitude up and my protein-bar breakfast down.

The large chamber is stacked with bodies, torn to pieces like the ones in the corridor. As we make our way down the stairs from the upper balcony the stench gets worse. The blood is inches deep on the floor between the pews, still wet and viscous in places.

I look around and the full horror of the place sinks in. This pile of reeking flesh was not too long ago a group of living human beings. Men, women and children. Families. Co-workers. Lovers. Friends. Alive and breathing until they met death at the hands of an unforgiving enemy. An enemy that would not stop until all life in this place had been quenched.

Even though the chances are slim, we still need to search the room for survivors. The odds of anyone having lived through the slaughter and then escaped death from suffocation or blood-poisoning in this place are virtually zero. But, like most people on this planet would claim, miracles do happen.

"I'm not going out there." Finn shakes his great shaggy head.

"Yes, you are. It's just a bunch of dead guys. There's nothing to be afraid of."

"Thorfinn, son of Ragnvald –"

"– is never afraid, yes, I know, so what the fuck are you griping about? Come on."

We break out our respirators and carefully make our way out into the room. Walking is difficult in the carnage. Everywhere there are bodies or parts of bodies, and no matter how hard we try to avoid it, stepping on some of them is unavoidable. Slipping and stumbling we make our way to the altar where most of the bodies are gathered. They are piled five layers deep in places and most of them are only ever going to be identified by dental records or DNA-matching. We search every nook and cranny of the hall for a live one but find none. Our target is not among the dead, either.

"Who would do something like this?" Wagner finally gasps through his mask, his eyes wild behind the reinforced glass shield.

"I don't know, Finn, I don't know." I'm not a big fan of the Redeemers, and I usually don't want to get involved in shit like this, but when someone starts killing children I can't look the other way. There are some things you just don't do and expect to get away with. The people who did this are going down. No matter who they are.

My dark thoughts are interrupted when Wagner steps on a severed arm and slips in the mess. With a roar he goes crashing into the putrefying pile of corpses. Bodies come tumbling down on top of him with the wettest, nastiest sound you could never imagine. Skulls collide, elbows snap, rib-cages crack and bury him in dead people's remains.

"*Fuck-fuck-fuck-fuck*," I hear him screaming beneath the corpses. I lunge forward and dig through the pile. I search for his hand and find many, wet and cold and slippery. Then his massive slab of a hand comes shooting out of the gore and I grab him around the wrist and heave with all my might. With superhuman effort I manage to haul him from the pile and back on his feet.

"*Fuck-fuck-fuck*," is all he screams as he desperately wipes the muck from his face. He's covered in blood, faeces, and the juices of rotting corpses and there are pieces of people in his hair and beard. I can bet you my mother's wedding ring he's happy he's wearing a full face mask. Even through the mask I can taste the putrefaction in the air. I tear a piece of bloodstained cloth from the altar and wipe the carbon glass shield for him.

His eyes are huge and bulging behind the mask.

"*Fuck*, that was bad," he gasps, barely able to breathe.

"Aw, come on, you big baby. You've had worse." I need him to focus. Whoever did this could still be around, and if they are, Wagner's screaming will have alerted them to our presence. We need to get going. There is nothing we can do for these people, and our only chance to find out what happened here is to find some surveillance feeds.

Wagner goes into a long tirade in his native Norse, but I'm not listening. Something has caught my eye under the pile of corpses. When I pulled Wagner free, some of the bodies got dislodged and scattered across the floor. Underneath one of them is something small, round, and brass-coloured. Why the hell is there a spent cartridge beneath the bodies? These people were unarmed and they don't look like gunshot victims.

Or do they?

Wagner's oaths recede into the background as I crouch down in the mess and start examining the bodies. For the first time I truly see them, and not what my shocked brain tells me to see.

These cuts are surgical. The people in this chamber have been sliced with something incredibly sharp, not at all like the armed men in the corridor who had been torn apart. On closer inspection, I realise all of these corpses show bullet wounds in addition to the cuts, and from their relative positions it's clear the bullet wounds came first. Now, why would someone first gun down all these people and then go to the horrible trouble of cutting them up with knives? It doesn't make any sense. No sense at all.

Unless…

Unless the people who did this wanted to cover up their presence here by blaming whoever or whatever killed the guards outside. Horrifying though they were, the corpses in the corridors were soldiers, killed in battle. These people were civilians, slaughtered in cold blood. Besides, these people seem to have died more recently than the ones outside. About a day later, I'd say. Some of the blood is still wet.

What the hell is going on here? What have we got ourselves into? Damn you, Gray. This was supposed to be a simple kidnapping operation, not a bloody mystery bug hunt.

"Wagner, quit griping. Work to do." I get back up from my crouch. There's no need to inform Wagner of this new development. He's spooked enough as it is from his close encounter with the dead. "We need to find their surveillance centre and grab ourselves some feeds."

As we leave the room and enter the corridor, I let out the breath I never knew I held. I've never been happier to enter a dark, confined space filled with who knows what in the way of automated defence systems. I don't care. Them I can deal with.

Finding the surveillance centre is easy.

Unfortunately, someone has beaten us to it. The place is shot to shit. Looking around, it's soon obvious that not a single storage device has survived, and I very much doubt we can salvage a single terabyte of data from any of these machines. *Shit.*

Someone broke into this bunker and went to a lot of trouble to make sure that no-one can find out what really happened here. Which makes it imperative that we do.

We bring out the floorplans for the bunker and soon find the backup storage unit. It's in what looks like a sealed security locker in the hall not too far from the main surveillance centre. It's easy to find.

"Wagner, do your stuff." I wave at the small reinforced door in the wall. Wagner grunts and slides his great knife in the crack between the door and the doorframe. He heaves on it, and the muscles ripple across his back, making his tattoos move like an animated movie. The tendons stand out like ropes in his neck as he slowly forces the door open. I can't help being a little impressed.

Inside are row upon row of surveillance racks. The stuff is old, but it looks like it's been well maintained and as far as I can tell most of the lights that should blink are blinking.

Of course the data turns out to be quantum encrypted.

That shouldn't prove too much of a problem. Q.E. was hot stuff during the war forty years ago, but after the discoveries in the Antares accelerator, these days any kid with a console can crack it. Gray's geeks will have it open in no time at all, leaving us the chance of making it home in time for a beer tonight. I really need to get drunk after this mess.

"OK, Finn. We got what we came for." I drop the memory cube in a chest pocket. "We're out of here."

"Fuck yeah."

* * *

The next robot sentry is just around the corner, but this time we come prepared. As soon as we spot it, Wagner is there with another fragmentation grenade and he barely stops to adjust his aim before letting it sail through the air. He times the throw perfectly and the grenade detonates in the air, a metre below the machine. It's blown it into a thousand razor sharp pieces of shrapnel and fizzing electronics.

The target destroyed, I step around the corner and discover an unexpected bonus effect of the explosion. The blast has thrown open a door next to the turret. I cast a quick glance inside to make sure it's empty, then prepare to move along when something makes me stop in mid-stride. Wagner bumps into me from behind, almost knocking me off my feet.

"Watch where you're going, asshole," Wagner says in that rumbling voice of his.

"Watch it yourself, big guy. I'm point man, you follow my lead." He gives me a strange look of contempt and I continue quickly, "Anyhow, look at this." I prod the door with the barrel of my PDW and it falls off the frame, the hinges destroyed in the blast.

Inside is a smallish room, devoid of any decorations or furnishings except a big Redeemer banner covering one wall and an overturned camera tripod. On the floor are the torn remains of three men in once white clothes and headgear. And an excessive amount of blood.

Watching the recognition slowly creep across Wagner's face is almost funny, and I can't help smiling at the sight. This is the room where they shot the video.

One of the men still holds the curved knife and I squat and carefully pry it from his cold, dead fingers. The DNA in the dried blood on the blade could give us a name for our man. As I straighten to get back up, something else catches my eye and I freeze. Written on the wall in the blood of the fallen, like a severely messed up child's finger painting, is a message.

A message that changes everything.

I'm coming for you Gray.

So much for not getting involved.

The Creature

The creature is feasting on something raw and bloody, half submerged in the sand in front of his eyes. It's an arm, torn to shreds by rifle fire. There's a watch strapped to it. His watch. His arm.

His mouth tastes of blood and sand.

He tries to roll over in the shallow water and discovers the arm is no longer part of his body. Where it used to attach there is only a bloody stump, covered in sand and dirt. The black tendons and sinews that used to move it hang like dead worms from his flesh. Fuck. That complicates matters.

With difficulty he manages to roll over on his back and checks his chest and abdomen for damage. Apart from the arm there's only a dozen punctures from small-arms fire. Some of them are still bleeding, but they are already scarring over. The new skin is raw and brittle, and he can feel bullets grinding against bone deep inside. He has had worse. The arm will still take some time and resources to regrow.

He's lying on the beach of the raging river beneath the waterfall. The spray from the fall is heavy in the air, and everything is moist and cool now that the sun has dipped beneath the mountains. Over the rim of the waterfall far above he can see a black column of fat oily smoke rolling skywards, reaching for the heavens. Above it all, Arcadia is still burning in the sky. The world has been burning for hours, and the oxygen in the atmosphere is now almost used up, and the planet will soon be a dead shell. A black tombworld for the millions of souls he released. What a glorious memorial to the Cherubim's victory over the Terrans.

Thoughts of his men bring back the memories of the massacre.

With a dark heart he remembers how his faithful soldiers flocked to him, shielded him with their bodies even as they were torn to pieces by the metal storm. He remembers how he grabbed their hands, and he remembers how they grabbed his back. He remembers how they pushed him over the edge of the waterfall to safety, and he remembers the drop. The impact. The darkness. Light. Bubbles. Water everywhere. He remembers how the river engulfed him, drew him down, rolled him, crushed him against the rocks deep below, and he remembers thinking it was a just punishment for failing his men. He should have seen Gray's betrayal coming. He should have saved them. He should have died in their stead, but he didn't, and now it's up to him to avenge them.

The howling of great engines above brings him back to the present.

A dark military flier comes in low over the river. Its jets thrash the trees into a frenzy and he is peppered with fallen twigs and leaves. As it moves slowly downriver, the shouts of Gray's mercenaries move up the riverbed, closing in on his position. He can't stay here.

He knows Gray cannot afford to let him live, and so his only hope of getting off this moon is fooling the hired muscle into believing he's dead. If he's fast enough he can get to Gray before the old man realizes he got away.

His bare hands will crush Gray's body, and his knowledge will crush the man's standing. Gray will die in both flesh and reputation, and the general will savour every moment. He will eat Gray's heart and make the old man watch. Gray's suffering will be legendary.

The approaching mercenaries and the detached arm give him an idea. The little creature scuttles off as he grabs the severed limb and rolls over on his back.

"Hey," he shouts to the heavens. There's a rise in the voices of the soldiers and the flier banks around and heads back up the valley. He gets up on his haunches. It's an awkward move with only one arm.

"Hey, over here," he shouts and then dashes off into the jungle. He dives into cover behind a tree just as the mercenaries open fire. The noise is deafening. Trees and roots and fruits are turned into splinters as the bullets carve their deadly trails through the forest. As he had hoped, the flier opens fire with all it's got and the beach and the nearby forest explode under the heavy ordnance, leaving a deep crater in the wet ground.

Without waiting for the debris to settle he gets to his feet and throws the severed arm onto the beach. It will be found; conclusions will be drawn. And he will have time to get away.

* * *

Gray's mercenaries emerge from the jungle on a wide line, weapons at the ready. Meridian moves silently around them, keeping out of their line of sight as he circles them. The soldiers look warily about them as if hunting a great beast of the forest. And they are not far off.

The deadliest thing in the forests on the general's home world of Elysium is the carnosaur. Fifteen tonnes of rage armed with foot-long claws, teeth the length of a man's arm, and a spine of razor-sharp ivory spikes crowning its back. The carnosaur is the greatest predator on all the known worlds.

Meridian killed his first carnosaur when he was a nine.

He wasn't supposed to kill it. They were meant to evade them, to prove to their tutors that they had learnt the skills necessary to master the jungle at night. The test was simple. Survive in the forest until the sun rose and you passed. No points for second place.

As night settled over them that night, he could hear the other boys screaming one by one as the creatures of the night got to them. Some of them he thought he recognised by their voices, and he knew he would never see them again. He didn't care. He found the whole exercise boring. Evading the great, lumbering beasts was no sport, so he decided to try and kill one, just for fun. The easiest way to get to one would be while it was feeding, and the closest source of food was his squad brothers.

He settled down to wait in the highest branches of the tree where Jeremiah had made camp. Jer was one of the tough guys of the brood. He liked hurting the smaller boys and relished bullying them around. To little Caspar, Jeremiah was a god.

A head taller than Caspar, Jer was a natural leader. Little Caspar had watched him, and he had learnt, and he had practised in front of the mirror in his cell at night. He had mastered the skills, and he knew that he would one day be a great leader of men. Jeremiah would not. Jeremiah would die that night.

It was so simple. All he had to do was wait for Jer to fall asleep on his branch from exhaustion. Then he climbed down from his hideaway, cut Jeremiah's hamstrings, and pushed him from the tree. Before the poor boy understood what had happened to him, his terrified screams brought the carnosaur.

They found little Caspar the next morning, sitting smiling in a shaft of sunlight on the creature's bony skull, his angelic face war-painted with its stinking blood.

When they found out what he'd done to Jeremiah they were stunned. Then they gave him a squad.

* * *

The memory brings a smile to his face as he silently crouches in the foliage behind the line of soldiers of fortune. The flier hovers in the air above. It tears at their clothes with its jet engines, it deafens their ears with noise, and blinds their eyes with whirling dust. Amateurs. Fucking amateurs. He's close enough to feel the sting of debris from the flier's jets and, it's too bad he can't kill them. It would be so easy. But, for his plan to work, they all need to live and report their findings to Gray.

He watches them converge on the beach. They move slowly up to the crater, weapons at the ready. One of them looks inside while the rest of them turn around and cover the area with their weapons. They are not taking any chances.

"We got him," the man calls to his comrades and the general can see their shoulders relax. "Direct hit. There's just an arm left of him. Fucking A." He can hear their harsh laughter even above the howling of the jets.

The general smiles. They will not be laughing when Gray finds out they let him get away.

Silently, he turns away and makes his way through the jungle, back to the waterfall. The ancient rock is slick with lichen, but it's rough and full of hand- and footholds. He uses the waterfall as cover and climbs up the overhang behind the sheets of water. It's slow going with only one arm, but he is in no hurry. His ride has not yet arrived.

When he reaches the top he raises his head over the rim and surveys the scene of the slaughter. A few heavily armed guards stand around a pile of the bloody remains of his beloved Cherubim.

The sickly sweet smell of roasted flesh hangs on the air.

Next to the corpses is a much smaller pile of blackened orbs. The severed and burnt heads of his men. A bloody machete is stuck in the dry earth next to the pile.

He locks the pain deep inside his chest where he can use it to fuel his hatred, and settles down to wait for his ticket off this forsaken moon.

* * *

When night falls and the lights on the meat-patrol flier come on, Meridian gets ready to move.

Paramedics in white HazMat suits have long since finished lifting the decapitated Cherubim into wooden coffins and are starting to load them onto the flier for transport back to Elysium and their military funeral. Gray's mercenaries are not paid to ask questions, but even they would find it strange if the bodies of dead soldiers were left for the creatures of the night.

There are only a few coffins left and the pilot has already turned on the engines, no doubt hoping to be back home in time for dinner. Meridian waits for the paramedics to pick up another coffin and carry it away before making his move. Under the cover of darkness, he crawls up to the coffin furthest from the light. He slides the blade of his knife under the lid and gives it a careful heave. The cheap lock squeaks as it breaks and he freezes. Precious seconds tick by as he waits for the soldiers to come investigate, but the whine of the jets warming up must have drowned out the noise.

Soon he has the lid open. The smell inside is horrible, even though the body is sealed in a white body bag. He ignores the stench and crawls inside to lie down on the slick and cold body of one of his men. One of his friends.

He closes the lid and snaps it shut.

It's not a second too soon.

He hears muffled voices through the wood and feels the coffin being carelessly hoisted from the ground.

"Fuck, this one's heavy," one of the paramedics say.

"Shut up and move," another voice replies, and he feels the coffin being carried away.

A few moments later the coffin is dropped unceremoniously onto a metal floor.

"Who were these guys?" he hears the first voice asking.

"No idea," replies the second voice.

"I heard they were special forces who got caught by the Arcadians and executed," says a third voice.

"I never heard of Arcadians beheading prisoners," says the second voice.

"What the hell? Are you a Terran sympathizer or something?" says the first voice.

"Fuck no, I'm just saying."

"Shut up and get the last ones on board. We need to go," calls a fourth voice from further away.

"Yes sir," calls voice one. The sounds of receding footsteps echo through the hull, and the general is left on his own in the darkness and the silence. He unzips the body bag beneath him and wriggles inside like a travesty of a man snuggling up to his lover. It is not pleasant, but it is necessary. He must rebuild his body, and his brother will not mind giving up his dead flesh.

As the engines engage and the flier rises into the air he feels his body start to heal. One final time he rides into battle with his brothers. To vengeance.

Gray will not see this coming.

Good Locks and an Apple a Day

I'm coming for you Gray.

The writing was on the wall.

Clearly, Gray is not telling me everything about this mission, and that disturbs me. Without all the pieces I can't solve this puzzle, so for the time being I think I'll leave Gray out of the loop.

And so, once Winger's chopper pick-up gets us safely back in the city, I send Wagner out to find us a neutral hacker while I go to find a doctor to see to my shot-up face. Now, here I am, back under the oppressing Ceiling of the Bottoms, leaning against the concrete wall outside a G-porn theatre, sucking a snake grass pipe and listening to the news blaring from the small TV of a rickety fast food stall.

There's a disorienting buzz in my head and a really bad feeling in my gut, and it's not the sweet smoke of the snake grass. This whole mess feels like it might blow up in my face at any moment and get us all killed, and I haven't got a fucking clue about what's going on.

"... Cardinal Santoro returned earlier today from the conclave at Kandahar. The talks went well, according to a church spokesperson..."

Good for him.

I pour the rest of the tasteless beer down my throat and drop the empty bottle next to its dry brothers. The cut shop across the street is just the kind of place I'm looking for. Not too fancy, not too shabby, and random enough not to have been bugged by our competition. The last thing I need now is another showdown with the Combine. After last month I've had enough of them for a lifetime. The light is still on behind the boards covering the single ground-floor window. It's late, and the doctor should be going to bed at any moment now.

"... the police report a man jumped from his tenth storey apartment this afternoon after losing large sums of money at a black market gambling hall. According to neighbours, the man is a well-known professor of astronomy and has never had problems with gambling before. It's a warning to all of us that you cannot serve both God and Mammon. In other news..."

Poor bastard. I crack another beer from the six-pack at my feet. My guess is the guy discovered something celestial that went against the church doctrines and the inquisition got to him. This place is so fucked up.

I watch the crowd of late-night revellers through the pipe smoke as I wait. Sad as this place may be, this is where you come to have fun in Masada. The church has outlawed just about every vice you could think of, but they turn a blind eye and a deaf ear to what happens down in the Bottoms. Cardinal Santoro is smart enough to realise that if people are not allowed their little depravities every now and then they will eventually explode and revolt. This way the people even get to feel they are spitting oppression in the eye when they go out drinking and whoring. What most of them don't realise is that everything that happens down here is by the cardinal's leave. Everybody has to pay tithe, so sayeth the law, even if you run your business nowhere near the law. Apparently God has decided it is so. Very kind of him to see to the recent financial troubles of his church.

The shop-front of the clinic is no more than a narrow door in the massive concrete wall, crammed between a titty bar and a grimy grocers. Not the best place to put your shop if you want to attract customers. Unless you are targeting a niche market that seldom lives long enough to get bladder problems or arthritis. Customers that tend to chronically suffer from more exotic ailments like multiple stabbings and perforating gunshot wounds. People like me.

It's long after closing hours, but that shouldn't be a problem. Late hours and a gunshot wound usually means a lot of cash is about to change hands, and I've yet to find a doctor who'd say no to the extra income. Since auto-diagnosis machines became cheap and reliable enough, the pay in the health business is not as good as it used to be. When the machines took over the day-to-day dispensing of pills, the human doctors had to turn their scalpels elsewhere to bring in the dough.

And there's my cue.

The light in the window goes out and it's time for me to move. I take a last drag on the pipe, tap it out against the heel of my combat boot, and push off from the wall. Like a good boy, I look carefully both ways before crossing the street. The people of this city drive like they believe death by car crash is the quickest way to paradise.

I make it to the other side with nothing to show for having risked my life except a good soak from the rusty rain, and I take cover against the downpour in the doorway. The sounds of traffic and human voices intermingle, all working together to provide a pleasant metropolitan soundtrack celebrating life and commerce. The ubiquitous street preachers are everywhere on the sidewalks, dampening the spirits of everyone around them with their doomsday tales about how the end of the world is nigh. Is it just me, or are they unusually fervent tonight?

"The lord Jesus Christ has returned. The day of judgement is upon us." A crazy-eyed, straggly-bearded guy wearing nothing but a soaked, transparent, and unpleasantly clingy nightgown stumbles down the street between honking cars, trying to outshout the traffic with his prophecies. Stuff like that execution video tends to spread like wildfire on the feeds. Especially in a place like Masada, the Christian equivalent of a savannah at the end of an unusually hot dry season. Everybody is waiting for the saviour to return one of these days.

When I push the buzzer next to the door, nothing happens, and I have to resort to the old-fashioned way of requesting entry to the premises. Pounding the door for a full minute gives me nothing for my efforts except a sore palm and strange looks from passersby.

"Can't you see the place is closed?" a drunk guy shouts at me. "Fuck off and try again in the morning."

I flip him the finger, and he moves along screaming abuse as his friends drag him away to avoid a fight. Too bad, I could use some exercise.

Another minute of pounding and the light turns on again inside the shop.

"I'm coming, I'm bloody coming," shouts a gravelly voice from inside. It sounds like the good doctor is a man in his late seventies who has spent his entire life disregarding his own advice about giving up whisky and cigarettes. He opens the door and as always I'm surprised to find my mental image smashed, ground into the dirt and pissed upon by reality.

The doctor turns out to be a man in his early thirties, with fair hair standing on end, and your average olive complexion. He looks unfairly fit and healthy for a guy who lives and works in a place like this, and he must be very fond of whisky and cigarettes to get that cool voice.

"Do you know what fucking time it is?" He clears his throat as he looks at me from behind the safety of numerous security chains. His gaze flicks from my eyes to the bloody bandage around my head and back. "I see. Come back in the fucking morning. I'm closed."

I say nothing. Instead I pass him a wad of bills and a business card. He takes the money, rifles through the pile, and sighs. Then he reads the card.

He's good. It's barely noticeable, but the momentary pause and short intake of breath tells me he's understood the implications of the title and company name on that card.

"You had me at the money. No need to hammer the point home, Mr. Let me guess. Gunshot wound to the face? Or have you always been this pretty?" He inspects my soaked and bloody bandage as he removes the chains and opens the door. I hang back, waiting for him to invite me in.

"Well, come the fuck in and close the damn door behind you. What are you? A damn vampire that has to be bloody invited or you'll fucking explode? Well, consider yourself bloody invited. I hope this is a goddamn matter of national security or I swear to God I'll kill you myself."

I step across the threshold with a tiny smile deep inside. You can't be too careful these days. Had he been in the employ of one of our competition and had recognized me he would just have let me in and murdered me during treatment. Instead he seems to be exactly what he looks like; a down-at-luck, tired-as-hell, hard-working idealist with a mouth foul enough to embarrass many a dockworker. I like this guy.

"Someone got jealous of my pretty face and decided to do something about it." I step into his office and the doctor closes the door behind me and engages the electronic locks before putting all the ancient security chains back into place. In a neighbourhood like this I can't blame him. Good locks and an apple a day keeps the doctor away as my old man used to say. They will do you no good if you're locked with the doctor on the inside, though.

The doctor motions towards a white vinyl examination table in the middle of the cramped room. "Please, sit down, Mr…?"

"Nonya." I remove my jacket.

"Mr Nonya? Nonya as in…"

"Nonya business." I sit on the edge of the table.

"Right… Got it. No more small talk." He mimes a zipper closing his lips with long fingers and turns on the sharp lights over the table.

"Well then, let's have a look at you," the doctor says, not entirely unsympathetically.

He starts by removing the bandage Wagner wound around my head. It stings like hell when he tears the soggy bandage from the crusted blood on my face. The bleeding has stopped, but the gauze is red with my blood when it comes off. Still, not as much as I feared. I might still live to die another day. When this crap is over, I'm taking all my back pay and going on all-inclusive holiday to the beaches at San Cristobal. Preferably with a busty blonde or two on my arm.

"That doesn't look so bad." He twists my head this way and that. "There's some minor bruising but I don't think this will even need stitches."

"Say what?"

"Have a look." He hands me a small mirror and I can see for myself that there's a lot of dried blood but no deeper cuts. And here I was, thinking I'd been seriously hurt. I look like shit though. About the only part of my face I recognize under the bruises is the brown of my eyes, and even that looks a bit off.

"I'm going to do a scan just the same, to see if there is any deeper trauma. From the looks of it, you got off lightly. No major damage to the brain." He shines a small torch into my eyes. "Unless you used to be a damn bundle of joy and the epitome of courtesy before you got shot, in which case I'd say there has been some major fucking damage done. If the scan shows nothing of interest, you will be out of here in no time."

"Great, but do you think you could hurry this up a little? I've got places to be, things to do. People to hurt."

"The scan only takes a bloody minute. Patience is a virtue, you know. So says the good book." It sounds like he actually believes it. "Lie down."

"Sir, yes sir." I do as he asks and the clinical smells of disinfectants and lingering death envelop me like the waters receive a drowning man as I lie down. To me the smells of a doctor's office always remind me of the first time I drank myself senseless. Someone had an older brother who knew someone who got us a bottle of medical-grade firewater, and ever since then the smell of pure alcohol makes me remember that night. It was the night I kissed Akinyi. She was the cutest girl in class and I was very much in love with her. I wonder what became of her. Probably became a too-young mother raising five kids by different fathers on her own. The curse of the pretty ones. At a young age they discover they don't have to do anything to get ahead in the world. People just give them what they want, until one day when life catches up with them and they realise there are much younger, prettier girls around. And the kids need new clothes.

The doctor takes out an antiquated keyboard and punches a few commands. A mechanical arm with what looks like a miniature grenade-launcher at the end moves into view from somewhere beneath the table. I must have flinched because the doc puts a very soft hand on my shoulder. Why do doctors always have soft hands?

"Relax. This is not going to hurt. If you promise me not to cry you will get a plastic toy afterwards."

"I can't fucking wait."

The machine moves around my head in a slow arc, making a low-pitched humming sound while the doctor punches in new commands as he watches a holo-screen. I relax on the vinyl surface of the table, trying to make myself comfortable.

"How come, doctor, that you, apparently a man of God, has got such bad language? Isn't swearing a sin?"

"Oh, the good lord doesn't mind a bad word every now and then. He cares about what's in your heart, and my heart is clean as the insides of a fucking autoclave."

"Interesting philosophy. That your own interpretation of the book?"

"Who's to say what's right and what's wrong? The cardinal has his version of the truth, and I have mine. No harm done as long as we pay obedience to the one true God."

"Whatever you say doc. Each to his own, live and let live and all the rest of the yada-yada, I suppose."

"Interesting philosophy." He adjusts a knob on the scanner for some arcane medical purpose. Then again, he could be doing it just for show for all I know. "Is that your own interpretation?" There's only a hint of sarcasm in his voice.

I can't help a small smile and he goes on. "You don't strike me as a man who would turn the other cheek, Mr Nonya." He continues to analyse the images from the scanner as he talks.

I shrug, drawing an irritated look from the good doctor that tells me to lie still. "Well, I try. I believe in giving people a second chance. But I'm also a follower of the ancient truth of three-strikes-you're-out. Fool me once, shame on you. Fool me twice, shame on me. Fool me three times and that's the last thing you'll ever do. So far, you're doing alright, doc."

He doesn't look away from the screen, but I can see a small smile playing at the corner of his lips. "I always thought that saying went 'Fool me once, shame on you. Fool me – you can't get fooled again'." I can't help but smile. A religious man with a sense of humour? What on earth will they think of next?

The scan is almost over when his smile disappears and he hits a button to retrace the scan, leaning closer to the screen.

"Now, what the hell was that?"

"What?"

He doesn't reply but runs the machine back and forth a couple of times, adding resolution to the three-dimensional image.

"Fuck me sideways, that's weird."

"What?"

He sits back, scratching his forehead while looking at the image. The light from the screen illuminates his face from beneath, giving it an almost comically ominous sheen. His body hides the holo-screen from me so I can't see what he's seeing.

"What?"

"You might want to see this."

"Why?" I swing my legs over the side of the table and sit up.

He turns to me. "There's a fucking machine in your head."

Old Bottle of Scotch and a Wooden Spoon

"What?"

"There's a machine in your head."

"What the hell are you talking about?"

Why would there be a machine in my head? What kind of machine? Who put it there?

So many questions. So many answers not coming my way.

"Look." The doc swings the screen around, and sure enough, rendered in bright, friendly red, a decidedly mechanical-looking item is lodged at the base of my brain. He twists the 3D image around to make it perfectly clear that the machine really is located inside my body and is not an optical illusion. It's the size of a golf ball, perfectly spherical, and anchored to the bone on the underside of my skull with short metallic legs. I reach up a trembling hand and touch the back of my head. I can barely feel it under the skin.

"Now, this might sound bloody funny, but have you been abducted by aliens lately?" the doctor asks. "Because that is the only rational explanation I can come up with. Does it hurt?"

"No, it bloody well doesn't hurt. If it did I would have gone to the doctor sooner. And a friendlier one at that."

"Sticks and stones, my friend. Sticks and stones."

"How long has it been there?" I stroke the skin over the implant.

"From the looks of it, it's been there for quite some time. At least a couple of years, judging by the lack of scar tissue."

"What the...?" I try to remember when something like that might have been inserted, but I can't think of a single time I've been sedated over the last few years.

"Now, what do you want to do about it?" the doctor asks. "Is it supposed to be there?"

"No, it's bloody well not supposed to be there."

I grab the lapel of his white coat, pull him halfway out of his chair, and put my nose in his face to really drive the point home. "And I want you to make it not be there anymore. Understand?"

"OK, OK. Jesus, Mary and Joseph and all the apostles and the angels of heaven, you've got a seriously lousy temper, man."

"Wouldn't you, if you'd just been shot in the face, insulted by your doctor and then learnt that you've got a fucking machine in your head?"

"Fair enough. I think I'm going to have to do some serious digging if I'm going to get that thing out." He pushes his chair back from the desk and picks up a clear plastic panel from a side table. It turns into a screen displaying the 3D image from the scanner as he holds it in front of my neck. "It's not located too close to the spine," he says as he moves the panel around, getting a feel for the location of the thing, "so I should be able to do it without paralysing you or turning you into a vegetable."

Well, whoop dee-fucking-doo.

"Do it, doc."

"It's gonna cost you."

"Just do it. I want that bloody thing out."

"Alright." The doc gets up and walks over to an hermetically sealed cabinet. He pulls on a pair of latex gloves from a dispenser before opening the doors, and I can see it's full of medical equipment. The stuff that first catches my eye is his first-rate collection of cutting tools. I use several of those myself in my daily trade, and I can tell the good doctor really knows his knives. If I had found that impressive array of slicing tools in anyone else's closet, I'd start to think he was moonlighting as a serial killer. I realise I don't know the doctor that well. Maybe this was not such a good idea after all.

He removes a set of small stainless-steel scalpels and a big pair of vicious-looking pliers from the wall of the cabinet. At times like these a vivid imagination is a curse.

He brings his finds back and places them on a stainless-steel tray along with some other medical paraphernalia. Then he stands peering down at me, a troubled look on his face.

"Right, I'd recommend anaesthetisation for this procedure, but the choice is all yours," he says as he picks up one of the scalpels and inspects its sharpness with his rubber-clad thumb. Apparently satisfied, he places the scalpel back on the tray and looks me straight in the eye, one eyebrow raised inquiringly.

The idea of being unconscious in the operating theatre of a doctor I just met doesn't particularly appeal to me, and even less so after I've seen his impressive collection of knives. I want to be awake if something happens. That metal thing could be about to demand to be taken to our fucking leaders, for all I know.

"No thanks, I think I'll go for a local."

"Thank God for that, at least. For a moment there I thought you were going to go for the old bottle of scotch and a wooden spoon to bite down on." His laughter is just a tad high-pitched, and his forehead wears a thin veneer of perspiration. He's nervous, and I can understand why.

"OK, lie down on your stomach and we will have that thing out in no time." The bravado is hardly convincing, but I do as he asks. He picks up an auto injector from the tray. It trembles slightly in his grip.

"This might sting a bit," he says as he puts a rubber gloved hand on the back of my neck and applies the injector. The cold steel against my skin is uncomfortably reminiscent of all the times someone has put a gun to my head, but it's not too bad. I'm used to that.

He's not lying. It does sting a bit.

But then the whole back of my head disappears in a vague fuzzy cloud, and it takes a while before I realise the scraping sounds I'm hearing is the doctor cutting my flesh open.

"How does it look doc?" I've got my cheek pressed against the antiseptic vinyl cover of the bed and speaking is difficult.

"This is not the work of an amateur, I'll tell you that much. I'll know more when I get… all the way… down to…" The sound of metal on metal, muffled by blood and tissue, tells me he's found it.

"Well, hello there. OK, let's see if we can get this bloody thing out."

"What do you see doc? Talk to me."

"It's a metal sphere, about three centimetres in diameter, anchored to the bone of your skull with some kind of metal legs, probably titanium. I'm going to try cutting the legs to remove the object."

I see him grab the big pair of pliers from the tray before it disappears from view. Then my whole head jerks as he cuts the legs one by one. The sound inside my head is not something I care to describe.

"OK, just one more and we're done."

Finally, the thing comes out with a wet cracking sound. "There." The doctor holds it up into the light, to all the world the perfect image of a happy obstetrician proudly presenting the newborn to the world.

"What is it, doc?"

"I haven't got a fucking clue. It looks military, though."

"Give it here." I prop myself up on my elbows and reach out a hand. With obvious relief he drops the ball into my hand and applies a cotton wad to the back of my head. I can feel something running down my neck.

The ball is warm and slick with blood, and underneath the muck its surface is a dull gunmetal grey. There's a tiny pinprick of red light blinking at one pole, indicating the thing is active. Why would you put a blinking light on a thing intended for implantation? The answer is simple: It was not intended for implantation at all because I realise I've seen one of these before.

It's a remote-controlled detonator. You usually find them in the firing mechanism of nuclear warheads. What the hell is a nuke detonator doing inside my head?

"Can I keep this?" I ask the doc as he starts sewing up the big hole at the base of my skull, the stitches only felt as a dull yanking in my numb skin. "For luck?"

"Be my guest." I can tell from the shudder in his voice that the thing has scared him. And I haven't even told him what it is. Hell, the thing has got me spooked too. Has it always been there? Do we all get them implanted at birth? No, then we would know about them. People do brain scans all the time. First sign of a headache and people scan for tumours, just because they can. No, it's got to be targeted at me. But by who? And why?

I don't know, but I am going to find out. The people who put it there are going to provide me with some answers, whether they want to or not.

These things invariably come with a built-in tracking device, allowing the people in charge to know where a particular nuke is at any given moment.

Chances are that whoever put it there is tracking it, and I can save myself some legwork by letting them come to me.

Meanwhile, I'll just hang on to it. Maybe I can trace the serial number stamped on it, but I won't hold my breath. If they have the resources to get their hands on high military tech like this and have it implanted without me noticing, they will have no problems erasing their tracks. The necessary resources and know-how point to one of the other corporations. The church has the skills, but what would be their motive?

I engage the safety to disarm it in case someone has the sudden urge to trigger it. It would cut me in half if I had in in my pocket when it went.

"Are we done here, doc?" I ask.

The doc pulls off his bloody gloves and throws them in the trash. The back of my neck is starting to pulse dully with pain through the anesthetic. I dread waking up to that pain tomorrow.

"First I'll need to thaw you a new patch of skin to cover that hole in your head." He takes a swab and wipes some of the fresh blood from my neck and smears it on the sensor of a handheld blood analyser. "And that…" he looks at the reading from the machine, waiting for the beep, "…shouldn't be too hard. You are lucky enough to have the most compatible blood-type and gene-map in the known universe. I have plenty of spare parts for you."

He removes what I assume is the vacuum packed skin graft from a shelf packed with similar items and places it in another odd looking machine.

"We have a couple of minutes before the graft is ready. How about a cup of coffee? I'm buying." He's clearly fighting hard to keep his voice under control, and I can see his hand trembling as he wipes the sweat from his forehead with a tissue. Even though he doesn't understand what he's gotten himself mixed up in, he's smart enough to understand that it is bigger than him. Potentially the kind of thing people get disappeared over.

"I guess a whisky would be out of the question?"

"Correct. It doesn't go well with the anesthetic." He leans over to the coffee dispenser placed next to the scanner and presses speed dial. As we wait in silence for the cup to fill, I look at the guy and I've got to admit he handles the situation admirably. His hands shiver and he's sweating profusely, but that's about it.

When the cup is full, he picks it up with only a slight tremble, takes a sip, makes a face and puts the cup down again. It smells good, though.

He kneads his hands together like a freezing man rubs out a chill, seemingly fascinated by the actions of his own extremities. Then he looks up again.

"Are you going to kill me?"

"Depends on whether you ask any more stupid questions."

There's a weak beep from the thawing machine and a short pause from the doctor. "OK, then. Let's do this."

The skin graft is cold and slimy against the back of my head as he lays it out over the sewn up hole in my neck. Then he places a wad of gauze over it and tapes it in place. "There, we're done." He quickly wipes the blood from my neck.

I swing my legs over the side of the table and reach for my jacket.

"Thanks, doc." I pay him generously and add a big tip. "For the pension fund."

He lets out his breath and his body relaxes. "You're welcome." He must have realised that money for the pension fund means I'm not going to retire him on the spot.

"With that I could close my shop tomorrow." He nods at the pile of cash in his hand. "Take damn good care, Mr Nonya. Nice not having you here tonight."

"You're catching on fast, doc." I jump to the floor. "Take care." We shake hands and nod at each other. There is a strange look in his eyes. A mixture of worry for his patient and relief that I'm leaving. The doctor is a good man, but he is not a brave one.

After I close the door behind me and step out into the neon-painted night, I hear all the locks engage behind me before the security chains are pulled back into place. To protect against thieves or to protect against me I don't know, but I don't blame him. I realise I never even learnt his name.

I take a look at the chronograph on my wrist-pad. Witching hour. Still a couple of hours to spend before I have to get back to Wagner and his hacker. From somewhere off in the distance the muffled sound of automatic gunfire echoes down the underground. I step out into the rusty rain to find a bar on this night of knives and mysteries. I don't think I've ever needed a whisky more than I do right now.

The metal sphere is heavy in my pocket.

She Came Recommended

A couple of hours later, I'm back in the bar where I met Wagner. I'm halfway down my first bottle of whisky for the night, I'm in a lousy mood, and I'm still no closer to figuring out what this mess is about or who is behind any of it.

There are just too many questions buzzing around in my head, the whisky is not helping, and the pounding bass lines are doing nothing to improve my headache. The place where the doctor removed the sphere itches like hell. It's almost tingling. I hope it won't get infected.

Who killed all those people in the bunker? And where is the murdered prophet now? The obvious answer is that someone went in, killed everyone and made off with the guy. But who? The church or another sect who wanted to lay their hands on the saviour would be the obvious choice. It could be one of the other corporations, I guess, but my money's on the church. They have both the motive and the resources to pull off something like that. But why the slaughter?

And what the hell does Gray want with the guy? Apparently they have had some dealings in the past, and Gray must have done something to piss the guy off.

And then there's the detonator in my head. Why didn't Gray's doctors find it when they patched me up last week? They must have seen it. Unless they are in on it.

This is exactly the reason why I don't want to get involved in these things. It's always too bloody complicated. Thank the powers that be for whisky. I take a big drink from my glass and let the smoky taste of peat burn my worries away.

All I know right now is that we need to hack that memory cube to see if there are any clues on the video feeds from the bunker and then find a geneticist who can analyse the DNA on the knife.

Then we just have to find the bastard.

I type a quick status report to Gray on my wristband communicator. I just want to let him know we're back in town and that we might have a lead to follow up. I don't want to tell him any specifics before I know if I can trust him. A couple of seconds later a chime tells me Gray is online. He's obviously not asleep yet. Old people tend to sleep very little I've noticed, and Gray is very old. I pick up the call.

"Excellent, Asher. Come on in and we'll get on it."

Sorry, Gray, no can do.

"It's safer if I handle it alone, boss. We don't want any traces of this pointing back to the company." It sounds very convincing to me.

"Good thinking. That's why I pay you the big bucks." He sounds a bit strange. Maybe he saw through my little lie after all.

"Find out what you can, Asher. Money is not an option."

I like the sound of that.

"Already on it, boss." I hang up.

As if on cue, Wagner steps into the bar, stooping to get his massive bulk through the doorway. In tow he's got a girl in her late twenties, early thirties. Small, cute, spiky red hair, tight body and an attitude to match. She's wearing a short padded leather jacket over a thin white tank top, grey army-issue fatigue trousers and over-sized combat boots. Standard street girl attire, completed by black leather gloves.

The shiny Nishin console protruding from a tattered gym-bag over her shoulder is something of a surprise. That's Wagner's hacker? I'm not one for stereotyping, but she's a little too close to a teenage geek-boy's wet dreams for comfort, and I'm starting to think Wagner has been duped. People like her don't exist in the real world. The whole sexy-street-girl-slash-expert-hacker ploy has been done to death, and I don't buy it for a second.

"Finn, over here," I call over the ludicrously loud music and wave them over.

Wagner slides in opposite me. The girl remains standing, glaring at me.

"She came recommended," Wagner announces apologetically in his thick Norse accent, waving a ham-sized fist in her direction by way of introduction. "She's supposed to be some kind of wiz with the computers."

He keeps waving his hand in the air, miming something I take to be search gestures. Searching for porn is as far as Wagner's net skills go.

I lean back and give her a good once-over, taking great care to give her my best horse-trader's look. Her features look more Asian than the bland multi-cultural melting pot of the Elysian norm, with perhaps a dash of ancestral Africa thrown in for good measure. Several tattoos peek out from the sleeves of the jacket and I realise I was wrong. She's not cute, she's drop-dead adorable, but I know her type. She's just another rich kid, blinded by the night, playing anarchist. She probably doesn't dare buy razors for fear of slashing her wrists in a tantrum of defiant angst. Why the hell did Wagner bring her?

"Fuck this, I'm leaving." She throws her hands in the air. "I didn't come here to be drooled over by some creepy guy." She turns on the worn heels of her army boots and walks away between the tables, presenting us with a tantalising look at a very perky behind. Damn. Maybe I was mistaken and she really does know what she's doing. This girl is a pro.

"Did you say you were a hacker or a hooker?" I call after her receding back-side. That brings her to a halt under a red spotlight.

"No, I didn't," she shouts in return, her back still towards us, head turned to one side, red fringe falling across her forehead in a carefully nonchalant tangle. She shifts her weight to one leg, showing off more of that alluring behind. "Why?"

"If you're as good with that console as you are with the theatrics, the job's yours."

Damn, I want to squeeze that ass.

"The pay any good?" She turns around, all signs of theatre gone. She's all business as she comes walking back to the booth, with a careful swagger in her step as if walking a tightrope or a catwalk. There's also a dangerous glint in her baby browns that actually gets to me. There's more to this girl than meets the eye. Mental note to self: don't underestimate her.

"Ten K for cracking the protection on this." I hold the scratched memory cube up into the light, shaking it like a box of matches under the battered lamp hanging low over the table. "Shouldn't take you more than twenty minutes or so if you're any good." I set the cube down in the middle of the table and lean back against the seat. "That's a lot of credits per second."

"Twenty minutes, huh?"

"Or thereabouts."

"Why don't you crack it yourself, then, if you're such an expert on computer security?" She crosses her arms and stands looking down at me expectantly. The lamp illuminates her from her sweet cleavage down, leaving her face in shadow. Why do I get the feeling that it's very much intentional?

The way she holds her arms a little awkwardly tells me she's wearing something bulky in a shoulder holster under the leather jacket. A packing hacker. Interesting. Pimps usually don't allow that. Their paying customers tend to die unexpectedly when they do.

"Maybe I just enjoy paying obscene amounts of cash to rude people for doing routine stuff?" The fact that she didn't even flinch at the mention of the insane pay tells me she's already sold on the job. Ten K might not get her out of the Bottoms, but if she can hide it from her pimp it will make her life a lot easier.

"OK, I'll do it. But not here. I need the stuff at my place. I'll bring it back to you tomorrow, cracked and cleaned."

Nice try. I give her a lopsided smile.

"I don't think so. We spent a lot of blood, sweat, and tears getting hold of this little baby, and where it goes, we go."

She considers this for a moment, then shrugs.

"Fine, but the food and beer's on you, and no going through my panty-drawers."

I smile again, for real this time. "Deal." I extend my hand. At first she looks at it as if considering turning down the whole deal just to avoid shaking it, but then she reluctantly takes it in hers. The firm grip through the glove is a bit of a surprise. It seems like some of these kids actually work out. Good for them.

I hold her gaze for a couple of seconds longer than is comfortable but she doesn't even blink. We shake and when I let go she snatches her hand back and rubs it on her thigh. Odd. I may be a sleazeball, but I'm not that slimy.

"Shit man, you're hot." She says.

"Thanks."

"No, I mean you're burning up. Are you sick?"

"Nope, I'm healthy as a horse."

Wagner looks ill at ease. The girl just glares at me and keeps rubbing her thigh. She's got some sort of problem, but as long as she's good, I don't have a problem with her problems.

"Is your place nearby?" I ask her.

"First of all, I'm going to the ladies'. And no, you can't come. Then you drive me to my place, I crack your feed, you pay me and we go our separate ways. No hassle, no funny business. And no French benefits. I have friends who know I am here and they will come looking for me if I don't contact them at a certain time. They are the kind of people you don't want to mess with, even if you consider yourself some kind of tough, ex-military hard-ass. Clear?"

I laugh under my breath. "As hyperdiamond. I'm Asher Perez, by the way, and this here's Thorfinn Wagner." Wagner nods at her. She ignores him.

"I'm Suki."

"Suki what?"

"Just Suki." She looks defiantly at me, daring me to make something of it.

Poor girl. No family name means no family. No rich kid then.

"See you in a bit then, 'Just Suki'." I smile and give her a mock salute as she heads to the ladies'. She leaves behind a faint perfume of leather and strawberries. I like her smell.

"Damn it, Finn. Where did you find this kid?" I turn back to Wagner as the restroom door closes on her pert behind. "I didn't know you were one for the ladies." I toast him with a tip of my grimy tumbler and take a long swallow of the piss-coloured, foul-tasting, and insanely expensive whisky.

The Norse are not much for romantic love. Physical strength is what they get off on, and only another Goliath has that in sufficient amounts to impress. Since there are very few Goliath women and they all live at the court of the Jarl on Nifelheim, the rest of them have to make do with each other. Watching two Goliath warriors go at it is an interesting experience. It's not so much making love as a wrestling match to the death between two mountains of muscle. There's no dishonour for the winner, and Goliath porn has an avid fan base.

As a rule, the priests are smart enough not to openly question the Goliaths' choice of bedfellows, but there has been the occasional fire-and-brimstone zealot preaching the hell awaiting all sodomizers. There are not as many of them around as there used to be. The ones who persevere invariably end up on the receiving end of that which they so fervently preach against and no doubt secretly desire. Too bad for them they are already dead by then and their corpses left for the lizards.

"I'm not. I didn't. She found me. I put out a contract and she applied."

"A contract?" I groan. "Why didn't you buy a bloody primetime feed-spot or shout it from the roof of the cathedral while you were at it? This is supposed to be a low-profile job, remember?"

Wagner just shrugs his mountainous shoulders. "Got us a hacker, didn't I?"

I take a deep breath, and slowly let it out again.

"Whatever. If she's any good, we'll be on our way in an hour or so anyway."

Out of the corner of my eye I see the door to the bathroom open and our new pet hacker emerges. That was quick.

She heads for the exit. "You coming or what?" she calls over her shoulder.

I look at Wagner. Wagner looks back. I sink the last of my whisky, make a face, and slam the glass on the tabletop. "Yeah, we're coming." I grab the bottle.

We get up and follow her out of the bar.

The Burial

The burial is beautiful. He knows it is, even if he can't see it. The Elysian army are masters of the far-from-subtle art of military funerals, and he has seen enough of them to know what goes on outside the coffin. From the soft patter on the polished wood, he can tell it's raining. The angels are crying for him and his men. They will soon be crying with joy as he executes his revenge on Nero Praetorius Gray. The blood of the betrayer shall flow tonight.

From outside, the muffled sound of synchronised volleys of rifle fire reach him.

There will be no mourning wives, parents, or children at this funeral because his men have none. Will Gray be there? Probably not. By now he will have learnt that Meridian's body was never retrieved after the slaughter, and he will be very careful about appearing in public until it has been found. There's no way for him to know the general is already back on Elysium, but he won't be taking any chances.

That means Meridian will have to bring the fight to Gray. Many innocent people will die, and that fills the general with sadness. He is not human, but still he swore to protect them, and protect them he did. He gave them a few more precious years to live their ordinary lives in peace, but it will not last. The Terrans will return, and they will return with a vengeance. The Terran senate cannot allow this insubordination to continue. News of the victory over the Terran forces and their Arcadian lackeys will spread across the young empire of humanity and the other colonies will start to reconsider their fragile peace with Earth. That cannot be allowed, and an example must be made. When the limping force returns to Earth with news of defeat, the senate will have no choice but to send a new fleet. A bigger fleet. One which will not be defeated. If they don't, the colonies will revolt and humanity will be plunged into civil war.

The golden dream that was the Unification turned out to be nothing more than yet another coup by power-hungry men in suits. In time, all such empires must come crumbling down under their own weight, and that time is fast approaching for the Terran Commonwealth. It's a rule of nature.

The general jostles as the coffin is lifted and carried to its final resting place. Like the countless military graves he has seen, he knows it will be a precise rectangle of darkness, freshly dug in the immaculately mowed lawn of the perfectly ordered cemetery. He knows there will be a simple white cross engraved with a name and date of death. No date of birth on these crosses, though. That would raise too many eyebrows.

There's a jolt when the coffin comes to rest on the dark soil at the bottom of the grave, and Meridian draws a deep breath in preparation for what is to come.

The first shovelful of wet, heavy dirt is thrown on the lid and he suppresses the urge to scream, to let them know he is down here. Shovel after shovel is dumped over the coffin, the sound increasingly muffled by the mounting layers of dirt. Eventually all sound is extinguished and he is left on his own in the darkness. The only sound is the soft rush of blood in his ears and the gentle hiss of the bodybag around him as he shifts position and starts to explore his prison. Even though there is not much left of the other body in the bag he can hardly move. He unzips the bodybag and pulls the knife from its sheath on his forearm.

The regrown arm works perfectly.

It's a good blade. Gray gave it to him when he was born. They all got one. It's the very blade he used to cut the hamstrings of young Jeremiah all those years ago. It is the same blade he used so many times on countless battlefields, taking countless lives. Now it will serve him again as he digs his way back topside, and it will serve him yet again when he kills Gray.

It's a good blade, and every time he draws it he does so with a sense of pride. This time is no different. The feeling of the cold steel in his hand is comforting, like meeting an old friend and knowing everything will be alright again.

The total darkness inside the coffin smells of expensive satin with an overlay of fresh death. Even his extremely sensitive eyes are blind, but he doesn't need to see. He lets his hands wander over the smooth satin lining, hunting for the seam of the lid. There's no need to panic and waste precious oxygen. It's just a matter of waiting for the night to fall and for the mourners to go home. Gray will be there when he gets up. Gray has been there for a very long time.

The general starts counting.

One-one thousand.

Two-one thousand.

Three-one thousand.

He can taste the flesh of his dead brother on his breath.

* * *

After an hour has passed, night has fallen above and he sets about his task. It's funny that humans still after all these years are so superstitious about cemeteries after dark. Someone once said they are the safest place to be since everyone there is dead. But why take the chance, right?

He has used his spare time well and carved the wood of the coffin until only the barest amount of timber separates him from the masses of dirt above. He's not worried about being crushed. He's only worried about getting stuck, but he has faith in his strength. Say what you want about Gray, but he never does anything half-hearted.

Taking a deep breath, he steels his resolve and stabs the knife through the final layer of lacquered wood and the dirt comes crashing down into the coffin. It fills his mouth, his nose, and his eyes even though he tries to keep them shut. The dirt tastes and smells of death. Generations of rotting corpses have made the soil rich and fertile. He feels a worm wriggle in his mouth and tries to spit it out, but the pressure of the dirt is too great.

The earth is wet and heavy, making it hard to dig, but he is strong, and he is patient. Slowly, very slowly, he pulls the earth down into the hollow of the coffin, giving himself room to claw his way towards the surface The knife in his hand works as both shovel and pickaxe. After only a minute his hands are bleeding freely, the wounds healing almost as fast as they are inflicted.

The air in his lungs is getting stale, but still he battles on against the earth, moving upward, centimetre by centimetre. Every powerful muscle in his body screams with the exertion and yet he struggles on.

With a final push, the knife breaks through into open air and he claws his way up into the rain. The wet soil sucks him back down and tries to keep him below, but he is stronger than the ground. He pulls in a mighty breath of moist night air. It smells of all the flowers and the animals of the night, mixed with the unmistakable reek of humanity. The lights of the city are close, and he can hear the sounds of everyday life over the sound of the rain.

Everyday life. How strange that sounds. The way ordinary people go to work in the morning, leaving the kids at the kindergarten on the way. They sit in their offices all day, shuffle their data and have a cup of coffee with their colleagues. Perhaps they flirt with an intern. In the evening they pick up the kids and go home to dinner. They have no idea about what men like Meridian and the Cherubim are doing in their name. They don't want to know. All so normal and enviable. And then they die.

The rain washes the mud off him, and the white parade uniform regains some of its lustre as the non-stick surface does its best to clean itself from the dirt. He gets up on one knee, making sure there is no one around. The rain has made sure the cemetery is empty tonight.

He gives a silent salute to the crosses of his fallen brothers, and then he sets out across the sodden lawn towards the city lights. Only briefly does he note there is one grave less than there ought to be. So they didn't manage to piece everyone back together. Too bad.

He starts out walking, then goes into a quick jog, and then into an all-out sprint, water splashing around his boots with every step. A low rumble starts building deep in his chest. As he runs down the cobbled path towards the edge of the cemetery the rumble raises into a roar. When he vaults the tall cemetery gate, the roar turns into a primal scream of rage.

Vengeance has no patience.

Obvious Pride in her Handiwork

We take the car to Suki's place in the low end of the Bottoms. Like most such areas across the settled universe, it's famous for its cheap booze and even cheaper whores. I wonder which lured Suki here? It could also be the cheap rents.

Vagrants around oil-drum fires, flickering Neo-N signs, stoned-out kids on sofas on the sidewalk, you name it, it's all here. The depressing atmosphere is made even more crushing by the presence of the Ceiling, omnipresent and unforgiving, a mere twenty metres above our heads. Down here it's always midnight. Witching hour. Party hour.

The traffic lights shift in our favour as we reach each intersection. They're perfectly synchronized by our car's low-level but still highly illegal AI as it whispers silently to the city hub across the net.

As we drive slowly up the street towards Suki's address it starts to rain again from the upper levels of the city. Like cockroaches, the natives scurry back under the dirty tarps hanging from spars bolted to the buildings. As we glide past like a shark through a shoal of herring, they start to follow us. I can almost hear their brains working, weighing the reward of robbery against the danger of messing with someone who can afford a car like ours. Before they can decide on a course of action, we stop outside Suki's block. When Wagner steps out and they realise just how close to death they are, the crowd scatters faster than you can say 'survival of the fittest'. One of them even starts to whistle.

I mean, come on.

When I turn off the engine, the only sound in the car is the rusty rain pattering on the smoked glass roof. Suki gets out without a word. As I follow her into the warm night, the scent of wet rust and offal envelops me like a sodden blanket.

I make a show of switching on the anti-personnel systems of the car, raising the remote high in the air before pushing the button. I savour the massive bass-kick to the chest as the sub-sonics engage. An evil blue sheen flickers into existence over the car, draping it in a baleful halo of electric current. Like the AI, it's not entirely legal, but highly effective.

If we're lucky, everyone will think Suki scored big and found herself some high-class customers for the night and just ignore us. Rich kids and cheating CEOs come here all the time to sow their royal oats and beat some undeserving prostitute senseless. To further the appearance of slumming upper crust, we leave the heavy artillery in the car. It's potentially a bad call, but we've seen no indications that anyone that counts is taking an interest in us. So far so good. We should be out of here in no time with the information stored on that cube.

Famous last words.

Suki opens the wood-look polymer door for us using an old-fashioned metal key. Jeez, this really is a backwards area. The high-ceilinged foyer inside is just as dirty and run-down as you might expect. Decorated in once-splendid faux nineteenth century Gothic, the hall is now a mess of decay. The wallpaper is moist and crumbling, the carpets are worn through, the stairs look like they might fall apart at a glance, and the wall-mounted lights don't work at all. The only illumination comes from a dim streetlight outside, falling through the tall stained-glass windows above the door, still miraculously intact.

Like most buildings in the Bottoms, the whole place smells of dust and mildew. This one has its own signature perfume of sour rat piss from the carpet mixed with the musk from a group of old leather armchairs mouldering away in a corner.

Suki closes the door behind us and locks it.

"Nice place," I say as my eyes quickly adapt to the darkness.

"Dark as hell," Wagner chips in, not adding much above stating the obvious, as usual.

Suki pulls out a flashlight and turns it on, revealing far more than necessary of the ruined hallway.

"This way." She waves for us to follow her up the stairs. "The elevator's been out for years."

Besides, it looks like someone's been living in it for a while. A dirty mattress sticks out between the broken doors and I can hear rhythmic grunts from inside. Someone got lucky tonight.

Her apartment is on the fourth floor. No name on the door, no indication at all that anyone lives there except a set of shiny new locks. It's probably a good idea for a cute girl like Suki to keep a low profile in a dump like this.

"Welcome to my place," she says as she opens the door, pulls off her leather jacket, and throws it on the bed. I was right. She's wearing an automatic pistol in a shoulder holster. Maybe she just wears it for show, who knows. Personal protection as a fashion statement. Stranger fads have come and gone over the years, and I'm too old to try to keep up with what's hot and what's not.

The place is small, even by Masada standards. Like most apartments in Masada, it's made from a single piece of once-white polymer plastic. They're cast in the off-world mega-factories in the Belt, then hauled here and glued together with other similar units to form a building. The single room is barely large enough to fit a bed recessed into the wall, a table rising from the floor in the centre, a single chair and a kitchen unit. A door at the kitchen end probably leads to the bathroom. There are no windows, and the only illumination is an overhead strip light. Since building space is in such short supply in Masada, the prices of real estate are skyrocketing. Places like these are the only ones ordinary people like us can afford.

The walls and ceiling sport several suspicious-looking stains, and the scratches in the floor are filled with decades of dust and dirt. She hasn't even bothered trying to cheer the place up with colourful cushions like any normal girl would.

"It's not much, but it's home," she says in an offhand way, casually excusing the place. Like all of us living in places like these, she's no doubt kidding herself that it's only temporary and that she will soon be moving on to greener pastures. It never happens.

"I like what you've done with the place," I say in a sad effort at humour. To my surprise, that actually gets the flicker of a grudging smile from her.

"Fuck you," she replies a millisecond later, back in character as the streetwise hacker.

"Any time, anywhere," I reply, the old joke never getting tired.

"Not going to happen, grandpa," she gives me the finger and sits down at the desk, deliberately pulling her gun from its holster and placing it beside her, pointed in my general direction. It's a strange gun of indeterminate origin and I've never seen one like it before.

"Do you want me to crack this thing or not?" She waggles the memory cube at me.

"Please, do." I reply.

After making sure the place is secured, Wagner sets his massive frame down on the edge of the bed. He pulls his trunk-like legs up, hugs them to his chest, and freezes up in that eerie Norse way. The king of the trolls, turned to stone by the rising sun. Freezing up like that is just one of the irritating habits Goliaths have. It's probably great for preserving energy on that ice-ball moon of theirs, but it freaks people out.

"Alright, let's see what we have here." She pulls a tangle of cables from a drawer in the wall behind her and dumps them unceremoniously on the small table. One end of the tangle remains in the drawer, supposedly connected to her main processing cores, or whatever these kids use to do this kind of stuff. Then she snaps the cube into some sort of interface connected to the cables, and pulls the console from her gym bag. It looks like one of the new top-of-the-line Nishin Combine Amagiri units. The ones that are not on the market yet. I recognise it from the prototype we tried to steal from them last year. Impressive. This girl has got some serious connections.

She plugs what looks like a random cable from the tangle into the console and waves some arcane patterns in the air above it, and the console springs to life. Behind her, lights come on in the drawer as information about the cube appears in the amber mist of the three-dimensional console interface. Whatever she's doing, it looks good.

"OK... Standard quantum encryption, terabyte key-size, layered architecture..." She scrolls through page after page of techno babble. "Quite basic stuff. I can definitely crack it, but it will take a while. This stuff is old, but it's pretty sophisticated for its time. Military, by any chance?"

"Need to know basis," I reply, shaking my head. "No need to know."

"Like hell. If you tell me something about this piece of junk and give me a hint of what I'm looking for I might be able to do it faster. That means I will be rid of you and your giant frozen friend over there," she nods in Wagner's direction, "a little faster. So yes, I do need to know." She glares at me, daring me to contradict her.

"Fine, fine." I back down. "Yes, it's military. We lifted it from an old bunker and we believe it contains the surveillance video from the bunker's camera systems. Something happened there that our employer is very interested in."

"Well, why didn't you bloody say so? With video I have to use an entirely different approach. I might have wasted hours applying the wrong algorithms to this crap. You need to fucking talk to me, mister."

"Sorry," I say sheepishly for lack of anything better to say.

"Look," she says in a marginally less hostile way, "I'm going to be busy for a while. Why not send out the big guy to get us something to eat?" She is already deep into the digital innards of the cube. Orange blocks of digits and symbols flash by in the holographic display over her console, adding some colour to the drab room. I realise I'm hungry again.

"Wagner, work to do." I kick the foot of the motionless giant and he snaps out of his paralysis, ready for action. "You heard the lady. Go get us something to eat. And bring a crate of beer."

Wagner grumbles as he gets up, but he knows his place in the pecking order, and as long as he thinks I'm top dog, he will let me get away with it. Not a second longer.

"Scandinavian for me," Suki calls from the console without looking up.

"Scandinavian will be great," I tell Wagner and beam him some cash from my wrist console. The thought of some juicy meatballs gets my saliva flowing and I realise I'm starving.

He nods and steps out of the cramped apartment, probably glad to be out of there. To a Goliath a place like Suki's must feel awfully claustrophobic.

"Alright, sit back and relax, Perez," Suki says when we're alone. "This is a long way from finished."

I look around for a suitable space to sit – the only one I can find except for the toilet is the bed and I lie down on it. It's not too hard and not too soft. Goldilocks would feel right at home. I can't help wondering if our girl has had sex on it lately.

"So, how long have you been a hacker for hire?" I ask her, just to make conversation.

"All my life," she replies with her eyes on the holo-screen, fingers busy with some obscure controls in the glowing interface.

"Why not get a regular job working for a company?"

"The money's worse, the hours are worse, and I would have to do what others tell me to do. You tell me."

"Point."

"Look, Perez, or whatever your name is." She looks up from her work, a scowl on her face. "Shut up while I tell my friends I'm still alive, OK?"

"By all means. We don't want them barging in to rescue you or something."

She reroutes the input from her console to her communicator and types out a brief message. "Now they know we're here and that so far nothing is wrong," she says. Her eyes go back to the display and her fingers start flipping between pages in the holographic display again. "If I don't call again in an hour, they will come."

I raise my hands in a gesture of surrender. "Fine with me." She doesn't care. She's working.

We remain silent for a while, our breathing and the occasional tap of her fingernails on the tabletop the only sound in the room.

"So, what do you do when you're not hacking military data feeds?" I finally ask when I get too bored staring at the Rorschach stains on the ceiling of the bed alcove. They all look like dead people anyway.

"Look, mister..." She looks up from her chore.

"Perez."

She sighs deeply. "OK. Look. Perez. If you wanted conversation you should have hired a geisha. You pay for a hacker, you get a hacker."

"Don't hackers ever talk?"

"Not this one. Shut the fuck up or get out." She seems jumpy over something.

"Fine, I'll shut up."

"Fine." She's already back at her tapping.

Where's Wagner with the food when you need him? Now would be a perfect time to show up and break the ice, but no such luck. That only happens in carefully scripted sitcoms and novels. I settle down for another long, boring wait.

I'm surprised when, two minutes later, she leans back and stretches her arms above her head in a silent victory salute. Her eyes are still on the display. "Got it."

"It's done?" I ask, getting up to stand behind her. That was fast.

"No, I just got a strain of the fucking plague."

I look uncomprehendingly at her.

"Of course it's done, want to see it?" She takes obvious pride in her handiwork.

"No, erase it," I reply coldly.

"Seriously?" Her finger hovers over the delete button, her eyes boring into mine.

"No, just kidding. Of course I want to bloody see it. Play it."

She pokes a virtual controller and the hologram over the console transforms into a low-quality 2D image. It shows a big church hall, complete with pews and crucifixes and a few praying individuals. Seeing it again sends a shiver down my spine.

"That's not the view we want. Are there other feeds?"

She pokes another controller and a whole page of images fade into existence in the air above the table. I scan them and find the one we want.

"That one." I point to a display showing a small room with a battle flag on the wall. "Can you show a time-lapse of the last two weeks or so?"

"Can do."

She moves two sliders in the air and the selected camera view jumps back in time and then begins to fast forward. The room looks like it doubles as a storage area when it's not used for staging ritual executions. For a long time we see nothing but people coming and going with crates, cartons and boxes. Then, one day, the room is cleared out, the banner is hung on the wall, and all the lights are turned on.

"Here we go," I say and bend over the table to get a better look as she switches back to real time. In the corner of my eye I see her lean away from me and her hand going for the gun on the table, but then she stops herself. Interest in what is happening on the screen apparently overrides her aversion to me.

On the screen, three men haul a fourth man into the room and push him down on his knees in front of a camera. This time the view of the action is from above and behind, which should give us an interesting angle on what happens after the official feed ended.

"What the hell?" she asks, glancing suspiciously at me as the men step behind their victim, unable to avert her eyes from the drama playing out before us. She gasps and looks away when the knife does its swift work taking the man's life. "Are you fucking kidding me?" She looks at me rather than the screen.

I don't reply but nod at the screen when we get to the interesting part. She turns back to the feed.

The dead man gets to his feet and without a moment's hesitation kills his three captors, ripping them apart with his bare hands.

"What just happened?" I breathe. Even Wagner couldn't do that, and this guy is definitely no Goliath. Besides, he's just had his throat cut. It has to be fake. But why?

"I have no idea," Suki replies quietly. Then she turns to me with a strange look in her eyes. "But he kind of looks like you."

The hell he does. I'm much better looking.

Suki goes for her communicator, doubtless to call in her friends to come rescue her from something she doesn't want to get mixed up in. I don't blame her.

At that very instant the door comes crashing open and there is Wagner in the doorway. He's got his huge automatic pistol pointing down the hallway and a crate of beer under his arm.

"Get out, we're under attack."

What the hell is Suki talking about? He doesn't look anything like me.

Their Bastard Offspring

Wagner drops the crate of beer – sending a fortune in prohibited beverages foaming all over the place – and takes cover behind the door frame. The boom of his gun mates with staccato bursts of automatic fire from the hallway, and their bastard offspring echoes around the old building. The air fills with smoke and shrapnel, and I grab Suki by the arm and haul her from the desk.

"What the hell are you doing?" she shouts.

"I'm saving your life. We need to get out of here." I grab her console and thrust it into her arms. If we don't get out, we will die in here.

"No fucking way. It's you they want. Just leave me and go."

"They know you're involved. You're coming with us." I grab her bag off the floor and throw it at her as I pull my gun and check there's a bullet in the chamber.

She stuffs the console in the bag and grabs the gun from the table as I shove her toward Wagner.

I slap the big guy on the shoulder and point my hand across the hallway. He nods. I hold up three fingers, then rapidly lower them, one by one. As I close my fist I lean around the door post and open fire at random down the hall. Wagner hauls Suki across the corridor, kicks in the opposite door and takes up position in the opening. Behind him I can see the two female residents sitting screaming in bed, arms around each other, sheets ineptly pulled up to protect their nakedness. Down the corridor, four operatives are moving in and firing in a perfectly choreographed way that implies some serious military training. They are dressed in black, like ninjas, if ninjas were covered from head to foot in some kind of highly mobile armour, the likes of which I've never seen before. Their faces are hidden behind red hyperdiamond shields. These guys are not your average street hoodlums, and I'm thinking corporate strike team or church muscle, both of whom have valid reason to be interested in us. Either way, they're bad news.

"Fall back," I call to Wagner as I open fire again to cover him. I see the lead ninja take a couple of rounds in the chest without flinching. Damnit. That is some heavyweight armour they're wearing. Our small-calibre fire is not likely to cause them any serious damage, and I curse the decision to leave the heavy gear in the car. I sure as hell wish I had the Aitchenkai with me right now.

Under the cover of my fire, Wagner backs down the hallway, pushing Suki behind him toward the fire escape at the end of the corridor. Had Wagner not surprised the ninjas when he came back early with the beer they would have caught us in a death trap in Suki's apartment. Meeting an armed Goliath must have thrown them off their game, and we still have a couple of seconds before they realise they are only taking small arms fire. Somewhere a baby starts crying.

As Wagner opens fire, I make a run for it and dash past him and Suki toward the fire escape. If we can get out into the maze of the Bottoms we'll have a chance of slipping away. The fire escape is just a big window that opens onto an outside balcony and I don't even stop to kick it out. Instead I fire a volley of hollow-points into it and let my momentum carry me through. The glass explodes and glitters like diamonds around me as I fall and I land with a jarring impact on the steel mesh outside. Unfortunately the fire escape is old, and the welding was probably not top notch to begin with. When I crash into the railing, the ancient metal gives way and I bounce over the edge and find myself in free-fall.

Years of training and a finely honed survival instinct kick in and I twist around in the air. I throw my left arm out and grab the edge of the metal flooring with fingers steeled by adrenaline and the inevitability of death if I lose my grip. A sharp jolt, excruciating pain in my shoulder, and I'm dangling four storeys above the street. Somehow I manage to get a leg up over the edge and haul myself back onto the fire escape. I keep low to stay away from the bullets flying from the broken window and take cover to the left of the shattered glass. A quick glance inside tells me Wagner is still holed up in the doorway where I left him. Suki is cowering behind him, hugging the bag with her console to her chest.

"Suki. Over here," I shout as I open fire once more at the ninjas. She is not hard to convince and comes running down the hallway with bullets whizzing around her. She dives through the window and lands hard on the platform next to me. I grab her around the waist and pull her up against the wall behind me.

I eject the empty magazine and slide in a new one before risking another peek inside. Wagner is pinned down in the doorway, and when I open fire and force the ninjas to take cover he comes bounding toward me in slow motion, the floor of the old building shaking with every thundering step. I manage to squeeze off a few more rounds before he fills my entire field of view. One of the ninjas takes a bullet in the face but keeps on coming.

Wagner squeezes through the window, and even above the gunfire I hear the thuds of bullets punching into his flesh. As big as he is, Wagner is by no means unstoppable. I've seen Goliaths take an insane amount of punishment and remain standing – after all the Norse breed for strength, not brains – but even Wagner has his limits.

"Go," Wagner shouts over the gunfire as he hunches down on the other side of the window. I motion for Suki to climb down the ladder to the next level. As she descends, I send a grateful thought to the long dead architect of this place who chose not to cheat but decided to go for the regulation plascrete in the building. If he hadn't, we would have been shot to shit through the walls by now.

"You OK?" I shout to Wagner over the noise, my own gun adding thunder to that of the Goliath's. The front of Wagner's T-shirt is red with blood and his long hair and beard are all sticky with gore, making him look even crazier than he is.

"Fucking go," he shouts back. I risk another quick glance into the corridor and see the ninjas closing in. They've taken up defensive positions in the doorway Wagner just left. At the moment they seem to be reloading, only one of them firing in our direction to keep us down. It's either that or they are waiting for the cavalry to arrive. If they are corporate or church they will have a backup team stationed in the street, and I scan the alleys below for another strike team. There's nothing. Instead my eye catches movement in an open window across the street, close to the Ceiling. It could be the reflection of light in a sniper scope.

"Sniper," I shout, an instant too late, and Wagner bellows like a stuck bull as he takes a round in the back. I jump down the enclosed ladder and as I land I return the sniper's fire, only hoping to throw him off his aim. I won't be able to hurt him if he's wearing that armour. A sniper is not standard corporate or church tactics. Who the hell are these guys?

"I'm taking fire here," Wagner shouts down at me.

"I know. Get the hell out of there."

"How?"

He's right. There's no way he's going to fit down the enclosed ladder. The guy who designed this place really was a sucker for regulations, and the regulations didn't say anything about Goliaths. Wagner has reloaded and fires off a quick volley into the hallway to keep the ninjas away while I desperately scan our surroundings, trying to find him an exit.

"That balcony over there." I point it out. It's on the opposite building, one storey below us and a good five metres away. The difference in altitude should make it possible for someone with Wagner's strength to reach it.

"Are you fucking crazy?" Wagner yells at me.

"Do or die, brother," I shout back and another bullet from the sniper persuades him to give it a go. I fire another round at the sniper to mess up his aim, and Wagner goes for it. He gets up, takes a few bounding strides down the length of the platform and launches into the air, arms flailing like a first grader in a schoolyard fight. At first it looks like he's going to make it, but his momentum is not what it should have been. The amount of blood dripping through the metal grid above tells me why.

He's taken some heavy damage, and even a monster like Wagner has got to feel the pain and shock of a dozen hits. To really drive the point home, another bullet from the sniper's rifle tears through his shoulder in mid-air, painting a crimson ribbon in the air.

Wagner misses the balcony by a metre and his outstretched hand clutches at nothing as he plunges to the street far below. A drop like that will kill even Wagner, and I watch in horror as he falls.

One second he's falling, the next he's crashing into a balcony below his target, his massive bulk pulling the entire structure out of the wall. Masonry and rusted metal tear free and join him on his rendezvous with the street. He plunges on to the next balcony where he lands hard on his side. The balcony creaks, but it holds. Without waiting to see if he's alive, I follow Suki down the next ladder, firing the last bullets in my magazine at the sniper. With Wagner out of sight, the sniper's fire is once again concentrated on me.

Suki pounds down the ladder to the last landing with me close behind. High velocity bullets whistle through the air and shower us with concrete as they explode against the wall. Someone smacks me with a baseball bat in the thigh, and for an instant I'm disoriented. Then I realise I just got shot. Fuck.

I throw the remote to Suki. "Here, start the car." She catches it and punches the button to fire up the engine as I quickly assess the damage. It can't be too bad or I would be passing out already. I test the leg and find I can still stand on it. Out in the street, the blue field over the car flickers out as the powerful engine kicks into life. I gingerly lean on my injured leg and realise I can still use it.

Wagner is back on his feet on the opposite balcony, now level with us. The ninjas pour out on the fire escape above, exchanging fire with Wagner, and I realise we will never make it to our ride alive. From their elevated positions the sniper and the ninjas will cut us down like rubber ducks in a shooting gallery. We're dead.

A sudden loud creaking from above gives me an idea.

The platform where the ninjas are standing has taken some heavy punishment but has so far held its own against gravity. When I lean out over the railing and let a few well-placed hollow-points cut one of the already bent and creaking supports, the poor thing gives up the ghost and the ninjas are tipped into space.

"Wagner, to the car," I shout.

"Got it."

He grabs the railing and swings his gargantuan body over it and drops the three metres to the street. His powerful legs absorb the impact easily and he makes a run for the car. He leaves a trail of blood behind him on the dirty asphalt. Not waiting around to see where the ninjas went, I kick the rusty folding ladder down from its resting place on our landing. The thing goes crashing to the street and we slide down it to the filthy alley below. My injured leg sends a brief spike of pain into my brain and then is quiet, like it's only reminding me of its existence. Thank the powers of evolution for the invention of adrenaline.

Wagner has reached the car and gets in. He guns the engine and then lets all the hundreds upon hundreds of horse powers loose. The broad wheels spin against the cracked asphalt before finding purchase, and the armoured car comes roaring down the alley towards us.

Wagner has retrieved his toys and as he fishtails the car around to shield us he rolls down the window and opens fire on the sniper's position with the heavy artillery. The rhythmic pounding of his autocannon thunders around the neighbourhood, and the façade explodes as round after round of .50 calibre shells tear the building apart. Ricochets bounce off the Ceiling above, raining sparks over the street. I pull the back door open and push Suki in before diving after her.

"Go, go, go."

Wagner doesn't hear me over the noise and keeps firing at the building. The interior of the car fills up with burning-hot shell-casings.

"Wagner, get us out of here." My mouth tastes of gunpowder and dried saliva. If we weren't sitting in Gray's expensive car I would spit on the floor.

Something in my voice finally gets through to him and he pulls the cannon back in. The car now reeks of hot metal and gunpowder, and there's blood everywhere on the luxury upholstery, wet and sticky. Grey will have our hides for messing up his ride, but we can deal with that later. Wagner steps on it and I'm pushed into the back seat, the mighty roar of the engine only a soft rumble inside the soundproofed compartment.

As we drift sideways around the corner I look behind us and see no trace of the ninjas but something tells me we haven't seen the last of them. In the distance I can already hear the sounds of approaching police sirens echoing down the artificial caves of the Bottoms.

Next to me in the back seat, Suki sits in stunned silence, staring at the gun in her lap. She hasn't fired a single shot.

Now what the hell was that all about?

Classic Masada Sob Story

"What the hell was that all about?" Wagner says from his post at the edge of the self-supporting camouflage tarp we've thrown over the car. We've parked under the half fallen trunk of a giant moss-draped tree deep in the park. The darkness under the trees is buzzing with the sounds of life. Our yet-to-rise twin suns are already bouncing their light off the Ring, bathing everything in a soft glow, turning the jungle into a magical cave of wonders. The park is nothing compared to the wilderness of the real jungle below, but it's still a beautiful place. It's also pretty damn warm and damp, and we're all sweating profusely. Even in the gloom under the trees I can tell Suki's top is almost transparent and I find it hard to keep my eyes away.

"I have no idea, but my money's on the Church" I stretch my wounded leg out through the open passenger-seat door, trying to get a feel for the damage. It's not too bad, obviously, since I can still use it. The damp under the trees is probably not doing me any good, but I think I'll live. The leg is actually feeling better already.

Wagner is in a far worse state, and I can only hope the very basic medical attention I've managed to administer will at least keep his wounds from going infected.

"Considering who we are looking for, the Church would be the obvious choice, don't you think?"

"But why kill us?" Wagner complains. "Why not just go after the guy themselves?" Pretty astute thinking for Wagner.

"Maybe they are willing to spend some brass getting rid of the opposition? Perhaps they don't want people to know Jesus has returned yet? Who knows how those guys think. Does it matter?"

I see Wagner do the Norse sign against evil at the mention of the J-word. He has always been a bit superstitious.

"Maybe they just didn't like your ugly faces?" Suki puts in from the open back door of the car. She's resting her chin on her pulled-up knees, hugging her legs. Her spiky hair is putting up a hell of a fight against the early morning damp, and so far it's coming out on top. She's a regular poster-girl for hair products.

She hasn't said many words since we escaped the ninjas, and I can't say I blame her. Getting shot at is no fun for anybody, and when it's your first time you are entitled to feel a little miffed about it. The first time is always a bit special as they say.

"In Wagner's case I don't blame them, but yours truly?" I pretend to look at my reflection in the outside rear-view mirror and shake my head. "I don't think so. They knew what they were doing and no one goes to that much trouble to put a cap in your ass because they think you're ugly. Not even someone as ugly as Wagner." I turn to Goliath. "No offence, big guy."

"Offence taken, asshole," Wagner flips me a massive finger. Deep down below the gruff exterior I know he enjoys the banter. He's just getting better and better at hiding it.

"So, you think those ninjas decided to off us just because we saw that video?" Suki looks skeptically at me between the headrest and the door. "Was that thing even for real?" She looks not half as distraught as I thought she would. Either the shock of the firefight really got to her, or she is one tough cookie.

"As far as we can tell, that feed is the real deal. I have no idea how he could survive that, and I really don't care."

"Why not?"

"We are not paid to care." I shrug. "Our job is to bring the guy in."

Suki makes a strangled noise and covers her head with her arms. "Just listen to yourself. You are so full of macho bullshit it's coming out of your ears." She looks up again. "Don't you need to know why you're looking for this guy? It might have some 'operational impact' or some other military implication." She waggles the quotation marks in the air with her fingers.

"Not really. Our job is to do what we're told and not ask questions. Ask too many questions in our line of work and you'll find yourself breathing through a hole in your chest."

"And I suppose you learnt that the hard way in the army?" The way she says army indicates she would be far from impressed if I started trading war stories with Wagner.

"I was never in the army," I reply a little too defensively. She's starting to get to me. Hell, I don't have to explain myself to her.

"Why not? It would be right up your alley."

"I have an authority problem."

"Well, you could have fooled me, Mr Gung-Ho Macho Bullshit."

"He couldn't pass the security check," Wagner chips in with obvious glee. He's really been in a lousy mood these last few days. "Bad blood."

"I bet he has."

"Well, screw you both over a slow fire. I didn't make it into the army, so what? I consider that a good thing."

"Is he always such an asshole?" Suki asks of Wagner, ignoring me.

"Only when he's awake."

Now it's my turn to flip Wagner the finger. "Ha fucking ha." He ignores me.

"You know what I think?" Suki asks Wagner, still not bothering to acknowledge me. "I think he's one of those people who are reborn as assholes over and over again, getting better at it every time."

Wagner just hums and gazes off into the distance, to all the world looking like he's pondering something profound, and making quite a good job of it.

"Come on, no one's born an asshole," I object.

"I'm just saying; maybe it's in your genes to be an asshole." Suki shrugs and finally looks at me.

"OK, I had a crap childhood, so what? We still have a say in who we become. I'm an asshole by choice."

"Fair enough, but maybe you chose that because of your childhood?"

"What? This gonna be one of those 'What came first, the bullet or the gun' arguments?"

Suki is looking oddly at me. I stare at her, matching her gaze for gaze. The moment drags on, starting to turn uncomfortable. What the hell is she on about?

"The gun." A deep rumble from Wagner.

"What?"

"What?"

We both turn to the big guy, perfectly synchronised.

"The gun came first."

I just stare at him, my mind taking a second to catch up and realise what he's talking about. If it wasn't Wagner, I'd say it was a perfectly timed ice breaker. Since it is Wagner, it's just another classic example of the inner workings of the Goliath mind, but the tension is broken and I can't help but smile.

"Finn, you are just about the thickest person I know. But I like you anyway."

"Fuck you," the giant replies, but I can tell he's beginning to thaw. Hell, even Suki can't hide a tiny smile, and I think we are going to be all right.

"So, tell me something about yourself, Perez. Where were you born?" Suki asks, obviously in a better mood and willing to share some stories in this sudden new atmosphere of glasnost.

"On the big A."

"You got out in time."

"Not all of us." I suck on a tooth for a while. Not sure if I want to share, but what the hell. "My parents were red wine intellectuals. My father used to lecture me about how there will come a time when you have to stand up for your beliefs and be ready to die for the truth. The usual yada-yada. He got what he wanted. He was executed in the square of our eco-village with the rest of the avant-garde in a government black ops raid. The Terrans claimed a terrorist group used our village as cover. My mom and I watched from a nearby hill as they burned it to the ground along with all my friends and their families. The soldiers shot anyone who tried to run.

My mom bought us passage on a ship to Elysium with the only coin available to her. Years later she told me my father had been a rebel. The fact the Terrans were right doesn't make what they did any less wrong." I shrug.

Suki looks at me, perhaps with a little more interest than before.

"How about you?" I ask her.

"Me? Nothing original." She looks away. "I grew up in Masada, my mother was a hooker, my father a construction worker out on the Antares Particle accelerator. He got the Shivers like everyone else and died a catatonic junkie when I was twelve. I decided to follow in my mother's footsteps rather than my father's. At least that way I had a chance of living to see thirty. Discovered I had a knack for computers when my pimp got knifed and couldn't do his books, and here I am." Now it's her turn to shrug.

Classic Masada sob story, and a little too rehearsed, like something carefully assembled to cover a bigger shame. What could she be hiding if that is her cover story?

"From your foul mouth I take it you're not a particularly frequent church-goer," I observe. "That can be dangerous for a lone girl in a place like this."

She looks away. "I can take care of myself."

Oh, I bet you can, little girl.

She turns back again, a strange look in her eye. "You don't strike me as a Godhead either, Perez. If you listen to most people in this dump, that means there is nothing to stop you from raping children or burning worlds. How can you be a good guy when you don't worship Jesus?"

Wagner growls from his post at the mention of the name-that-must-not-be-mentioned. "Shut up. The trolls will hear you." We pointedly ignore him.

"It's funny you should say that, because I always found it odd how most people on this planet can actually be quite decent people when they do." I look her deep in the eye. She stares back until a small smile forms at the corner of her mouth. Our views on organized religion measured and found compatible, some common ground at last, she turns her attention to Wagner.

"What about you, Wagner?" Suki calls to the giant. "What's your background? Where do you come from?"

"Nifelheim. Joined the Einherjar when I was fourteen." He closes his fist and taps his heart. "Youngest accepted recruit ever. Fought in the Corporate Wars on every side for twenty years. Drafted by Gray Industries, now Mr Gray's personal bodyguard. I work with that asshole sometimes." He nods in my direction.

"And you know you love it, big guy," I smile. "OK, now that we have traded life stories, perhaps we can get back to work. We still have no idea what those bloody ninjas wanted, and I never thought I would say this, but I really want to find Jesus."

There Wagner goes and does the sign again and mutters something under his breath.

"Once we bring him in we can go to ground, lie low and leave the Church alone for a while. Gray Industries has the resources to keep us off the radar until the church forgets about us."

"Well, that's great and all, but you have no idea where he is. I assume you have some kind of genius plan?" Suki seems skeptical of my powers of deduction.

"As a matter of fact, I do. Here's my five cents. We don't know where he is, but I think we can hazard a guess or two of where he's going. Considering who he seems to think he is, I'm willing to bet he's going to contact one of the shadier sects."

"Why not the church?" Suki asks. A valid question. The church would seem like the obvious choice.

"Because that would put him at a disadvantage. The church is too powerful. Even if he is who he says he is, and I'm not saying he is, they would lock him up and experiment on him just to make sure. Two and a half millennia ago people might take your word for it when you claimed to be the immortal son of God, but today people would require some kind of proof. That proof would most likely include more resurrections. Repeatability, you know. No, if I were him I'd go to one of the more powerful sects and try to persuade them of my identity. There are plenty of crazy crews out there who would jump at a chance to be the progenitors of the Second Coming."

"Oh, yeah? How come you know so much about sect psychology?"

"Keeping tabs on those bastards is part of my job. They are always out to bomb or kidnap people like Gray."

"OK, sounds reasonable, I guess, but how are you going to find which sect he's gone to? There are at least a dozen possibles."

"We'll just have to visit them, one by one."

"We? Now hold your horses, mister. There is no we here. I'm out of here as soon as we're back in the city."

"Really? Have you forgotten about those ninjas? They know where you live, girl. By now they probably know where you buy your panties and the names of all your regular johns. Hell, they might even have started killing their way through them to find out if one of them knows where you are."

"Like I would care." She shrugs. "So, what are you saying? That I'm safer with you?"

"We can protect you."

"You can also get me fucking killed. What would they want with me? I don't know anything."

"You know what's on that feed. That is about as much as I and Finn know, and apparently it's enough for them to want to kill us."

"Well, I still don't think I'm safer with you. You may think you are the toughest thing since hypercarbon, but did you not notice the effect your bullets had on those guys? Fucking zero, if my memory serves me right."

Why do I get the feeling she's stalling for something?

"Well, that's just because we didn't bring the good stuff to that fight. Next time we will be prepared, and they will not catch us unawares again." I really hope that's true. "Now, do you think you could have another look at the data on that cube and see if there's anything else we need to know?"

"I could try." She takes her console out of her bag and starts it up. This is something she knows how to do, and it seems she's anxious to show off her skills.

Perhaps she's worried we might kill her when she's no longer useful to us.

* * *

Ten minutes later, Suki has found something.

Did You Just Do Something?

She waves me over and I hobble around to the back door where I lean over her to see the screen. I rest my arm on the top of the door to take the weight off my bad leg and the position gives me a very alluring view of her damp cleavage.

"I fucking hope that's a gun in your pocket," she says without looking up. Is it that obvious?

Sweat drips from the tip of my nose and splatters on her console. I'm close enough to feel her warmth and I notice she still smells of strawberries. I tear myself back to the task at hand.

"So, what did you find?"

"First, there's this." She opens a file and spins the view for me to get a better look. It's another feed from the bunker.

The screen flickers and then into the great church hall where we found all those bodies. In this video those people are still alive and well and praying. There's the sound of a door slamming open. Shouting voices order everyone to move up against the altar and a team of heavily armed soldiers enter the frame. They are not wearing unit insignia or other identifiers, but the way they move and the equipment they're using screams church strike team. When I see who's commanding them my suspicions are confirmed. High inquisitor Borgia is a very recognizable man. So I was right. It was them all along.

The congregation is herded into a crowd in front of the cross and the soldiers form a firing line in front of them. An old man who is obviously some kind of minister steps out to reason with the assailants. He gets a rifle butt in the face and drops to the floor. As the crowd starts screaming, the soldiers open fire, cutting them down quickly and mercilessly. Then the knives come out and the real slaughter begins.

"Kill it," I order Suki, and she reaches out and stops the replay.

"Why?" Is all she asks, staring at the dead screen.

"Why? They didn't want any witnesses to what happened after the execution. Why, I don't know. But I'm going to find out. Whatever it is, it's big. Church government black ops big. There's more?"

"Yes." She shows me another feed. This time of something that looks like a high security storage area. A metal door rumbles open and the Prophet enters, covered in blood from head to foot and breathing hard. He moves up to one of storage lockers in the back wall, and it's clearly obvious that he knows what he's looking for. From a canvas shoulder bag he pulls two access cards, one of them still cuffed to the severed hand of its rightful owner. He inserts them into identical slots on each side of the locker and the door pops open. He removes something the size of a baby's head from the locker and puts it in his bag and leaves.

"So he was there to steal something…" I muse. "Can you find out what was in that locker?"

She flips the display towards her again, flicks a couple of virtual switches in the glowing interface and pulls up an item list of some kind. "I did a scan of their inventories. They have a lot of nasty shit in there."

"Of course they do, it's a military bunker."

"There's nothing special left in there that you couldn't buy on the black market with sufficient funds. Except for one thing. This." She turns the screen around to show me what she's found.

I look at the readout where her finger is pointing.

That can't be right.

The sweat on my back turns cold.

There's no way they would have one of those things just lying around like that. No fucking way in hell.

Then again, they did promise they would bring about Armageddon.

"From the look on your face I take it you know what that thing is." Suki looks at me with a mixture of intrigue and dread on her face. "So do I."

Really? This little street-girl is full of surprises. She must be watching a lot of quiz-shows.

"What the hell is an Archangel doing in the hands of the Church of Christ the Redeemer?" Wagner groans from his watch at the edge of the tarp. "One more time and I'll…"

Suki looks at me like I might have the answer to my own question. I haven't got the foggiest.

All I know is that security people like me have screaming nightmares about stuff like it. Whatever else you might think about those things, you have to admit they are aptly named.

The Archangel really is a nasty piece of kit. Murderously effective, yet so simple only a true sociopath or an engineer could have thought it up. It's basically a hollow metal shell containing a dormant cloud of self-replicating nanites calibrated for human flesh. Drop it into the midst of an enemy army and the nanobots will consume the soldiers in hours, leaving only pieces of bone and gore on the ground. The perfect weapon to destroy your enemy without collateral damage in the form of buildings, machinery and wildlife. The green choice for the ecologically conscious warlord. Assuming you feel no affinity with your own species, it's the perfect weapon of mass destruction.

The guys who designed it weren't stupid. To protect their own side, the nanites are programmed to self-destruct when exposed to a magnetic field with a particular oscillation rate. Carry a small generator that emits the correct field and you can walk through the carnage unharmed.

If just one of those nanites gets under your skin, it multiplies using trace elements in your body to build evil little twins of itself. They will consume your flesh in minutes before spreading to the next victim. Since they go from the outside in you have quite some time to enjoy the view of your body being eaten down to the bone before you die.

Imagine what would happen if someone detonated one of those things in a major city with a space port. Bye bye, human race.

That is why these things were never used in the war, not even against the Terrans, and all self-replicating nano-technology was banned forever. Instead of receiving the acclaim they expected, the inventors were tried and publicly and messily executed for crimes against humanity. A clear warning to everyone who might be interested in taking up their line of research again.

Until now, all the grenades were presumed destroyed.

"It's no longer in the hands of the Redeemers," I remind her sadly. "We're fucked."

In my line of work you get to utter those two words a lot, but this time I think we really might be. All of us. "Unless..."

"Unless what?" Suki looks at me, a kindling hope in her eyes.

"Unless we can do a gene trace on this." I pull out the knife from in its protective plastic bag from my pocket.

"What the hell is that?"

"The knife they used to kill the Prophet."

"What? You've had his DNA all along, and you didn't tell me?"

"Why should I? You're a hooker. And I didn't know I could trust you. I'm still not sure I can, but we're running out of options. We need to sequence his blood and see if we can pick up his DNA trail."

"I know an old guy who could help you with that."

"What? A client of yours just happens to be a geneticist with a gene sequencer?"

"Sort of."

"Great. Just great. An ageing john is going to help us track down Jesus?"

"By Odin's beard, stop doing that," Wagner howls.

Suki just shrugs and looks down at a sharp ping from her console.

"Hang on." She's typing furiously.

"What now?"

"Now what the..."

"What?" I don't like the sound of this.

"Oh no. No, no, no."

"What's going on, Suki?" This does not sound good. How can this crap just keep getting worse? I don't want to be a hero anymore.

"Someone has locked on to my signal."

"What? Can they do that?"

"I told you so," Wagner calls.

"These are no fucking trolls. They shouldn't be able to... OK, let's see how you like this, you bastards."

She pounds some furious commands into the console and the whole display goes dead.

"What the...?"

"Is it supposed to do that?" I point at the dead display.

"Fuck no." She bats my fingers away. "The bastards cut my signal. They shouldn't be able to do that. What the hell is going on here?" She's pushing buttons on her dead console, trying to elicit a response from the machine.

I grab her shoulder and spin her around to face me. "They're on to us. How the hell did that happen?"

Her console is restarting, chiming happily to indicate it's once again ready for action. Suki is already back where she left off, her line of thought unbroken.

"There must have been a... Yes. There it is. Big as a bloody barn door. Why didn't I see it?"

"See what?"

"There's a trigger on those vids. The first time we watched them, we were at my place, behind my firewalls." She's obviously thinking out loud, so I let her ramble on. "But this time the signal got through to them. Why the hell didn't I think to look for triggers this time? Like a bloody rookie. And now they have a lock on us. Fuck."

"Who are 'they'?"

"I don't know, but I should be able to do a reverse trace on them. From that I should be able to..." She's typing as she's talking. "Well, hello to you, Mr Church Hacker fuck." She flips her finger at the console.

Bad news. If the church went to all the trouble to put a wire on those vids, they no doubt have a strike team standing by to deploy when the wire is triggered. Meaning we are fast running out of time.

My communicator buzzes again. Gray is trying to call me. Screw that. I cut him off. A couple of seconds later it chimes with a text message.

Found anything?

Gray is really starting to piss me off.

"Guys. Gray's techs report there's a hell of a spike in comms traffic from the Church," Wagner calls, holding a finger to the communicator in his ear. "Did you just do something?"

"Damn. They're moving fast. We have to get out of here. Wagner. Torch the car."

"On it." Wagner is already hauling bags of kit from the trunk.

"Does this shit happen to you a lot?" Suki asks.

"Story of my life, babe. Waste the console."

She just stares at me.

"I said, waste it. They can track us through it." In the distance the sound of approaching helicopters can be heard. Fuck, they move fast.

"But my brother gave me this core."

Now, what does her brother do for a living to be able to buy his prostitute sister a top of the line hacking core? And why don't I have brothers like that?

"I have no idea who you are girl or what you're up to, but that will have to wait. Waste it." I catch the kit bag Wagner throws me and he hoists his own over his shoulder.

"Alright, alright." She tears the main core from the console and the display disintegrates into nothing. Then she pulls out the cube and throws the core and the dead console on the ground and crushes them under the heel of her boot. She stamps them into the wet ground and looks defiantly at me from under her wet fringe.

"There. Happy now?"

"Like a dog with two dicks." I reach out for the cube and she hands it over with clenched jaws. "Now let's get the hell out of here before this place starts swarming with Church muscle."

I push Suki hard in the direction of the trees and take off after her.

I hear the explosion from the car a fraction of a second before the scorching pressure wave kicks me in the back and throws me into the undergrowth. I wonder briefly what Gray will say about us blowing up his car.

The sound of the approaching helicopters turns into a screaming roar as the black birds come in low over the park. Their automated gun-pods track every motion in the area.

Damn, we don't need this.

My Private One-Man Army

The helicopters converge on the burning car, giving us precious seconds to make ourselves scarce. In the empty park we stand out like clowns at a funeral, and if they brought dogs we will need to get very creative if we are to escape this shit with our lives. We have to find a new set of wheels and get back into the city where we can blend in. And we have to do it fast.

The church obviously wants the Prophet real bad if they go to all this trouble to track down anyone who sees that video. They can't be entertaining the idea that he is who he says he is, can they? I mean, come on.

It's still pitch dark under the trees, but the weak light from the rising Hope-A reflecting off the low clouds is just enough to guide us through the thick underbrush. Wagner leads, a night scope jammed over his face and the headset in his ear. Suki tags along behind him and I make up the rear, the Aitchenkai PDW a comfort and a welcome weight in my hands. This is my element. This is what I do. But I don't like the odds this time. Three, maybe four helicopters, carrying at least a dozen well-trained policemen each and possibly dogs, against the three of us. We're outnumbered and outgunned a dozen to one.

I run up the broad trunk of the fallen tree above us to get a better view.

Out in the field I see the choppers set down and heavily armed men pour out. Damn it. These are professional soldiers, not cops. And they are not regular army operators either. These are Red Guards. Apparently the ninjas they sent weren't enough, and hunting us down has gone from being a covert strike op to a full-scale military campaign. I'm a little proud of that.

The powerful floodlights on the choppers illuminate the exhaust from the turbines, making the rapidly advancing Red Guards look like wraiths. The crimson spotter beams on their helmets that have given them their name add to the image of sinister beings from another world. One of the shadows is much bigger than the others and moves with a dangerous grace and terrifying sense of purpose. Through a brief hole in the smoke, I catch a glimpse of a scarlet cloak and I know who he is. Wearing red to a jungle fight is not only a serious fashion fuck-up. It's also very stupid, unless you are insanely proud of your own abilities and are willing to give your victims a needlessly fair chance, because you're a glutton for sport. Indulging two deadly sins and hoping to get away with it in the service of the cardinal can only be done by one man. The one they call the Sumerian. Jasper Constantine Borgia, the Witch Hunter, high inquisitor of the holy church, and a law unto himself. If he's here, they are taking this very seriously indeed. Over the sounds of the rotors, I hear the baying of big dogs. Damn it. What have I done to deserve this?

"Finn, we need to find a stream and lose those dogs," I call to the giant over the comms line.

"Got it."

As we dash off into the undergrowth, the choppers take off again, spreading out over the park to provide aerial surveillance for their troops on the ground. Those birds are carrying some of the most advanced sensors known to man, and I have no illusions of fooling them for very long. Our only hope lies in moving fast and making it into the city to find somewhere to hole up and let this shit storm blow over.

"Stream," Wagner calls from the communicator in my ear. About time something went our way this morning. Without breaking stride, Wagner jumps down the high bank and lands with a huge splash in the shallow stream. Then he motions for Suki to follow him. She hesitates for only a second before jumping. She lands hard in the gravel and loses her balance and almost falls over in the water. Ignoring her, Wagner covers the bank with his huge autocannon. Goliaths have no pity for the weak, and bothering to help a girl regain her footing in a cold stream would be seen as softness. Suki is left to fend for herself.

I jump down after them, landing next to Suki. Instead of helping her regain her balance, I push her into the muddy stream.

"What the f –" is all she has time to say before the water receives her and she goes under. When she surfaces again she is furious.

"What the hell are you doing?" she spits at me, still retaining enough self-control to keep her voice down. I don't reply but instead throw myself into the water, staying under the surface long enough to feel the cool water trickle into every nook and cranny of my clothing. When I surface, Suki is glaring at me. When Wagner follows my lead and soaks himself, the coin drops.

"Thermal camouflage? Really? Do you think mud and water will fool the heat sensors on those helicopters?"

"For a while, unless we stand around here arguing long enough to dry up. Wagner, if you please?" I point the way down the stream in the general direction of the city, and the giant nods and sets off as fast as his damaged body allows.

Despite the insane price of real estate in Masada, the wilderness of the park has been left in the pristine condition it was when the first settlers arrived on Elysium. The official reason is to provide the inhabitants of the city somewhere to relax and get away from the stress of the megacity. Everyone knows the real reason is because the overhang it's on is not structurally safe to build skyscrapers on.

A stream is perfect for covering scent trails and heat signatures, but it does shit-all for visual detection. When we round a bend in the stream, one of the choppers comes roaring over the treetops. One of the automated gun pods spots us, makes a split-second decision, and opens fire. The world around us explodes into walls of water as two thousand .50 calibre rounds a minute cut like a saw through the forest. The helicopter is moving fast and it only has time for a short burst before it's gone over the other side of the gully. We have mere seconds before they return, and they will no doubt call the other choppers, and then we will be severely fucked. There's only one thing to do.

"Finn, take it out."

"Will do."

In the first rays of the rising sun Wagner drops his bag into the creek and gets down on one knee. From the bag he pulls out a rocket launcher and quickly assembles it. I can do that in my sleep in total darkness, and so can Wagner, but I can't help shouting at him all the same.

"Get a move on. It's coming."

"Fuck you," Wagner snaps at me and shoulders the weapon. His thick arms ripple with muscle under the tattoos.

The chopper has made a wide turn and is coming straight up the creek, providing us with as narrow a silhouette as possible. Amazing design really, the helicopter. It has looked basically the same for centuries. Innovations in materials have made them lighter, stronger and more heavily armed and armoured, but the general design has remained unchanged. Like the car and the handgun, there's no need to improve on an already perfect concept. But while the chopper is an ancient design, the weapon in Wagner's hands is not.

He barely looks into the viewfinder of the launcher before pulling the trigger. The missile screams towards the chopper, and, with a satisfying *whoomp*, it strikes the most vulnerable part of the machine, right under the rotor blades. The armour on that bird is thicker than my thigh and had Wagner hit the fuselage, the chopper would just have shrugged it off. The explosion tears one of the eight blades off, causing the rotor to go dangerously unstable. The chopper is thrown off course just as it opens fire with both of its forward-facing gun pods. The hail of bullets misses us by a couple of metres. Had we been in their way, there would have been nothing left for them to mop up.

The pilot struggles with the unresponsive machine, trying to bring it back under control and fails miserably. It veers off at a dangerous angle and exits stage left. There's a massive explosion and a great fireball rises into the dawn sky.

"Great shot, Finn, now let's get the hell out of here. They are going to be pretty pissed about that."

"Can we go and count the corpses?"

"No, damn it, we cannot go and count the corpses. What the hell is the matter with you?" Wagner growls and throws the launcher back into the bag and slings it over his shoulder.

My private one-man army.

Following the river is no longer an option, and we head off into the woods again. As far as I can tell, we're about two clicks from the wall separating the city from the park. The wall is not there so much to keep people out as to keep the wildlife in. All the really dangerous animals in the park have long since been exterminated, but there's still a lot of critters in here the authorities would rather keep away from the streets and restaurants of the city.

The jungle is very dense and the going is slow and tiring. Suki looks like she's on the verge of collapsing, and Wagner's size is a huge disadvantage in the thick undergrowth. The jolly giant is starting to look weary. "Wagner, hold," I call. He stops and looks back through the foliage.

In the not-too-far distance we hear the choppers circling around the stream where they lost us, widening their search patterns with every turn. Soon they will be on us again, but for the time being we are safe under the huge ferns of the jungle. We gather under the umbrella of a big mushroom-like plant.

"Assessment time," I say as I get down on one knee in the deep moss. The warming jungle wraps us in a blanket of comforting earthen smells that provide a deceptive sense of calm and harmony. Nothing could be further from the truth.

Wagner and Suki get down too, obviously grateful for the respite from the arduous struggle through the jungle.

"These are not the same guys we saw last night," Suki gasps between ragged breaths.

"How can you tell?" I ask.

"Well, they are not wearing that fancy armour, for one thing. And they are much less coordinated." So now she's an expert on military tactics too. She's right though. These guys are good, as befits the Red Guard, but they lack the deadly purpose of those ninjas last night.

"OK. So, a different outfit this time, but now at least now we know it's the church that's behind this. Wagner?"

"At least two more birds." The giant pants, his huge chest heaving like a bellows. The guy really needs to exercise more. I feel winded, but not nearly in the shape of Wagner or Suki. All those hours in the gym seem to have paid off. "Two, maybe three squads on the ground," Wagner continues, "at least one of them a K9-patrol."

"Sounds about right," I nod. "Bad news: I believe Borgia is leading those men." The look on Suki's face mirrors my own feelings on the subject. "Yes, I know he's got this badass reputation, but he's only one man. If we're clever, we can outsmart them."

The look on Wagner's face says he doesn't want to outsmart anyone. He wants to challenge Borgia to a duel. He's been boring me about it for years. Borgia is probably the only man legally present on the planet who could give Wagner a run for his money in a one-on-one fight.

Legally, in this case, is relative. Borgia is pushing the limit on drug-enhanced body modifications, but being the champion of the cardinal means some rules can be bent in the service of a higher cause. I've got to admit it would be an interesting fight. Centuries of selective Goliath breeding against the latest advances in steroids and boosters. The ultimate fight between nature and science.

Where Wagner has the advantage of brawn, Borgia's got the brains. Maybe one day Wagner will get his wish, but not today if I can help it.

Suki chips in. "I think I heard cars unloading from the choppers."

That's good news. If we could commandeer a vehicle we should have a chance of making it to the city alive.

"Those cars sound like our exit. We need to get our hands on one of them."

"Get our hands on one?" Suki pants, still winded. "How are you going to do that? Do our realities overlap even in the slightest? Because in my reality we are outnumbered ten to one, and they have all the hardware. Are you just going to walk up and ask them nicely to hand over the keys?"

"Oh, no," I reply, a plan already forming in my mind. "This is not going to be very nice at all."

The Reckoning

The reckoning begins with the guard at the entrance to the Gray Tower's underground car park. The general vaguely remembers the man from a security briefing a couple of months ago where he had the guts to question some regulation or other. Average grades, average skills. Nothing to stand out in his profile, but then, a man with average grades in Gray's service would make top of the class in most other security forces without breaking a sweat. At Gray Industries, it puts you in charge of the parking garage. The guard is not a smart man, but a good one. The kind that could destroy the world with their trust.

The guard's smile turns into an amusedly quizzical look when he notices the general's soaked and mud-stained dress uniform. The smile freezes into a grimace of incomprehension when the knife slashes his throat from ear to ear. There's no need for the general to be subtle. They will soon know he is here, and leaving one of them alive now means he will just have to face the same man later, armed and ready. Much better to take out as many as he can before word of his presence gets around and they start hunting him.

Reaching over the counter of the guard booth, he finds the Gray Industries standard issue submachine gun in its easy-access holder. He mechanically checks the clip, a smile of pride flashing over his face as he notes it is full. He was responsible for putting the security procedures into place during the construction of the Gray Tower, and it pleases him immensely to see they are still enforced.

He hauls the rapidly expiring guard over to the elevator, where he holds the guard's face in front of the retina scanner and calls the elevator. Meridian drops the soon-to-be corpse, steps inside the elevator and punches the button for the fifth floor. According to the guard's security level, that's as far as the man's clearance will take him. It's not as far as the general would have liked, but that can't be helped. He still has a few minutes before they learn he's here, and he intends to use those minutes well.

On the fifth floor, he gets out and quickly looks around, calling the map of the place from his perfect memory, weighing his options. Priority one is camouflage. The ruined parade uniform got him through the entrance on sheer surprise value, but once inside the building it makes him stand out like a recently resurrected war hero in an office tower. More suitable clothing will buy him a couple of extra minutes. Every second he can get will bring him one step closer to Nero Praetorius Gray.

And that is all that matters.

* * *

A couple of doors down on his right is the room he's looking for: the guards' locker-room. The door slides open to his stolen key-card and he enters, his SMG shouldered and ready for action. At this time of day, the room should be empty. He's in luck.

He quickly swipes the card over the locks of the twenty or so security lockers in the room, hoping the card will open one of them. No such luck.

No matter. These are not weapons lockers, and he forces one of them open with his knife. The locker opens on a sad snapshot of a human life. On the inside of the door is taped a small flexible screen, continuously rolling images of a seemingly happy family. A reasonably pretty woman, two handsome enough children, and what is probably the real gem of the man's existence: a shiny, brand new sports car with the kids in the back seat. It's painfully obvious the car is the real point of focus, the children just an excuse for taking the picture and putting it on his locker door. The general can sympathise with the man. A good car is a valuable tool, children are just another generation of cannon fodder.

The war is over, and the man's children will grow up in a time of peace. Will they be ready when the Terrans return for round two? Or will their generation have talked themselves into believing peace is the new default? Maybe one or both of them will take up arms against the enemy in the inevitable war to end all wars, but he doubts it.

In the locker is a crisp, dark grey uniform, fresh from the laundries. The general quickly slips out of his messed-up uniform and pulls on the thick, grey one-piece coverall. A quick look at his reflection in the mirror-screen on the wall tells him the coverall fits him reasonably well. Once again he thanks his creator for making him average in size and looks. The general is not a handsome man, but neither is he hideous. He's neither black, nor white, but, like most people on the planet, he's somewhere in between. At a party you would talk to him and find him likeable enough, but the next day you would have forgotten all about him. There's nothing about him that stands out, and that's the whole point.

Tactically, it makes perfect sense. In the murder and insurgency business, standing out in a crowd is the last thing you want to do. Being of average height and weight also has the purely practical advantage of giving him a greater chance of scavenging gear that fits when the need arises in the field. Gray left nothing to chance when he designed his perfect warriors.

Slinging the SMG over his shoulder, he pulls on the grey cap of the building's security forces and pushes the locker closed behind him. With a little luck the broken lock will not be noticed for a while yet.

Getting out into the corridor again he almost collides with another guard coming up the hallway. The guy starts to say something rude but the general's blade quickly cuts the anger out of his voice. The man's final words are the usual bubbling pleadings for help and spluttered denial at an undeserved, inevitable, and quickly approaching end.

Two down, a building-full to go.

* * *

Five minutes later, the alarm goes off. Of course it's not an audible alarm. That would be too much of a signal to an intruder, but he knows every routine of this building. He put them into place.

A security team jogging past him down the corridor, weapons at the ready, tells him everything he needs to know. They head for the nearest elevator station, quickly slip inside, and before the door closes he sees one of them press the button for the garage floor.

They have found the first guard.

Had they found the guy in the locker room three floors down, they would have posted sentries at every elevator and staircase to prevent the intruder from moving around the building. At the moment they must still think he's somewhere in the lower levels, and he needs to make as much headway up the floors as he possibly can before they realise their error. Because when they learn who is in the building, his going will be getting tougher. A lot tougher.

* * *

He's almost halfway up the Gray Tower when the general alarm sounds. This time it's an all-out aural and visual alarm screaming its message in howling klaxons and flashing strobes. No need for secrecy anymore. From here on up it will be open warfare. His element. This is what he was designed for. For too many years as a general he's been distanced from the killing on the fields, and he has missed it. But no more. It feels great to get his hands dirty again.

Wall to wall, room to room, floor to floor he will fight them if he has to. He will fight them all the way to the top of the tower, where Gray will be waiting for him. Until tonight, all the battles the general has fought have been someone else's battles, but not this one. For the first time in his life there's no strategic goal, no greater good. Tonight he's fighting only for himself and the honour of his men.

This time it's personal.

* * *

The heavily armed team keeping him pinned down in the doorway with their rifle fire is good, as they should be. They are highly trained marksmen, every single one of them, but that is not his real problem. His problem is time. The soldiers have all the time in the world to wait for backup, and they know it. They preserve their ammunition and keep him in his place with carefully placed bursts of lead, and he can't afford to stay there. He reckons the time has come to get up close and personal.

He quickly leans out around the corner and fires off the last of his clip at the guard's positions. Then he crosses the intervening ten metres to the guards' position in the short interval before they poke their heads back out from cover, taking them by total surprise. He can still feel a few random bullets tear chunks out of his barely healed body as they reflexively fire their weapons in his direction.

Under his torn skin, the enhanced tendons and muscles writhe like glistening black snakes. To their eyes he must look like something out of ancient cyborg mythology, the unholy marriage of man and machine that just keeps coming at them through the bullet storm.

He doesn't hold it against them when hard eyes widen in terror as his hand closes around a throat and tears it out.

He doesn't hold it against them when they squeal in horror as he runs his knife arm straight through the body of a man, impaling him and taking out the man behind as well.

He doesn't hold it against them when they vomit in mortal fear as he tears his knife arm free in a splatter of steaming blood and guts.

The guards are hard men, and they fight well to the very end. He would not be shamed standing beside them on a battlefield had the cards of fate fallen otherwise. As they die in a tornado of steel and blood, he feels their kinship. They are brothers, like all soldiers are brothers.

He doesn't hate them. He kills them because he has to.

They stand between him and Gray, and so they have to die.

* * *

The general walks down the hall, firing a heavy assault rifle from each hand into the doorways he passes, killing indiscriminately. There shouldn't be any civilians in the building any more, and if there are, they are expendable.

As long as the end is just, the cost is justifiable. That's another of the mantras they taught them at the academy, and it has always been his guiding principle. What he and the Cherubim did to Arcadia was the ultimate application of that doctrine. As long as the end is just, the cost is justifiable.

Ending the long war and bringing peace was what everyone wanted, and he brought peace. Then Gray betrayed him and had his men executed. Executed for bringing peace.

He owes it to his men to bring judgement upon Gray for that betrayal. What happens after that is immaterial. All that remains now is vengeance, and, compared to that, the cost of the lives of a hundred security guards is inconsequential. It actually has a kind of poetic justice to it. For every one of his precious Cherubim slain he will kill sevenfold, and then the scales of justice will be balanced. The thought brings a smile to his face, and the last thing the humans see as he guns them down is a serenely smiling angel of death. He mows them down like a farmer scything his crops.

Before them stands the Reaper, and it is harvest season.

Like a Blood-red Sail

"On my way," Wagner calls over the command net. I tense under the roots of the giant tree where I crouch next to Suki and tap her shoulder.

"Go."

"Don't fucking miss," she hisses with an accusing finger pointed at me as she backs out from cover and moves further down the track. She's got one of my spare guns in her hand, pointed expertly at the ground. Her own strange weapon is still in her shoulder holster.

"I won't."

Is it that time of the month, or is she always this pissed off? She's been giving me the evil eye all day, and I think it's a bit undeserved. Yes, we more or less kidnapped her. And yes, we got her involved in something that's very likely to get her killed. And we did make her trash her precious console, but come on? Then again, put like that and maybe it's not quite so undeserved after all. If we get through this, I'll apologise to her.

She runs twenty metres down the track and hides behind a large rock, and I can't help resting my eyes on her shapely behind as she goes. She's in some serious shape for a hacker, and the way she carries the gun tells me she's not a stranger to firearms. There is something about her that intrigues me. Something is not quite right about her, and I'll be damned if I don't find out what it is.

There's a soft chime from my wristband communicator and I look down to see a text message from Gray.

Is that you in the park? Talk to me.

Busy, I respond and turn off the sound to avoid giving my position away. I can hear the roar of a powerful engine approaching from around a bend in the track.

The first rays of the morning suns are filtering down through the thick canopy, reflecting off the iridescent wings of huge insects hovering between the trees. Water drips from every leaf, glittering like strewn diamonds on the moss. A whisper-thin mist hangs in the air, turning the rays of the suns into spears of gold and emerald.

Everything stings and itches. Damn, I hate the jungle.

Wagner comes running around the bend at breakneck speed, sweat flying from his long hair. Fifty metres behind him comes a wide, armoured buggy, bouncing wildly over the roots of the uneven track. It's gaining on him by the second, but it's still too far away to lay any accurate fire on him. That doesn't stop the gunner from trying, and he sends burst after burst after Wagner. Not very clever. The jungle is thick, but the mega-city is only a kilometre away and those shells are designed to pierce tank armour. The working classes of Masada will be gloating over morning news feeds of distraught upper-class citizens in expensive park-view apartments crying over their shattered windows and ruined crystal finery. I guess it's time for someone to step in to do his civic duty and take those clowns out before they manage to kill some unsuspecting pillar of society.

"Now," I shout. Wagner skids to a halt in the wet dirt and turns to face his pursuers, panting, and I can see the joy in their eyes. They're no doubt already spending the reward in their minds when I push a button and the powerful climbing winch whirls home the slack on the monofilament wire strung across the track. It decapitates the driver and gunner – along with his vehicle-mounted heavy machine gun – and they die with smiles on their faces. Not a bad way to go.

The car speeds on and Wagner takes a quick step towards it, plants a big foot on its hood and launches himself over it. He executes a perfect twist in the air and lands in a kneeling shooter's stance behind the vehicle, his rifle trained on the already dead crew. He moves surprisingly well for such a big man, but then he's been fighting all his life.

The headless commander is not impressed and drives the car into the nearest tree.

Suki jumps out of cover and runs toward the idling car with her gun aimed at the crew. I cover her, but I needn't have bothered.

"Clear," Wagner calls, holding up a hand and Suki responds in kind. "Clear."

The wire glints with tiny ruby crystals in the morning light, and I don't want any animals running into it on their way to eat the dead soldiers. "Get in." I shout as I use my momo-blade to cut it down. Wagner hurls the decapitated bodies from the vehicle and I jump into the command seat. There's blood everywhere and the smell of death assaults my senses, but there is no time to get squeamish. With a disgusted face and a brimstone oath, Suki gets in next to me. Wagner folds himself into the gunner's rearward facing position in the back as best he can in the impossibly small space.

"Drive, drive," Wagner calls even before he's strapped in.

"Hold on. This is going to get bumpy."

The engine roars into life as I step on the throttle. I back the vehicle up and then set off down the track in a spray of dirt and blood. In the rear-view mirror I see Wagner pull the autocannon from his big bag of toys. He rests the huge weapon on his knee, the safety off and a fresh five-hundred-round drum-clip inserted. I wouldn't want to be in the shoes of anyone trying to catch us from behind.

Hopefully, the switch of car crew will not have been noticed by the Red Guards. If we're really lucky the previous owners didn't radio in to central command, hoping instead to bag us themselves and claim the full bounty.

"If we can make it to the city we're home free," I shout over the roar of the engine to Suki. She looks far from convinced.

"Yeah? Wagner took out one of their bloody choppers. You think they will leave us alone after that?"

"They might," I respond as I broadside the car around a huge boulder sitting in the middle of the track. The car took some serious beating when the corpse crashed it, but it still handles remarkably well. Say what you want about the Red Guard, but their taste in hardware is hard to fault.

"Goddamn it." She stamps her feet in the narrow well. "You have no idea how much I do not need this crap right now."

What the hell is that supposed to mean?

"Oh, yeah? You think you're the only one who finds this whole business a pain in the ass? Why the hell have they sent the Red Guards after us? For seeing an obviously faked video? Come on."

The car bounces over a large bump in the road and for a breathless second we're airborne. Then we crash back down with a bone-jarring impact and the steering wheel twists wildly in my hands. The car fights like a raging bull trying to throw us off and pound us into the dust.

"Yes, it has to be fake," Suki replies, but she looks away, hiding her face. I can't help noticing something in her voice saying she's not totally convinced. She's not turning into a believer, is she?

* * *

"That was smooth," Wagner shouts over the roaring engine as we go swerving through a fishtail around another muddy curve on our way to freedom. The path snakes sharply to the left and I bring us sliding stylishly around the corner and straight into a roadblock.

"Say again?" I shout back as I frantically scan the wall of vehicles, weapons and manpower for an opening. There is none.

In front of us is what looks like a full platoon of Red Guards crouching behind four big-wheeled ATVs, weapons at the ready. Standing in front of them is Jasper Constantine Borgia, an assault rifle aimed straight between my eyes from fifty metres away. The goody-bloody-two-shoes crew of the buggy actually called us in before getting themselves perished. They should have gone for the fucking money.

I stamp hard on the brake and spin the wheel, using the momentum of the swerving car to force it into a mud-splattering slide. As the soldiers open fire we are already accelerating away from them as fast as the five hundred horsepower engine and the big fat tires can take us. The uneven ground of the track kicks the car repeatedly in the balls and I'm glad it's not my car. The second-hand value of this thing will be like sex next to the Greenwich meridian; fucking close to zero.

A bullet shatters the rear-view mirror and needle-sharp fragments of reinforced glass pierce my cheek. Then Wagner pulls the trigger on the autocannon and everything is drowned by the noise as he empties the whole clip in a single continuous burst of explosive-tipped munitions. I cast a quick glance behind us and see the entire roadblock disappear in a cloud of exploding metal, spraying dirt and torn flesh. There's a massive detonation as a tracer round ignites the fuel tank on one of the vehicles, turning a group of soldiers into human torches stumbling screaming around the carnage. Through divine intervention, pure luck, or supernatural skill, Borgia himself stands unharmed in the middle of the chaos. He calmly squeezes round after round after us. His heavy leather cloak flaps in the updraft from the conflagration like a blood-red sail, making a colourful counterpoint to the boiling smoke around him. That guy is one hard son of a bitch.

"Helicopter, six o'clock," Wagner shouts and points behind us. True enough, there above the trees is one of the black military choppers, nose down and gaining quickly on us.

"Fuck," Wagner shouts again as he fumbles the reload and drops the ammo-drum behind us and the rounds go scattering across the jungle trail.

"Tell me you have more of those," I call over my shoulder.

"Last one."

Shit.

Without ammo the autocannon is just a very lousy club.

"There's a side track coming up on our left," Suki shouts as she points out a fork in the road, coming up fast.

"Could be a dead end. Can't risk it."

"It's not. Take the damn exit." The rapidly approaching chopper leaves me no option.

"Got it."

It opens fire just as I twist the wheel and throw us into the narrow side-track. Dirt, roots and splintered rock go flying all over the place, and the noise is like the voice of God on a bad hangover.

"Get us the hell out of here." Wagner shouts from his exposed position. He dumps the useless AC overboard as if dumping ballast will make the car go faster. It's already running at the top of its performance curve.

"What do you think I'm doing?" I shout in reply as I concentrate on trying to keep the bouncing buggy from veering off the path and into one of the huge trees lining the track. I'm not much of a driver, but I like to think I drive better than a headless corpse.

The narrow track is actually no more than a wide animal trail, weaving around and under the roots of the gargantuan trees, but it leads downhill, which is good. That's the way the gate lies. As long as we're going downhill there's still a chance we might survive this shit. Suki got lucky with that exit. Damn lucky.

* * *

Roots and sharp rocks make it a seriously bumpy ride, but we make good speed. As we come hurtling out of the jungle a couple of hundred metres from the park gate, I cast a quick glance behind us and see the chopper off in the distance. It's still circling the area where we left the main track. They spot us instantly.

"*Ach.* Here they come again," Wagner shouts as he holds on to his seat with all his might.

The chopper closes in fast, but it's too far away to stop us as we race flat out for the gate across the well-mown grass of the military cemetery taking up this part of the park. Even the state-of-the-art targeting systems on the chopper find it hard to track our small and swerving vehicle, and their bullets fall harmlessly several car-lengths behind us. Finally, the gunner or the automatic systems decide the danger to innocent bystanders is too great and they cease fire. They'll have to put their trust in the conventional forces on the ground to stop us.

"We're gonna make it," Suki shouts.

Damn it girl, don't jinx it.

There's a police squad posted at the gate and they scramble into action as we approach, trying to get their weapons to bear on us. It's much too late, and we just keep our heads down and storm through them, terrified cops jumping out of our way to avoid getting mangled. The barrier blocking the road is only designed to keep ordinary vehicles out of the park and it barely jolts the armoured buggy as we crash through it. Pieces of the broken boom fly everywhere.

These are just regular street cops, and I almost feel sorry for them at the thrashing they will get for letting us get away. Some of them manage to get off a couple of shots, but they soon cease and desist, also afraid to harm innocent bystanders. They are not the bad guys here.

I take us storming up the wide ramp that leads into Masada proper and the beautiful sunrise turns into the artificial Neo-N twilight of the Bottoms.

Police sirens are already wailing in the distance, but we got away. Now all we have to do is dump the buggy and find Suki's old geneticist and we are back in the business of saving the world.

Time is running out, and we're still no closer to finding out who or what the Prophet is, or what he plans to do with that nano bomb. All we know is that he's somewhere in the city, carrying the nastiest weapon known to man, and we're not the only ones looking for him. If we don't find him, and find him soon, this city is fucked. Hell, the entire human race could be fucked.

Funny, I never saw myself as hero material.

A Man Named Oddgrim Morgenstern

Suki gets off the pay console in the back of the Chinese diner where we're holed up and comes back to our table.

Apparently her expert is an old Jew who's spent most of his life gathering and cross-referencing data from every genetics database ever assembled. What the old coot is searching for Suki doesn't know – or won't tell us – but whatever it is, it has taken him seventy years to gather the data. If anyone can help us with a gene trace, it should be him. The old guy sounds like a match made in heaven for us, and once again just a little too good to be true. What the hell is this girl up to, and why do I have the feeling I'm on the butt end of a joke here?

"He will see us right away," she says as she turns a lacquered black chair around, straddles it and rests her arms on the seat back. "His name is Strauss. Nimrod Strauss." She looks at me like the name is supposed to mean something to me. It does not.

"OK...?" I venture.

"Never heard of him?" She looks deep into my eyes.

"Should I?"

"No, I guess not. He's only famous among educated people."

"Ha, fucking ha." I pull a face at her. She apes it back.

Wagner jumps to his feet and pours the half-pint of beer in his glass down his throat. He smacks the jug back down on the table and piss-coloured liquid drips from the ends of his long moustache. "Ready, boss. Let's get out of this Chink dump."

Wagner doesn't like Chinese food. Wagner doesn't like Chinese people. In fact, Wagner doesn't like anybody who's not a Goliath. After centuries of intermingling, the rest of us have come pretty close to a homogenous human race, but for Wagner there's just something in his Teutonic genes that rebels on contact with other cultures. That's the reason why Goliaths make such splendid soldiers. It's also the main reason they are not allowed on the inner planets.

Suki stays seated.

"So, it's a go then?" she asks. "We go see Strauss, we ID this guy you're looking for, and then we're done? You let me go, and we're square?"

I take a moment to think about it. "Yes. If we can get a match on the blood on that knife and get a solid lead on the guy, we'll let you go. Then Wagner and I go find the guy, take him to Gray, cash in the finder's fee and go drink all night long and pass out in the arms of cheap hookers. You can stay for the party or leave as you please. How does that sound?" If we deliver the guy to Gray, there's no reason for anyone to go after Suki and she should be safe from those church ninjas.

"I'd skip the hooker bit if I were you, but the rest sounds fine to me. Let's go."

* * *

If you took every stereotypical Jew you've ever seen and boiled them down to their very essence – in a metaphorical sense, please – you would get this energetic geriatric. He looks more kosher than a bar mitzvah and was probably into his second set of false teeth when the world was born.

The building looks like it might have been around in those days too. It's a small settlement-era chapel on the outskirts of Southern Masada, complete with tall stained glass windows, worn pews, and an ancient altar. Dark stone walls disappear into a vaulted ceiling high above, shrouded in shadows where the weak light from the desk lamps on the altar won't reach. Everything smells of dust and old books.

The place is a complete hell from a security point of view, which is why I've put Wagner on securing the perimeter. Besides, Wagner is not very good with people of Strauss' people anyway, and we really need the cooperation of this old guy.

"So, who are you looking for?" The ancient man shuffles over to the altar, now used as an overcrowded work desk, and clears it of yellowed papers. His shrivelled old fingers move marginally faster than Tutankhamen's would. Fortunately, there's a console terminal under the layers of detritus. I was beginning to think this would be an old-fashioned shuffle-through-shit-loads-of-papers search, but it seems we're in luck. When he turns the terminal on and I hear the ancient start up sound my newborn hopes are suffocated in their cradle. We're going to be here awhile.

"We're looking for a murder victim."

He nods for me to go on.

"We have no idea who he is, the body has gone missing, and my employer wants us to find him really bad." Hiding the truth behind a half-truth, I've found, is always the best deception. You are not actually lying and that shows in your body language.

"A friend, perhaps, of your employer's?" Strauss asks as he puts on a pair of ancient glasses and shuffles over to what looks like an old refrigerator in the corner of the room. The vain old fool. Who wears glasses these days?

"He could be my employer's grandmother for all I know," I reply as we follow him across the room at a snail's pace. "I don't know, and I don't care. I'm just paid to find the body."

The old man sits on an ancient wheeled office-chair next to the refrigerator.

"Alright then, let's see what we can see." He pulls a pair of yellowed latex gloves from an antique cardboard container on the desk and puts them on. Damn, is there nothing in this place that was manufactured after the war?

A chime from across the room signals that the ancient computer has finally started up. Strauss opens the refrigerator door and the contraption turns out to house a top-modern Nishin gene splicer. Perhaps he does know his stuff after all.

"Have you got something of the victim's person with you?"

"Better. I've got the murder weapon," I reply and haul the knife in its plastic bag from my pack.

He takes it from me and holds it up to the light by one corner, his rheumy old eyes blinking behind the round spectacles. I can't tell if his hands are shivering in anticipation of the hunt or old age.

"Yes... Lots of good DNA here," he turns it this way and that, lightly running his gloved fingers over the crusted spots on the blade. "This looks like a ceremonial Redeemer knife." He looks at me out of the corner of his eye. "Was your man sacrificed, by any chance?"

"I wasn't there."

"I never said you were..." he replies and puts the bag into a transparent biohazard cabinet fitted with interior gloves to allow him to handle the sampling process. "Nasty people, the Redeemers." He puts his hands though the gloves and opens the bag, extracts the knife and places it on a tray inside the cabinet. Then he removes a cotton swab from an interior container and dips it in some kind of solution in a dirty jar. "Did you touch the blade when you put in in the bag?" His eyes are fixed on the procedure inside the cabinet, but I get the feeling his mind is focused on me.

"Why?"

"If so, you might have contaminated the sample with your own DNA. It might be unusable."

"Clever," Suki nods in agreement with the old man.

Crap. Could it really be that sensitive? The look on my face must have betrayed me. He smiles at me.

"Oh, don't you worry. We will just take a quick blood sample, and then we can separate your DNA from his DNA." He rubs the moistened swab over the crusted blade inside the cabinet as he speaks. The swab turns red as the powerful enzymes dissolve the blood and suck it up into the cotton.

Suki gives me the ancient "that's just typical of you" look, well-known to boyfriends and husbands across the settled universe.

"... and here we go." He puts the swab into a small vial and seals it. "Now into the machine with you..." He extracts the sample from the biohazard cabinet and places it in the gene-splicer.

"And off she goes." He pushes a button on top of the refrigerator with a flourish like a stage magician turning a handkerchief into a pigeon, but in slow motion. The machine hums to life.

"How long is this going to take?" I ask him.

"Not long. Not long. We will have time for a quick sampling." He motions for me to hold out a finger and scoots over on his chair. In his bony hand is a device that looks like the bastard love-child of a porcupine and a spyglass. A transparent vial is attached to all kinds of vicious-looking brass needles and a thin handle, and the whole contraption shivers worryingly in his feeble grip. That thing looks older than Strauss himself.

"Is this really necessary?" I ask, perhaps a little too quickly.

"Relax, young man. This will only hurt a minute."

A minute? But he's right. If we're going to catch this guy we need a verified sample of his blood.

"Ow." He pushes one of the larger needles into the tip of my thumb. Damn, that really hurts.

"Oh, don't be such a baby," Suki sighs.

"There. That wasn't so bad." He pulls the needle out after extracting a large drop of blood. I suck my thumb. He unscrews the vial from the device, places it in another compartment in the gene splicer, and hits a sequence of buttons to start the second analysis.

"This will only take a minute." The old man leans back in his chair and looks oddly at me. I get the feeling he's afraid of me.

"Well, don't mind me. Do you have a bathroom?" I ask the old man, mostly to stay out of his way, but I also realise I need to piss.

"Over there by the altar." He motions to a door to what could once have led to a small sacristy.

The bathroom is tiny, but it serves its purpose.

After I'm done, I wash my hands and splash cold water in my face, trying to exorcise the stink of blood, sweat and gunpowder. It doesn't work, but the cool water feels good on my skin. I rub my eyes with the heels of my hands, and something comes loose under one eyelid.

What the hell?

I look into the small mirror above the sink, and gently use the tip of my index finger to probe my eyeball. As I touch it, the whole lens slides sideways, and I realise there's a coloured contact lens in my eye. But I don't wear contacts.

I carefully pull the thing out, and my heart drops into a lava pit in my stomach along with my grasp on reality.

The iris behind the lens is an almost unearthly light blue. Like the Prophet's in the video.

For a long moment, I can't think.

Then I reach up and slowly remove the contact from my other eye. The same icy blue.

Fuck.

He looks like you.

Suki's words echo through my reeling mind, followed by the image of a bruised face in the doctor's mirror. A face I hardly recognized.

Was that me in the video all along? Am I chasing a ghost?

Without conscious thought I stumble out to Suki and the old man, the contacts like disgusting stigmata on the palms of my outstretched hands.

"What the hell is going on here?" I ask, vaguely ashamed of the crack in my voice.

Suki spins around and pulls the strange-looking gun from her shoulder holster and aims it straight between my eyes. "We were about to ask you the same thing."

She calls to Strauss over her shoulder. "You're absolutely certain?"

"I've referenced and cross referenced the samples. The result is indisputable."

"So it is confirmed?" Suki breathes. "It's him."

"One hundred percent," Strauss replies. He blinks. "They both are."

"What the hell are you talking about?" I shake my head to try to clear it. This is not making any sense at all. "Did you get a match, or didn't you?"

"Yes, we got a match," Strauss sighs. "The blood on the knife belongs to a certain Oddgrim Morgenstern."

"OK. I like the name." My attempted cool feels fake as hell and I can tell they don't buy it for a second, but it's all that remains of my sanity, and I cling to it like a tick. "Who is he?"

"He's you."

"No he's not."

Suki nods at the contacts in my outstretched hands. "Then what about those?"

I shake my head. "I don't know. I'm..." My thoughts trickle away into the widening cracks of my mind and I just stare at her. She looks back, the gun still in my face. After what feels like an eternity something crumbles behind her eyes. "Oh, fuck. You really had no idea, did you?"

"Idea about what?" I try hard to keep the pleading out of my voice. I fail.

"OK. Here it is," Suki goes on. "Your blood does not match either the blood type or the genetic markers of Asher Perez at all."

A feeble "what?" is all I manage.

"It is, however, a perfect match for a man thought forty years dead and buried."

"But that's impossible." I shake my head.

"Even more impossible," old man Strauss chips in from his chair, "it's also a one hundred percent match for that of Oddgrim Morgenstern." He points at some figures on his display. They tell me shit.

"What?"

"You and Morgenstern share the same DNA," Suki explains to me like I'm a retarded child.

A sudden thought strikes me. It's the perfectly rational explanation for everything they're saying. "You have mixed up the samples." The relief runs like cool water through my fevered bloodstream. I'm not going crazy. I smile at them. A crazy smile.

The old man shakes his head. "No, the results are correct. Your DNA is indistinguishable from that of Morgenstern's."

"So, you're saying what? That he's my evil twin?" Another feeble try at humour.

With a sad smile, Suki pulls back the hammer on her gun, emphasising the stupidity of doing anything rash. "No. You are the evil twin."

There's a sudden movement over by the door.

"Put the gun down," Wagner commands as he steps from the shadows, his huge handgun aimed at Suki's chest.

"Finn, am I glad to see you."

Suki is not so happy to see him. "No, Wagner. You put the gun down, or I put a bullet in your friend's head."

"You were not supposed to see that," Wagner nods at the screen, and I am not sure if he's addressing me or the others. "I am sorry."

"You knew about this?" Suki looks at Wagner, incredulity and anger chasing each other across her face.

"Knew what?" I shout to the room at large. "Wagner? Knew fucking what?" In frustration I pull my own gun and aim it at Wagner's face and, et voilà, we have ourselves a three-way Mexican standoff.

Old man Strauss rolls behind a filing cabinet. "Morgenstern, eh?" He pipes up. "Sounds Jewish."

I appreciate his attempt to lighten the mood, but when the guns come out, the Rubicon is kind of crossed.

"Nah, I don't think so," I reply, my gun on Wagner's ugly face and my eyes on Suki's strange weapon. "The guy thinks he's Jesus Christ reborn."

"Hmm. Jesus was a Jew, you know. He might be right."

I like the old man, but I ignore him and focus on the matter at hand.

So does Suki. "Wagner, if you know what's going on here, then you also know what kind of gun this is." She gestures at her odd-looking weapon with her free hand as she moves sideways, trying for a position where she can cover us both. "You know it will kill someone of his kind as easily as it will kill one of us. I don't want to do it, but put down your weapon, or I will drop him, right here, right now and forever." It sounds like she really means it.

"I can't do that." He shakes his great head. "I have orders."

Strauss makes another valiant attempt. "Did you know 'Morgenstern' *auf Deutsch* means Morningstar in English?" He peers at me around the cabinet, his eyes rendered big and round by his grimy spectacles like something out of an ancient cartoon.

"No. So?"

"Another famous bearer of that name was the Lightbringer. You'd know him as Lucifer. Perhaps it's not Jesus you are chasing. Perhaps you are chasing the Devil."

There's a twinkle in his eye, but I can't tell if he's making fun of me or if he's dead serious. And I get the feeling he's stalling for time. But time for what?

"Wagner, why the fuck is she doing this?" I call to my friend without taking my eyes off Suki and her gun.

"I have no idea."

"Swear it."

"On the hall of my fathers." He turns a fraction of a degree in my direction, for just an instant taking his eyes off Suki and that's all she needs.

"Now," she shouts before dropping to the ground.

Now what?

Behind my back the stained glass windows explode into the room, bringing two huge ninjas falling through the air, firing extended bursts of assault-rifle bullets right into Wagner's chest.

Everything goes downhill from there.

A Man of Manners

The ninjas roll as they touch down, sending long bursts in my direction. Their bullets tear chunks of stone out of the wall as they track me across the floor.

Wagner's body armour must have taken the brunt of the impact because he is still alive. He launches a massive kick into the small of the back of the closest ninja from his position on the floor. The impact would have killed an unprotected man, but the ninja looks merely winded. Still, it's enough, and Wagner takes advantage of the situation. He gets up, grabs the man by the balls and the scruff of the neck and hoists him high into the air. Then he slams him back down in a perfectly executed back breaker and the ninja's spine meets Wagner's extended knee with a horrible crack, like a rotten tree breaking. The body goes limp and Wagner throws it aside like a wet towel. He is truly magnificent when it comes to close combat.

I scramble for safety as the other ninja turns to fire at Wagner. As I reach the first bench, three more ninjas come swinging through the windows. The laser-pointers on their short, vicious-looking assault rifles sweep the room for targets and they all converge on Wagner where he stands over their dead comrade. He roars at them as all three open fire at close range. He bellows like a stuck pig as the bullets tear through his flesh.

Damn, I knew we should have brought the hardware this time. Don't we ever learn? If Wagner is to survive I have to do something, and do it fast.

"Hey, over here," I shout before crawling as fast as I can towards the aisle. Bullets chew the benches to splinters around me.

Suki yells over the gunfire. "No, don't kill him."

I like the sound of that.

"We need him alive."

And I don't like the sound of that. Need me alive for what?

Looking under the front bench, I see Wagner launch a devastating sweep-kick at the legs of his nearest adversary. He's not nearly fast enough and the ninja is already airborne when Wagner's leg passes harmlessly beneath him. How the hell are we supposed to beat these guys?

I reach the aisle and charge the ninjas as fast as I can, hoping to get in close enough for them to be unable to use their heavy weapons. They must not have expected me to do something that stupid because they are very slow to react. Leaving all fancy theatrics aside, I go for a vicious body tackle. I duck under the rifle of the closest man as he opens fire and shoulder him in the solar plexus. He goes down with me and I twist in the air to use my not inconsiderable bulk to crush the air from his lungs. As I had hoped, the suits are flexible to allow their wearers to move freely and there's a muffled crack from inside as his ribs break. I grab his helmeted head with both hands and roll him over my back. I twist and pull as hard as I can, hoping to remove the helmet and expose the vulnerable human beneath.

"Perez, no." Suki's shout is too late.

There's a sickening crunch from inside the suit and the man goes limp in my hands. A malfunction of the suit or the result of some other effect, I don't know, but the ninja is out of action.

Meanwhile, Wagner is sparring with one of the three remaining ninjas, trading blows that would easily kill a normal man. The ninjas crowd around Wagner like dogs around a bear. One of them jumps on his back and grabs his face from behind. In horrible slow motion I see armoured fingers pierce Wagner's eye and tear it out. My giant friend howls in mortal pain and falls to his knees. Deep in Wagner's throat the howl catches on what sounds like bubbling mud and he goes down. One of the ninjas raises the muzzle of his assault rifle and aims it at Wagner's temple. Not even a Goliath will survive a headshot at point blank range.

I need something to throw. I grab a dropped rifle from the floor and hurl it with all my strength. It strikes the weapon of the ninja hard, deflecting it just as he pulls the trigger and the burst punches holes in the filing cabinet behind which Strauss is hiding. Following up my attack, I close on the shooter and punch him in the kidneys. To my surprise he goes down like a sack of bricks and I use my momentary advantage to stomp him in the face. His helmet cracks and through the opening I see blood and bone poking through the skin. He's dead. Those suits are overrated.

The two remaining ninjas turn their fire on me. There's no way I can get away fast enough, but I drop to the floor anyway. Luck must be with me because only a handful of bullets find their targets. It still feels like I've been kicked in the side, and my already wounded thigh goes numb. I realise my only chance of survival is to use Wagner as a human shield, and I roll behind him as the ninjas open fire again. My big friend is back up on his knees when the bullets find him and he goes down for the third time. I lunge for the weapon of the closest ninja and catch the barrel, feeling the hot metal sear my skin. I yank it as hard as I can, pulling the man off balance towards me and manage to get my arm around his neck. The other man empties his magazine on us, knowing his bullets won't harm his comrade, and I feel my hand explode with pain. Several fingers are blown off, but the pain is a mere flash and then gone, fading into a bearable dull ache and I can still move. Adrenaline truly is a marvellous thing.

Not having Wagner's massive strength, I break the ninja's neck by pulling his head backwards, twisting, and rolling him over my shoulder. Another sickening crack from inside the suit and he's dead.

One man left, and he's out of bullets.

I let his dead friend drop to the floor and crack my neck, panting hard.

"Perez, no. Don't do it," Suki screams at me, but the ninja motions her to stay back. He throws his useless assault rifle to the floor where it clatters against a wall before he assumes a fighter's stance. He's been well trained.

"OK, let's do this," I say as I wipe blood from my mouth with the back of my hand.

Suki moves in between us, reaching out like a boxing referee. "Stop it."

"Get out of the way, Suki," I shout as we circle her, both of us looking for an opening.

The ninja reaches up and tears the helmet from his head. Beneath is an Asian-looking man in his mid-thirties, good looking, covered in sweat. His black, longish hair is plastered across his forehead.

"Suki, get out of the way," he orders her. "Let me kill the abomination."

"No, Marcus. We need him. He doesn't know what he is."

"The fuck he doesn't. Look what he did to Emund and the others." His hand sweeps the room, indicating the dead ninjas.

"He doesn't know his own strength," Suki shouts. "Please, don't do this, Marcus."

"Stay back." His armoured backhand smashes into her unprotected temple and she's hurled like a mitten across the room.

"You shouldn't hit girls, you know." I spit blood on the floor.

"Oh yeah? And what are you going to do about it, defiler?"

Defiler? Not even in the top ten most popular derogatives in a fight. Who the hell are these clowns?

I lunge forward, noting his surprise at my speed. He's still ready for my attack, blocks it and throws a counter punch at my head. I go for a dodge but end up blocking his fist with my head. Bad move. His heavy gauntlet smashes into my face, breaking my nose. Damn, this guy is fast. Pain explodes across my vision in a pyrotechnics display to rival any hallucinogen trip. Then it recedes like a colourful tide off a sandy beach, leaving only a vague memory of discomfort. Sensing his surprise when I don't go down, I use the millisecond respite to drop him with a quick kick to the knee.

I try to stomp the life from his face but he sees the move coming from a mile away and rolls out of the way. His knee must be broken because he stays down and instead tries to punch me in the balls. I catch his arm in a two-handed vise grip.

"Oh, no you don't." I slowly break his arm and he screams.

"And this one is for Wagner."

I crush his windpipe with a quick jab, and the fight goes out of him as the breath bubbles through his broken throat. His functioning hand claws at his flesh, trying ineffectually to clear his airways. It's over, and I let the pain and fatigue overcome me as I drop to my knees.

That's when I notice all the blood. I've been shot worse than I thought. My leg is a mess of torn flesh, and beneath the gore I can see pieces of metal protruding. My side is a nightmare of pulped meat. Crap.

I feel faint and I fall on my side as the world grows dark around the edges. So this is how I go. Not bad for an old man.

In blurring slow motion I see Suki run to the fallen ninja and hold his head up, ineffectually trying to ease his breathing. I roll over on my back to keep from having to watch Marcus die slowly of suffocation. Will his be the first in the long line of angry ghosts to welcome me into the afterlife?

* * *

I must have passed out because the darkness slowly clears and I wake.

Two moons shine through the shattered windows, draping me in a glowing blanket like something out of a Rembrandt painting. Suki walks slowly into the shaft of light, her boots echoing on the cold stone floor, dust motes swirling about her like fireflies. She stops beside me and stands looking down at me for a long time, face in darkness, her hair a spiked halo. In her hand is the odd-looking gun, pointing at the floor. The gun that will kill one of my kind as easily as one of them. Whatever the hell that means.

A quivering sigh and she gets down on her knees, careful not to touch the blood pooling on the flagstones. There's an awful lot of it.

"Oh, Perez." She shakes her head.

"Wagner?" I croak, struggling to get up on an elbow to get a look at the fallen giant, but my body doesn't respond as well as it used to.

"It's bad." She shakes her head again. "Real bad."

Fuck. I slump back into the cold blood.

"Why did it come to this?" She reaches out with her fingers as if to touch my face, but changes her mind. Her hand hangs frozen in the air between us until she lowers it onto the gun in her lap.

"Who are you, Suki?"

"I could ask you the same thing, Perez. If that really is your name."

"Who were they?" I gesture feebly at the dead ninjas.

For a long time she just looks at me, tears brimming in her eyes. When the tears finally fall, they drop like diamonds into the blood, and she starts talking.

"They were my family, Perez. My cousins, Edi, Gunnar and Jonas," she points them out to me, "and my two older brothers, Marcus and Emund."

She removes a tiny ear bud and lets it drop to the floor where it rolls away into the darkness, no longer needed.

"So that's how they found us so easily." I cough a mist of blood into the moonlight. Never a good sign. The taste of blood fills my mouth. How many times have I tasted my own blood in the last few days? Too many.

"They trained for this their entire lives, and you killed them. Just like that." She tries to snap her fingers but they slip silently in the blood on her hands, her eyes freezing on her fingertips as if mesmerised. She shivers with deep, silent sobs.

"Well, not just like that," I object, unable to mimic her gesture with my butchered hand. "They put up a hell of a fight."

She sighs and looks away into a distant place visible only to her.

"I know." Her eyes return to me. "I tried to stop them, but they wouldn't listen."

"Why were they trying to kill me? I've never done anything to you or your family."

"No." She shakes her head slowly. "Not you personally. But your kind has been our enemy since before history began."

"My kind? What the hell are you talking about? We're the same flesh and blood, Suki."

"That's where you're wrong, Perez. You are not one of us. Never have been, never will be. You may look like us, talk like us, and bleed like us, but you don't die like us. Just look at you now. With wounds like those you should be dead."

I look down at my broken and bleeding body.

"Well, I don't feel like dancing, if that's any consolation."

"Fuck you, Perez, I'm serious. You are not like us, but you are not like *them* either." She's slowly shaking her head. "You and Morgenstern are something new, something we've never seen before. Your genetic scores are off the charts, and that scares me."

"I am who I am." I try to shrug. It hurts like hell.

"I'm not so sure about that." She looks oddly at me. "I believe we all have a choice, Perez. We are not who we are. We are whoever we choose to be, and right now, you could be our only hope."

Hope of what?

The door explodes off its hinges in a cloud of cordite and ricocheting shrapnel. For a second I think Wagner has returned from the land of the dead. My dimming eyesight clears and I see His Most Revered Worthiness, the High Inquisitor Jasper Constantine Borgia bowing his head through the broken doorway with a huge assault rifle pointing at the floor. Oh, for fuck's sake. Does this crap never end?

"Secure the area," he orders the Red Guards spreading out behind him as he strides down the aisle. He steps over the bodies of the fallen ninjas and stops in front of me and Suki, where he hunches down in the middle of the blood. His massive leg-muscles stretch the coarse fabric of his combat trousers, making them creak. He rests his elbows on his mountain-sized knees, his long, black hair almost tickling my lips.

"So, you're Asher Perez." He tilts his head, trying to get a better look at me. "You're not an easy man to find." A respectful nod from the giant inquisitor.

"The pleasure is all yours, motherfucker." If I had the strength to spit on his boots I would.

"Ah, a man of manners." A quick smile touches his fleshy lips. He gets back up and turns to his men. "Bring this one, the girl and the Goliath. Find out who these clowns are," he gestures at the dead ninjas, "and kill the old man." His men move out behind him. Two of them grab Suki by the arms and haul her screaming to her feet as another man walks over to where Strauss is hiding behind his cabinet. The old man slowly gets down on his knees, hands clasped in his lap. He gazes bravely into the eyes of his executioner through his round spectacles. At the last moment his courage fails him and he opens his mouth to say something. I look away.

"No!" Suki's shout of denial is drowned by the sharp bang of a gun in the otherwise silent chamber. The noise rolls around the rafters until it finally dies out and all that can be heard is Suki's howling vows of bloody vengeance. Snot and spittle fly from her lips as the men drag her kicking and screaming down the aisle.

Massing all my remaining strength, I reach out a gory, fingerless hand toward Borgia, blood dripping on the floor between us. All I get for my trouble is a rifle-butt in the face, and my vision explodes into a hazy shade of nothing.

The Judgement

The judgement has begun. It's time for Gray to pay for his treason.

Standing outside the doors to Gray's penthouse office, the general takes a deep breath. The security camera above the door tracks his every move, and he knows Gray is on the other side, watching. He likes it that way. It gives Gray time to ponder his inevitable fate.

Blood is still dripping feebly from the general's torn flesh where it has not yet had time to seal around the slick black cords of his enhanced tendons and muscles. The blood dyes the thick carpet a rusty brown around him. Like everything in the Gray Tower, the carpet is expensive beyond measure, and it feels good to bleed all over it. All the wealth pumped into the construction of this tower is not going to protect Gray, and that makes the general smile. Things like that have always made him smile. Life's little ironies.

"What are you smiling about, Caspar?" A voice from a recessed speaker system. It's Gray.

"Nothing. Open the door, Gray." The general's tone is reasonable. Almost friendly.

"You know I can't do that." Meridian can almost hear the sad shake of Gray's head.

"I'm going to huff and I'm going to puff until I blow your door down, Gray. There's no use to hope for the security team. They're all dead."

"There's no way you can get through this door, General, and you know that. You helped me install it, remember." Gray's voice is calm, and there is not a trace of panic. He is confident in his security measures. He shouldn't be.

"Why don't we sit down and talk, Caspar? We never talk any more. We used to talk for hours, you and I. About life. About death. About who you would be when you grew up. Did you know the news feeds call you The Dread General? I quite like the sound of that."

"Yes, I heard that. Touching. I also heard of a back door to your office. A secret door. One that leads out onto the roof and a chopper platform."

Gray's silence speaks for itself. The back door was installed as a final safety measure by Gray to prevent him from ever being trapped in his hole. No one outside the building crew was to know about it. Within days of installing it, the members of the work crew were all killed in routine workplace accidents. It was a good thing they talked to the general before they died. The security of the Gray Tower was always his responsibility, and an unsecured door could have been a potential Trojan horse into the very heart of the Gray empire. It was his duty to find out about that door.

To prevent Gray from escaping through the front doors, the general pushes his assault rifle through the tall titanium handles. He bends the barrel into a loop to keep it from falling out if the doors are shaken from inside.

"Do you know what else they call you, Caspar?" Gray's voice is still soft and warm, but there is now a harsh note of urgency.

"There is a time for talk and there's a time for action, Gray, and your tricks of persuasion are not going to save you this time."

"They call you the Enemy of Man. How grand is that? We always knew you would be famous."

"Gray, I'm coming for you."

He doesn't even bother to destroy the camera as he walks to the nearest window. It overlooks the financial district of the city of Masada, far, far below. From this, the second tallest building in the city, he can see all the little lives going on below. Like ants unaware of the wars of men, they are unaware of the confrontation taking place above their tiny reality. People like those below always were unfit to manage their own world. That's one thing Gray has always been right about. You can't run a civilisation by compromising.

Meridian picks up one of the heavy lounge chairs and hurls it through the window. The reinforced glass explodes outward, sending a rain of razor shards tumbling into the city below. If the glass is even noticed down there, it will be written off as a freak incident. The impact of the chair will probably result in a police investigation, and unless the chair actually kills someone, the investigation will soon be dropped when the source of the unexpected projectile is discovered. Gray's name commands power in the world of men.

He climbs through the broken window and into the howling wind outside. At this altitude, the temperature is lower than the humid warmth of Masada's ground-level habitats, and the wind soothes the tatters of his skin. The replicating processes of his cells generate excessive amounts of waste heat, and he has always enjoyed a cool wind. He casts a quick glance down. Below him, the illuminated rooftop parks of the other skyscrapers glitter like islands in a dark ocean. It's beautiful.

As he moves off along the wide ledge at a brisk walk, he can hear the sirens still wailing inside, but no one heeds their call. Everybody's dead, and Gray is on his own.

A nightmare walks with him on the other side of the glass. A creature of metal and hyper-carbon, of slouching skin and glistening shreds of internal organs hanging out, torn by bullets, burnt by explosions. He ignores his reflection and moves on.

When he reaches the corner of the building, he looks up and finds the thick rope of cables from the communications array exactly where he remembers it to be. His memory has always been faultless. For better or worse, nothing he has ever seen, heard or done is ever lost to him. His nightmares are a nightmare.

The bunched cables provide him easy access to the roof. In seconds, he's standing on the helicopter platform, battered by the wind, chilled by a light drizzle from the darkening clouds above. The rescue chopper has no doubt been called, but it has not yet arrived. There is plenty of time.

He lopes across rain-slick concrete to the stairwell. The only thing rising above the flat roof is the distant spire of the cathedral. It crowns the steep pyramid of Northern Masada, like the Gray Tower crowns the Southern. The cathedral is the only building on the planet taller than the Gray Tower and thus the grandest building ever created by humankind.

He starts to descend the stairs to Gray's chambers.

"Caspar, wait." The voice of his creator comes from hidden speakers somewhere in the darkness. "You know I had to do what I did. You would have done the same thing if you were in my position." His words fill the narrow stairwell with their silky smooth insinuations. The voice of reason.

The voice of the Serpent.

"Oh, I know that, Gray. And you would have come for me, just like I come for you."

He reaches a hypercarbon door blocking his way. He knows this door is nowhere near as solid as the main entrance, and the general releases all his anger on it. The dull thump of flesh on metal is soon replaced by the clang of hypercarbon on hypercarbon as the skin and flesh on his knuckles is worn away. At the first strike the door shudders. At the second it dimples. After that it's just a matter of time until he wears his way through.

All the while Gray's voice is there with him in the stairwell, soothing, persuasive, ignored.

When the door finally gives in and the general steps into Gray's inner sanctum in a flurry of rain and wind, he finds the old man leaning on his great Terran oak desk. If the piece were for sale on the open market, the down payment alone would field a battalion for a month. What a waste.

"Welcome, World Burner, first among the fallen." Gray raises his arms in greeting, and the general pulls his knife from its wrist sheath. "Now now, Caspar. Put that thing away. There's no need for violence."

For a second he's tempted to do as Gray asks. There's no way for the old man to escape, and the general intends to savour this moment.

There's a momentary flicker to the side by Gray's otherwise steady gaze.

Something is wrong.

A whisper of sound behind the general alerts him to another presence in the room.

He spins, aiming to throw the knife at the unknown assailant, but it's too late.

A foot-long harpoon impales him through the stomach. A fraction of a second later, a million volts of current from a Carnosaur tranquilliser gun convulses over the wires between the weapon and the harpoon and on into the general's body. His every muscle locks into a rictus of pain, and, as he falls paralysed to the floor, his attacker steps from the shadows beside the door. The light from the single lamp on Gray's desk illuminates a strong, handsome face and broad shoulders.

He should have known. Solana stayed behind when they went to meet Gray on Persephone.

There was one grave missing at the cemetery.

"Well done as always, Major Solana." Gray leans back, steadying himself against the desk as he applauds the major.

"I'll hang on to this for now." Solana steps on the general's wrist and pries the knife from his fingers. The knife he has carried all his life. The loss of the knife hurts more than the deception.

Gray starts speaking again. "Now, I know you must be feeling surprised and not a little betrayed here, Caspar. You should know that the major was in my service long before he joined your precious Cherubim. He's been my eyes and ears all these years. You see, I always foresaw a time like this might come, and I needed someone on the inside to keep track of you. You are too good at what you do, and sometimes even my not inconsiderable assets have problems keeping you under observation. I should have put a tracer on you, like you do with children." Gray's smile is far from fatherly. "I created you, Caspar, and for want of a better word, I consider you my son. My precious, beautiful son, to whom I have given the gift of immortality. A precious gift indeed, and one which will make what I have in mind for you quite, quite bad."

The paralysis is slowly wearing off, but the general takes care to keep his limbs totally petrified while he waits for the return of full mobility. The barbs of the harpoon grind in his guts at the tiniest motion of the major's huge weapon. Solana won't look Meridian in the eye as he addresses his former commander.

"I'm sorry, General, that it had to come to this. I've served you faithfully all these years, and with great pride, but Mr Gray has always been my true captain."

"Enough of the pleasantries, Major. Let's get the General ready." He turns back to Meridian. "You see, Caspar, the very idea that you could come here, hoping to kill me, means I have to do something very nasty to you. No matter how useful you have been to me down the years. No matter that you won the war for me. No matter that you are my son. If people got the notion that I am a valid target, all the people I've crossed down the years would come crawling out from under their rocks to attack me. That would quickly get very tedious. So I'm sure you understand why your fate has to be a chilling reminder that Nero Praetorius Gray is not a man to be targeted. Since you're already officially dead, we will have to blame this little attack on some Terran infiltrator, but the lesson will still be valid. Your punishment will become famous throughout the underworld, yet no one but me and the major will ever know the full extent of your suffering. That is something that truly amuses me, and I will be thinking fondly of you in the years to come, knowing you are still hurting."

The time for action has almost come and the general readies for his attack. First he will kill the traitor major and then he will deal with Gray in the most horrible way imaginable.

"Major, I believe it is time." Gray nods at Meridian and Solana pulls the trigger on the tranquilliser gun again, sending another agonising surge of current through the mono-filament wires and on into the general's flesh.

This time the pain doesn't stop. Instead the major slowly cranks up the voltage, bringing Meridian to ever increasing levels of pain.

Eventually the general's mind goes mercifully black.

* * *

Darkness.

All around him total darkness.

Try as he might, he can't see a thing.

He can't move. His entire body is trapped in what feels like cast iron that does not give a millimetre as he tries to shift position. The only thing he can move is his tongue and his lips. Even his eyelids seem to be locked in place. He opens his parched mouth with a dry rustle of separating skin.

"Ah, you're back." Gray's voice comes from plugs inside his ears. "How good of you to rejoin us, General."

"Where am I?" His mouth is not yet fully responsive after the massive electrocution and his tongue stumbles over his teeth as he tries to speak.

"Ah, that is the ten-million-credit question, isn't it?" It's clear that Gray is dying to tell him, but wants to hold on to the secret for a moment longer, like a spoilt child. The man is quite mad, the general realises, and if the general had the capacity for fear he would now start to fear for his life. But general Caspar Batista Meridian has seen and dealt too much death to fear his own. Come in what form it may, death is just the cessation of life. He has lived more than most, and he leaves a legacy behind that will never be forgotten.

No, death holds no fear for general Meridian, even though he knows that for him it must come in some very special form. He has survived wounds that would have killed normal men, diseases that should have rotted his flesh, and torture that ought to have destroyed his mind. He is special. Gray made sure of that.

"Come on, Gray, cut the crap." Meridian coughs. "Tell me how I die. You know you won't make me beg for mercy."

"Who said anything about dying?" Gray's merry laugh is the scariest thing Meridian has ever heard, and then he can see.

A panel slides up before him and at first his eyes are blinded by the sharp light streaming through the widening crack. As his pupils contract to adjust for the brightness, he sees starlight that is far stronger than a starlit night on any planet. And then he sees the craft in which he's travelling.

It's a standard-size starship escape pod, crew space for one. And this one has been filled with plascrete, the strongest building material known to man, locking him in place in front of the tiny porthole window. The flight controls have been removed.

"Starting to get the picture now, General?" There's a vile smile in Gray's voice. "I will be checking in on you every now and then, to see how you're doing. At first we will have no problem communicating, but over time, the distance will begin to delay our talks. First a few easily ignored seconds between receiver and sender. Then minutes. Days. Weeks. Finally, years will pass between each sentence, but by then I am afraid you will be quite mad and not much fun at all. Goodbye, General. Enjoy your voyage into the great beyond." The line clicks and goes dead.

And then Caspar Batista Meridian, the Enemy of Man, the Dread General, the World Burner, begins to scream.

You Should Have Brought Him Instead

I dream of being dissected.
Laser scalpels slice my skin.
Rubber-gloved hands peel back my flesh.
I try to move, but I am paralysed.
A scream of silence and I awake.

* * *

First to pierce the oblivion is pain. My shoulders hurt like hell.

Next is the faraway sound of song, as of a giant choir chanting in unison.

I open my eyes and find myself in near total darkness, looking down my chest. Spittle dribbles down my chin. The darkness smells of dust and ancient stone. And death. A long way beneath my feet, a solitary pool of light reveals a worn stone floor, moving slowly in circles. I shake my head and realise it's me that's moving. I look up and see I'm suspended in mid-air, manacles around my wrists attached to chains disappearing into the darkness on either side of me, splaying me like the Vitruvian Man. The only source of light in the room is coming from somewhere high above and behind me. Oh great. Crucifixion, anyone?

"Hello, Asher." An amplified voice from the darkness.

"Hello." I look around, trying to locate the speaker. "Who the fuck are you?"

"Oh, you know me, Asher. You know me." A low chuckle from the shadows, echoing in what must be a vast chamber.

A man walks into the light far below and I realise that I do know him. The red cassock and silly hat kind of give it away. "Well, well, well, I'll be damned. If it isn't the great cardinal himself."

That explains the chanting. The Eternal Choir of the Masada cathedral is famous across the settled universe.

He bows to me. "Cardinal Dietmar Alejandro Santoro at your service."

"I'm flattered." The Santoros have held the cardinal's chair since the Settlement. Along with the Grays and the Nishii, they are the closest thing we have to royalty on Elysium. "Now, what the fuck am I doing here?" He wants something, or we wouldn't be having this conversation.

"Language, Asher, language," the cardinal scolds. "This is, after all, the House of the Lord. But I take it you are not a churchgoing man."

"I can't say that I am."

"Hmm." He seems to ponder something profound. "Tell me, Asher. How can people like you survive in a world without meaning, where everything is random?"

"It sounds better than a world ruled by a divine megalomaniac who will do anything to be worshipped by mere humans."

"Careful, Asher." There's a dangerous glint in his eyes and I realise he's not a man to be trifled with. "You could burn in hell for that."

"Yes, that *would* be random."

He purses his lips like he just ate a bad lemon and forces a deep breath. I press on.

"You want something from me, Cardinal, and I guess you didn't bring me here to discuss theology. Why am I still alive?"

He stands looking up at me for a long while. "I believe we have a common interest, you and I."

"Morgenstern."

"Yes."

"And this is the moment when you tell me to back off, or you'll have me killed?"

"On the contrary. I want you to help me find him."

"What do you want with him?"

"I thought that would be obvious."

"Oh, come on. You can't be serious."

"Of course not. The man is a homicidal maniac and should be put down, but he has an important part to play in what's going to happen over the next few days."

"If this is about the Archangel, I already know everything about it. Let me down and I will go stop him." I rattle the chains and feel my shoulders almost tear out of their sockets.

"Ah, but Morgenstern and the Archangel are only part of the problem. There is something bigger behind all this, Asher. Much bigger. In fact, it's so big I've decided to tell you some dangerous things about yourself and the world you think you live in."

I give him a very skeptical look and he goes on.

"You see, Asher, war is coming. The Terrans are back, and they are here to wipe us out."

"Oh, yeah? How come we haven't heard anything about it?"

"Because we only discovered them a couple of days ago. The sensor arrays on Erebus flagged an anomaly in a certain vector of space, which when analysed turned out to be a great fleet of Terran battleships braking into the system."

"Really? Some hobby astronomer would have seen them through his bedroom telescope and spread the word."

The cardinal smiles. "We've kept a lid on it."

A barely remembered news report on the apparent suicide of a professor of astronomy flashes through my mind. Ah.

"By now they are twelve hours out and will have long since launched the ramstrikes which we estimate will arrive within the next few hours."

"What?" This is bad. Genocide bad. "Why haven't you sounded the alarm? You've got to evacuate people. Run to the fucking hills."

"There is nothing I can do to prevent their deaths." He shrugs his bony shoulders. "Would you rather spend your final hours with your family and loved ones and be unknowingly wiped out in the blink of an eye, or die screaming in the congested streets, knowing there is not a single thing you can do to save your children from certain death?"

He has a point.

"When the Terran armies land, we are doomed, unless we have a powerful symbol to rally around. In Oddgrim Morgenstern we have the most powerful symbol of all. With Jesus Christ commanding our armies, we cannot lose."

"You know as well as I do that he is not Jesus Christ."

"Of course."

"So, who is he, really?"

"Well, let me tell you a story, Asher."

Oh, crap, here we go. Old people love to tell stories.

"There was once a great old man who ruled a grey kingdom from the top of a grey tower. The man had all the power in the lands, but there was one thing ailing him. He had no wife, he had no children and he was lonely. The people served his every whim, but none of them called him friend. So he decided to create one. A friend who was like himself. Smart. Powerful. Different. Someone to rule the grey kingdom after he was gone.

"He named his creation Morgenstern, the Light bringer, because he believed his new friend would bring the light back into his life." The cardinal laughs to himself.

"Hang on. Is this Nero Gray we're talking about? My employer?"

"The same."

"And he created Morgenstern? Cloned him, you mean?"

"Yes."

"Cloned him from what?"

"So many questions, Asher. That is inconsequential." He waves my question away. "When Gray finally realised Morgenstern was mad and sent the termination order, it was too late. Morgenstern second-guessed him and escaped. During the escape he killed twenty-seven of Gray's elite soldiers who stood in his way. At the time he was ten years old. Then he disappeared from the face of the planet."

"Well, you know what they say; children can be cruel."

The cardinal ignores me. "Oddgrim Morgenstern was no ordinary child. His body was a magnificent machine, designed and manufactured by Gray Industries. Like a cancer, the cells of his body divided at a vastly accelerated rate, but never out of control. And they never broke down or died. His body's defences had been improved by the introduction of nano-machines into his bloodstream. They aided his body's healing by cannibalising other resources, either internal or external, and allowed him to heal at a hundred times the normal human rate. They instantly sealed severed blood vessels and regrew lost body parts."

That would explain how he could survive having his throat cut, and I have a bad feeling about where this is going.

"Go on."

"In addition to the regeneration, his creators fitted him with some very impressive mechanical improvements. All major tendons and muscles in his body were replaced or reinforced with spring-loaded hypercarbon fibres, giving him the strength of a titan. As he grew, they cut him open again and again to adjust the enhancements. He could probably defeat a Goliath in unarmed combat. His nervous system was augmented too, giving him reflexes out of this world."

"Can he be killed?"

"Sever the head and the brain will eventually die from lack of oxygen." He shrugs. "That's about it."

"There can be only one, huh?"

"Hmm?" The cardinal gives me an uncomprehending look.

"Never mind. What happened? I know Gray. He doesn't like to be fucked over."

"No, he does not like to be fucked over, as you so eloquently put it. The Great War happened, and Gray's attention was diverted elsewhere. With the approval of the church, Gray Industries used their new technology to create a force of highly capable and immortal special forces soldiers to fight in the war. Time was of the essence, and they bred them fast and hard. They were instrumental in the destruction of Arcadia and thereby winning the war."

"Hang on." A memory of terminally boring high school history lessons in dusty classrooms rears its ugly head at the back of my mind. "Is this general Meridian and the Cherubim we're talking about?" Some of the kids in my class were actually impressed by what he did. They played Meridian and the Cherubim in the school yard.

"It is." He nods sagely.

"The psycho who turned on the ion drives of the *Gormenghast* in the atmosphere of Arcadia and burned himself and the planet to a crisp? The bastard in whose honour they raised a statue in Freedom Square?"

"The same."

"Was that Gray's doing?"

The cardinal nods. "And that, by the way, is the official version of what happened."

"Let me guess."

"You are correct. The general and his soldiers didn't die in the explosion. They got out before the ship entered the Arcadian atmosphere. They launched in their combat suits and fell to Earth – if you'll pardon the expression – on the small Arcadian moon of Persephone, where they met up with Gray. Gray knew he could never risk having his name associated with the operation, and he had General Meridian and his men executed on the spot. The general, of course, didn't die. He was a resourceful man and managed to escape. He hid among the bodies of his dead men and hitched a ride back to Elysium, where he was buried with honours. That night he dug his way out of his grave and killed his way up the Gray Tower, intending to destroy his maker."

"So it was Meridian who attacked the Gray Tower all those years ago. We always heard it was an Arcadian assassin."

"No Arcadian assassin would have got as far as the general did. He very nearly succeeded in his endeavour. He was only stopped at the last moment by Major Amon Solana, his own second-in-command who had been an agent of Gray's from the very beginning."

"It's so hard to find good help these days."

"Tell me about it. The punishment Gray visited upon the general was horrible. He plascreted Meridian into an escape pod and launched him into space." The cardinal raises his hands to heaven and goes into recital mode, like a bad Thespian playing to his last audience. "He laid hold on the dragon, that old serpent which is the Devil, and bound him a thousand years. And he cast him into the bottomless pit, that he should deceive the nations no more, till the thousand years should be fulfilled." He looks back. "Or something along those lines. Since the general couldn't die of starvation and he had no way of killing himself, he could only watch and scream as he drifted out of the solar system and into interstellar space. After a few years his mind was completely gone."

There is something about the story that rings true with me. I shiver and nod for him to go on.

"Then, a few weeks ago, the video of Morgenstern's execution and subsequent resurrection surfaced, and Gray knew his first-born had returned and was up to something. He also knew there was only one man in the universe who could ever catch Oddgrim Morgenstern, so he sent a salvage team into space, retrieved the general's body and brought it back to Elysium after almost forty years."

"Well, it sounds like Meridian is the guy you want to send after Morgenstern. You should have brought him instead."

The cardinal chuckles to himself again as if at some private joke. "Yes, I should have, shouldn't I."

He just stands there, looking up at me, the smile never leaving his face.

"What?"

He just keeps smiling and a cold shiver runs down my spine.

"Oh, yeah? Where is he then?"

Still that holy-ass smile. Oh, *come on.*

He tilts his head slightly to the side, nodding encouragingly as if to a child struggling to remember a difficult poem.

"Oh, for fuck's sake." He can't be serious.

"Yes, Asher. You know where he is."

"No, I don't." No way. No fucking way.

"Yes, you do."

"Really?"

"Yes, Asher. It's you."

An Encyclopedia of Scars

"Screw that. I know I'm no saint, but I'm not a zombie war criminal."

"That's what you think."

"And how is this possession or whatever supposed to have come about?"

"It was really very simple." The best delusions always are. "Thorfinn Wagner shot you in the back outside your apartment last week. Before you died, Gray did a brain-scan on you and imprinted it in the empty brain of the general."

Bang. A memory comes slamming back and lodges in my brain like a faulty rifle bolt.

I'm standing outside my apartment, my palm against the lock, when I hear a sound from behind. Thinking it's Wagner who's decided to come up for that drink anyway, I only half turn before taking three bullets in the back. The cold hard plastic of the door smacks me in the face as I fall. My cheek slides down the metal on the blood and bits of me splattered all over the glossy surface.

"How stupid," is the last thing I have time to think before darkness overcomes me. Shot in the back like a fucking newbie.

I never quite figured out how a simple street thug could get close enough to shoot me in the back. In my job you either develop a sixth sense for danger or you die. No one should be able to sneak up on me like that.

Unless, of course, I knew the attacker. What if it really was Wagner? His footsteps and pattern of breathing would not have triggered any warnings, leaving him free to gun me down. This time the memory goes on a second longer than before, and there he is, leaning over me, a look of regret on his huge, bearded face.

"Sorry, mate. Orders."

* * *

The cardinal is trying to mess with my mind, but I see through his deception. It's not even very clever.

"Your story is breaking down already, Cardinal. An imprint wears off after a few hours. People do it all the time at the virtua-shops."

"But those imprints are done on subjects with personalities already hardwired into place, and the fake persona is eventually rejected by the healthy brain. Imprint an empty or damaged vessel and the body will cling to the new personality, adopting it, so to speak."

Does it really work like that? I have no idea, but I'm beginning to think there is something really creepy going on here. Why go to all this elaborate trouble to trick me into going after a guy I'm already chasing?

"And Gray told you all this why?"

"He didn't. Most of I've known for a long time. The rest Thorfinn Wagner told me."

"Wagner's dead." If not, I'm going to kill him myself.

"He's not. He was in really bad shape when Borgia brought him in, but our physicians are very good. Apparently Wagner thought he owed you to tell someone the truth. He looked positively relieved to get it off his chest."

This story *would* explain why Wagner has been so grumpy lately.

"Look, cardinal, I like science fiction as much as the next guy, but I don't have time to hang around –"

"Funny."

"– Thanks – but I've got to go save the world."

"And you shall. But first you need to truly believe in yourself and your abilities."

"I do. I'm positively bad-ass."

"But you have no idea how truly bad-ass you really are, Asher, and that is why you need to listen to me. If you're going to stand a chance against Morgenstern, you need to realise your full potential."

"Look." I try to be reasonable. "Have you got anything even remotely resembling proof of these hare-brained ramblings? So far I have seen very little in the way of hard evidence of your claims."

"Have you not been unusually hungry these last few days?"

"I work out. I eat a lot."

"True. Or it could be the nano machines in your blood needing the extra fuel."

"You'll have to do better than that, or I'm out of here."

"Look at yourself." He points at my naked body. "There is nary a scratch on your magnificent body."

I look down at my chest, at my legs. He's right. My previously battered and bruised body is now as smooth and untarnished as the day I was born. But there could be another explanation for that.

"I'm not buying it. You could have kept me drugged for months to let me heal."

The cardinal nods in agreement. "Possible, but wouldn't a man in your profession wear an encyclopedia of scars on his body to tell the story of a life lived hard?"

He would. I do. I look down at my body again. Not a scratch. Not a single one. *What the hell?* But I refuse to give up so easily. "Scar removal is old news, cardinal. People have been doing it for centuries."

"And what about your hand?"

My torn hand looks fine. I wiggle my fingers. All five of them.

"You're the bloody church, Cardinal. You're bound to have a few magic tricks up your sleeve that you keep from the general public." I'm grasping at straws and he knows it.

"Playing hard to convince, I see, Asher. I guess a little demonstration is in order."

Why do I get the feeling he was hoping it would come to this?

He pulls a huge gun from somewhere in his cassock and aims it at my ribs. His thin, spotted hand shakes from the weight of the weapon, and there's a crooked smile on his withered lips.

"So this is how the Roman soldier felt before he ran the spear in our saviour's side."

"No, wait, I beli –"

Bang.

The impact is like being hit in the chest by a car. Strangely, there is no pain. Only the feeling of cold air where no cold air should be. For an eternity I can feel nothing, and then there's the trickle of warm blood down my stomach, over my naked crotch and thighs. Simultaneously I feel blood gushing down my back and between my buttocks from the large exit hole between my shoulders. I'm swaying in the chains, breathing in short desperate gasps, waiting for a pain that never comes. The cardinal stands gazing up at me with a curious look on his ancient face. In front of my eyes, the blood flow slows until there is only a trickle, and eventually it stops completely.

"*Now* do you believe me?" asks the cardinal.

"Or do you want me to shoot you again?"

Through Blood and Pain

He raises the gun. "I have plenty of ammunition and I can stand here shooting you all night, but we are in a hurry, so I would prefer you to take my word for it and accept who you are."

What the hell? If the cardinal is telling the truth, I am the most hated man in human history. The Enemy of Man, who burned a world of innocent men, women and children to win a war. A man thought dead and gone for forty years, who now turns out to be very much alive and kicking, and way too close to home for comfort. I would not be a man at all. I would be immortal. And I would not be alone.

I close my eyes and the nightmares come crashing back. Darkness. Stars. Screaming loneliness. I squeeze my eyes tighter and draw a shuddering breath.

Then I scream from the depths of my soul.

When I open my eyes, tears are streaming down my cheeks and the cardinal is looking kindly up at me.

"Do you believe me, Asher?"

I just look at him, so he shoots me again.

"*Godfuck*," I scream. "Stop *doing* that." The sound of the gun rolls around the huge chamber until it dies out. The bleeding stops again after a few seconds.

"You and Morgenstern are brothers, Asher. You are Abel to his Cain."

I cough up blood, but still there's no pain. "The way I remember it, Cain killed Abel." Blood drips from my lips.

A wide smile cracks his ancient face into a thousand crevices, and he splays his arms, the gun dangling from his withered fingers. "Payback time." The man is clearly insane.

And yet, there is an undeniable logic to his madness. His story would explain why I woke up in the alley outside that pub without knowing how I got there. The pain in my back would be from the intubation tubes of the life support pod. Clever of Gray to have Wagner shoot me in the back to explain that. And it would explain the coloured contact lenses.

They did it all to fool me I was still in my own body.

"Well, I can't see any better explanation right now, so I will have to take your word for it. Yes, I believe you, Cardinal Santoro."

He draws a sigh of relief and his ancient shoulders slump beneath his crimson cloak.

"Good. Good. Now, there are some things I need to discuss with you before I let you out to do God's work."

"Look, I don't want to come across as ungrateful, but could you get me the hell out of these chains first?" I shake my arms, drawing more pain from my protesting shoulders.

"Come a-cross… Your reputation as something of a comedian does not do you justice." There's a smile at the corner of his mouth. "But of course. My apologies."

He bows to me before speaking unheard commands into what must be a hidden microphone in his sleeve. With a jolt the chains come rattling out of the darkness and I fall to the floor three metres below. The hard stone comes up to meet me with a wet smack in the ass and I crumple naked and hurting in a pool of my own cold blood. For a long while I just lay there under the light, in the wetness, arms around my knees like a giant foetus. The pain in my arms as the blood returns is unbearable and I scream again.

The symbolism is almost laughably corny. *Rebirth.* Through blood and pain I am reborn into a new existence. I laugh the laugh of a madman. The cardinal just stands there, waiting.

Finally I get up on one shaking knee and look at the cardinal under bloody brows. "Where's Suki?"

"Who? The girl we brought in with you?"

"Yes."

"She has seen too much."

"What are you going to do to her?"

"Kill her, of course."

Bad idea. I really need to find out what her role is in all of this. She knows far more than she lets on and I have a feeling she is somehow connected to everything that has happened to me.

I get up from the floor.

"No, you won't. Bring her. If I go to find Morgenstern for you, she comes with me. And bring Wagner." I turn around and start walking away from the pool of light into the darkness.

The old man sighs and speaks orders into the microphone again. A short pause as he listens to the reply. "They are on their way."

"Great. Now, is there somewhere I could get some clothes and something to eat in this place?"

* * *

After an acolyte brings me a plate of food and some reasonably well-fitting army clothes, the cardinal bids me sit down in a plush leather armchair in his study. I sit. He remains standing.

The huge stained glass windows of the room are legendary. According to popular myth they came in on the *Gormenghast* with the first settlers and are among the oldest man-made objects on the planet. Priceless, obviously. They are also quite beautiful against the evening suns.

Trying not to think too hard on recent events, I strap on my communicator and busy myself with swiping away a bunch of missed calls and unread messages from Gray.

As you would expect, the cardinal's study is all dark woods, leather desk covers, old books, dimmed brass lamps and lush, dark green carpets. It smells that way too. Judging by the worn, yet classy, look that is impossible to fake, this stuff is all from Earth. I always knew the church was rich, but this is perverse.

"Do you drink, Asher?" the cardinal asks. He motions to a well-stocked liquor table next to the desk.

"Too often and too much," I reply, looking up from my communicator. "Whisky, if you've got it, bourbon if the alternative is death."

The cardinal pours two large drams from a crystal pitcher and hands me one. I down it and feel the smoky liquid burn my empty stomach. I hold out my glass for more. Without batting an eyelid he refills my glass. I'm guessing this is not some locally produced stuff, but rather a very expensive brand from Earth. Perhaps it's even Scottish. The cardinal has impeccable taste.

"Now, what did you need to discuss with me, Cardinal?"

"This, for instance." Like a stage magician he produces the spherical detonator the doctor cut from my skull. I gingerly rub the scar which is no longer there at the back of my neck. "Do you want me to tell you about it?"

Fuck yeah.

"Please, do."

"It's a security measure put into place by Gray." He holds the sphere up to the light, scrutinising it. "He's worried you might… stray." He puts it down on the table where it is mirrored in the darkly polished surface. I grab it and put it in my pocket. Better not alert Gray that I'm on to him just yet. The cardinal raises an eyebrow but doesn't say anything.

I look at him. "Stray?"

"In case the imprint wears off before you have completed your mission. Thorfinn Wagner was not only sent along to provide fire support. He was also sent to keep an eye on you. And to kill you, if the need arose. He had a remote detonator in his pocket when we brought him in."

"Hmm. Fancy that." I take a sip of the whisky and rest my glass on the wide leather armrest. "What are you going to do with Morgenstern after the war is over?" I look back at the old man. "People will want him to usher in a new kingdom of God or something. You know as well as I do, that that is not going to happen."

"After the war, when he has served his purpose, Oddgrim Morgenstern will die. Like Christ before him, he will die at the hands of a great oppressor."

"Are you planning to write a sequel to the New Testament?"

"Don't you think the son of God saving the land of the righteous from the forces of evil, followed by his subsequent execution, deserves a decent portrayal?"

I can't tell if he's serious or if he's pulling my leg.

"Sounds like a poor rip-off of the last book in the series if you ask me."

"We will find a way to put a new spin on it."

I just shake my head. Religion. Go figure.

"And who will get to play the ungrateful part of the executioner?" I ask, suspecting I already know the answer.

"Well, *you*, of course."

I knew it. "Me?" I scratch the stubble on my chin.

"Yes, you."

"Thanks, but no thanks."

"It has already been decided."

"By who?"

"By me."

"Don't I have a say in this?"

"No, Asher, you don't."

"But why me?"

"If anyone should kill the alleged son of God, it should be the World Burner. Morgenstern's death at the hands of the Enemy of Man will only serve to strengthen the beliefs of the faithful. It will be symbolic."

"And boost the sales of your third testament, no doubt. And what if I refuse?"

"Why would you? You know as well as I do that Morgenstern has to die. Why not let his death serve a higher purpose? Besides, I would hunt you down and destroy you." He flashes a quick smile at me. "And I would not be as merciful as Nero Gray." From the tone of his voice you might think he was discussing the cricket season.

I take another sip from my whisky. "It will only serve as a symbol if what you say is true and I really *am* the World Burner."

Bang. Out of nowhere comes another memory. Same room, same cardinal, another time.

* * *

He is pleading with me.

In my powered armour I am a head taller than him, and he has to crane his scrawny old neck to meet my gaze.

"No, General. The cost is too high. I cannot authorise such a waste of human lives, infidel or not."

"Signore, it has to be done, and you know that."

"But the loss of innocent lives would be incalculable," he says. Something resembling a smile flickers across his lips and flashes dangerously in his eyes before he gets it under control.

Like the glitter of starlight on a sharp-edged blade.

"It's a price we have to pay, Cardinal. I will take full responsibility for the operation."

He considers my words for a long while. Then he sighs.

"If you do this, you understand that your name will be reviled for all time, cursed and spat at for eternity?"

"I do, and it's a price I am willing to pay. I do this for the people of the Hope system. They have suffered under the yoke of Earth long enough. It's time we set them free."

"Well then, my son, there is nothing more for me to say, except 'Godspeed'. Tomorrow we wake to a new world order."

The cardinal walks over to a small stone basin by the wall. Like Pilate, he slowly washes his hands clean of all involvement in the operation. Then he walks out of the room, never once looking back.

But I know I saw that smile on his face.

* * *

Where the hell did that come from? I shake my head to clear it and realise something has been scratching at the back of my mind for a while. Like a rat trying to gnaw its way through my skull.

"Where are the other clones?"

"They're all dead. Killed by Gray on Persephone after the raid on Arcadia."

"All of them?"

"As far as I know."

"What happened to the second in command who brought down Meridian?"

"I suppose Gray had him killed after he had served his purpose." The cardinal shrugs.

"But you don't know for certain?"

"Not for certain, no." He shakes his head.

So that bastard could still be out there.

A knot of fury I can't explain tightens deep in my gut at the thought. *What the hell?* Is this the general rearing his ugly undead head? I fight down the bile rising in my throat and go on. "It sounds like you and Gray used to be bosom buddies. What happened?"

"We had a bit of a falling out after the war. He refused to acknowledge that only almighty God should have the power to create life. When he restarted his project to create more immortal soldiers, I had his scientists and everyone else who worked on the project executed."

"I can see how that could cause a falling out, yes. So –" I sip from my glass again, enjoying the sensation of the smoky liquid burning down my throat, – "what's in this for me?"

"How about the undying gratitude of the church and the people of Elysium?"

"Sorry. Not doing it for me."

"A sainthood?" The flicker of a smile at the corner of his lips.

"Come on."

"A chance to save a world in return for the one you burned?"

Ouch. That one hurt.

"That wasn't me." Technically. But he's got me and he knows it. He finishes his glass and sets it down carefully on the corner of his desk.

"And if you do this for me, I will make sure you will live out your life in splendour with all the comforts you could ever imagine."

No doubt. But my guess is that that life would be very brief and end rather abruptly. There is no reason for the cardinal to let me live after I've served my purpose, but my chances of short-term survival are far better if I play along for now. Gray will not be happy if I deliver Morgenstern to the church, but since my imminent survival hangs on this one decision, there's fuck all I can do at the moment. At least it buys me some time to find a way out of this bloody mess.

I force a winning smile. "A win-win situation if ever I saw one, Cardinal. You've got yourself a deal." I extend my hand to him, but he just looks at it from where he's standing, still leaning on the desk.

"I prefer not to sign any contracts, Asher, written or otherwise. Plausible deniability, and all that, you know."

"So *that's* how you manage to sleep at night. If only it were that easy for all of us." I look the old man deep in the eye but he just smiles. There is no emotion behind those pale eyes. None at all.

I shrug. "OK, your Eminence, how do I find Morgenstern? Masada is a big city."

He sheds the smile like outgrown skin.

"Ever since the release of that video, we've had traces running for Morgenstern's biometric data. We've caught him on a hundred different locations, and a statistical pattern of action has emerged."

"What's he doing?"

"He's visiting bible schools. We believe he is recruiting."

"Recruiting? Whom, and for what?" I plant my elbows on the armrests of the chair and steeple my fingers, tapping them lightly against my lips as I think. A gesture familiar to my body but alien to me. I shudder.

The cardinal goes on.

"According to the people we've interrogated, he's putting together an army."

"Why would he need an army?"

"We don't know, but find the man and you find his purpose. And do try to find out who told him about the Archangel. He has friends with knowledge they shouldn't have."

"OK, I'll ask him. But you haven't answered my question. How the hell am I supposed to find him?"

He looks reprovingly at me. "Language, my boy. He is scheduled to make a return visit to a particular school sometime tonight."

"OK, give me the name and I'll go bring him in."

"I wish I could. The problem is, our source hasn't yet told us the name of the place, and there are too many bible schools to stake them all out without raising suspicion."

"And who's this trustworthy source of yours?"

"A young man who overheard Morgenstern talking to a reverend. The young man got picked up by Borgia on his way home from school."

"I guess the young man's mother never told him not to talk to strangers."

"Borgia can be very persuasive when he wants to talk to someone."

"No doubt. Is he around?"

"Borgia?"

"No, the young man." Obviously.

"He's with the interrogator as we speak. The moment he breaks, we will know."

A dark presence looms at the back of my mind, and like in a dream, I hear myself speak. "Can I see him?" It's the creepiest feeling I've ever had.

"The young man?" I can't stop myself from nodding. "What, now?"

"Yes."

"Why would you want to do that?"

"We haven't got much time before the ramstrikes hit. Maybe I can persuade him to unburden his heart." I stand and down the last of the whisky. I'm not really sure I want to persuade anybody, but I'm not calling the shots here anymore.

The cardinal looks uncomprehendingly at me. Then he smiles.

"Ah. Welcome back, General Meridian."

Your Twisted Perversions

Standing outside the door to the torture chamber deep beneath the cathedral, I feel the chill of the place seeping through my bones. From the other side of the closed door, the muffled whimpers of a man in ultimate agony can be heard. I should be feeling apprehensive about what awaits me in that room, but I am not. It's like a blanket has been lowered over my mind, cushioning all emotion, leaving my intellect sharp as a knife.

The general is in the driver's seat.

"This will not be pretty," the cardinal warns me.

"It had better not be. Time is running out." My words from my mouth, but it's not me doing the talking.

In the bad light from the caged overhead lamps, the cardinal's face is unreadable, but I get the feeling he's not sure he should be down here with me at all at this time of night.

He holds a palm to the reinforced hypercarbon door and it rises into the ceiling without a sound. Inside is a scene straight out of hell. Like a blow to the gut, the stench of roasted flesh and human excrement assaults my senses. The air tastes of death.

Strapped to an operating table is what used to be a young man in the prime of his life. He stares unseeingly at the ceiling, chest barely moving as his shallow breath flutters through the remains of his body.

Arrayed on a large stainless steel tray next to the table are his arms and legs, severed and displayed within easy viewing distance. No doubt they have been cut from him piece by piece and placed there for him to contemplate as he refuses to spill what he knows.

The interrogator stands admiring his work, apparently very proud of himself. Like all men of his profession, he's an ugly bastard.

"Has he said anything?" I ask the interrogator.

"Who the fuck are *you*?" he replies.

"He's with me," the cardinal steps in, just in time to save the torturer from instant death.

The torturer scowls at me. "Not so far, but he will. I have never failed."

"I see you are a man of rare imagination where the body is concerned." I nod to the thing on the table. "But what about his mind?"

"His *mind*? There is no need to fuck with their minds. Pain breaks everyone."

"That is where you are wrong, my friend." Like most torturers, he is not a very intelligent man.

"May I?" I ask the cardinal, indicating the remains on the table. The cardinal nods.

The torturer starts to question the cardinal's permission, but the old man silences him with a look and I kneel next to the barely living carcass.

"Hello there," I whisper in the now exposed entrance to his ear cavity. The outer ear has been removed and is now displayed on the tray along with his other body parts. The stench is unbearable, but I steel myself and hear him whisper something, over and over.

"What's that, my friend?" I ask him, leaning closer, breathing shallowly.

He's whispering a single word on constant repeat. "Mercy. Mercy. Mercy."

Oh shit.

Oh fuck.

Could the torturer really be that stupid?

"What's he saying?" asks the cardinal.

"Mercy." I look up at the old man, a pained expression on my face.

"*Ha.* He's been repeating that over and over," the torturer scoffs. "I had hardly started on him when he began screaming for mercy. *You sad little fuck*," he shouts at the broken man on the table. The torturer really is very proud of himself.

I just stare at the him, silent rage bubbling in my chest. I take a deep breath and exhale slowly before addressing him, fighting to keep my anger under control.

"Are you aware that you might have doomed this world and your entire fucking race with your incompetence?" I get to my feet and move toward the man, forcing him to retreat.

"What the fuck are you talking about?" He holds out a hand to warn me to stay away. I don't care. He slaps me in the face, cracking my lip. I don't care.

The cardinal smacks his forehead with the palm of his hand and groans as the penny drops.

"What? *What?*" The torturer's gaze darts between me and his master. He backs away towards the still open doorway.

"You incompetent little *worm*," the cardinal hisses through clenched teeth as he palms the door shut before the retreating inquisitor can escape.

"Let me out. *Let me out.*" The torturer is brought to a halt with his back to the door. He dares not take his eyes off me, so he pounds his fists ineffectually on the solid hypercarbon behind him and turns to the cardinal, beseeching his master to let him go.

"Please open the door." The look on his face would be pitiable on another man.

The cardinal shakes his head as I close the distance on the torturer, who looks like he's trying to press himself through the indestructible material of the door.

"Your Eminence. What have I done? Tell me how I have displeased you."

"Do you know the names of the bible schools in this city?" I ask him, my face in his face, keeping my voice soft and conversational. He turns away, trying to escape my hot breath.

"Yes. Yes, of course I do. Everybody knows them. They're named after the knightly virtues." He's speaking quickly now, the words tripping over each other in their eagerness to please. "They are called stuff like Courage, Justice and…" It finally sinks in, the realisation spreading over his face like fire burning away a thin parchment of composure over a mask of howling fear. "Oh, fuck." He closes his eyes. "Oh, God. Oh, fuck." There are tears forming at the corners of his squeezed shut eyes and his lips tremble as he starts to sob silently.

"… and *Mercy*," I finish for him. "The school is named Mercy." I grab his throat and push him against the door. "He has been telling you the name all along, only you were too busy living out your twisted perversions to listen."

"I didn't realise. Your Eminence, I didn't…"

That's as far as he gets before my knife flashes through his throat, severing his jugular. I let go and he falls to his knees. He tries to stop the crimson torrent with his hands as breath bubbles out of his neck. It doesn't work. I can't say I blame the general for that. The bastard had it coming.

And then, as suddenly as he came, the general is gone again, and I am in control of my body once more. Maybe he just wanted to kill someone, who knows. I shiver, take a deep breath and take over where the general left off.

I wipe my knife on the torturer's shoulder before walking over to the man on the table. I gently tilt his head to the side so he can watch the agonising end of his tormentor. I put my hand on his forehead, soothing his burning skin. I can feel his pulse flutter in a swollen vein as his heart struggles to pump blood through his ruined body.

As the torturer desperately tries to contain the life pumping through his fingers, I raise my knife and show it to the man on the table. I raise a querying eyebrow. He whispers a single word, weak, but quite clear. "Please."

I plunge the tip of the knife deep into his heart, sending his sorry ass soul after his long since departed mind.

"Very humanitarian of you, Asher, but we're in a hurry," the cardinal urges, and I close the eyelids on the fresh corpse on the table. "You need to get going."

"Tell me about it."

We leave the torturer to bleed to death alone in his dungeon.

* * *

Back in the cardinal's chamber, he pours us another drink. We down the whisky without a word, the possible implications of the torturer's epic mistake too large and too dire for words.

The cardinal refills our glasses and walks over to his desk where he picks up a silk handkerchief that he brings to me where I sit in one of the deep leather armchairs.

"Thank you," I nod to him. The white cloth turns red as I dab at my broken lip. The bleeding has already stopped, of course, and instead I use the handkerchief to wipe the torturer's blood from my hands. There is still dried blood under my finger nails and in the creases of my palms, but it will have to do for now. I throw the handkerchief on the lacquered table where it comes to rest like a lone water lily on a dark pond.

"Who were those armoured men you killed in the old man's lab?" the cardinal asks out of nowhere, nearly catching me off guard.

"I have no idea," I lie convincingly. "I thought they were *your* guys."

"They're not." He sips from his glass.

"I realise that now."

To distract him from that particular line of questioning, I quickly change the subject.

"We found a lot of dead people in that bunker. We also found evidence that whoever broke in and killed them opened the doors, disabled the sentries and then reactivated everything again using old wartime overrides, known only to the church. Care to comment on that?" I sip from my glass, watching dried blood from my lip dissolve and swirl around in the amber liquid.

"You noticed that, did you?" The cardinal sighs and twirls his glass, looking into it as if trying to divine the future in the fine single malt. "Yes, that was unfortunate, but I couldn't afford any witnesses to Morgenstern's massacre of the residents. That wouldn't agree with the part I need him to play. I was hoping it would be written off as the work of an inquisitive raptor or something equally horrific."

"A raptor? Inside an impenetrable limpet bunker, four hundred metres up a sheer rock wall?"

"They can be awfully curious."

He looks up at me again, face set in stone. "Asher. The fate of this world hangs in the balance. A hundred lives is an acceptable price for the possible salvation of millions. Simple mathematics." He takes another sip from his glass.

"Only a psychopath could make that equation add up. There were kids in that place."

"They are with God in paradise now."

The conversational tone of his voice and the saintly look on his face is the scariest thing I have ever seen. If looks could kill, the old man's brains would be all over the wall, but he wears his righteousness like impenetrable armour, and he doesn't even flinch under my gaze. Eventually, I'm forced to look away.

"Fucking A." I shiver and shake my head as I look off into the distance, the whisky all but forgotten in my hand.

The cardinal moves on. "Why bring Wagner?"

"What?"

"I'm just curious. Why do you want to bring Wagner? He killed you."

"On Gray's orders. I can't hold that against him."

"Huh." The cardinal shakes his head in puzzlement. "Soldiers."

"Friends," I reply dryly.

"Endearing, I'm sure." He looks off into the distance, lost in some inner monologue. Then he snaps back to me.

"Do you want to work for me?"

"I believe we already agreed on that."

"We did? Yes." He looks a little mystified. "Quite."

Is he crazy? Crazy or not, there's something I need to know.

"This mind imprint or whatever it is..."

"Yes, what about it?"

"Will it... wear off?"

He looks at me for a long while.

"I don't know, my dear boy. I don't know."

Shit.

The cardinal goes on as if our little detour never happened. "And what about the girl who was with you?"

"Suki? What about her?"

"Are you sure you want her around?" He walks back to his desk and pulls out a drawer. "She had this on her when we brought her in." He pulls out Suki's strange gun and places it on the green leather desktop cover.

"A gun, so what?" I shrug. "Masada is a dangerous city."

"It's no ordinary gun." The cardinal rubs his hand on his red velvet cassock. "It was designed to kill people with your unique genetic setup."

"Like a silver bullet, you mean?"

"In a way." The cardinal nods. "One shot from this and your regenerative powers will turn on themselves, killing you in the most horribly painful way. I'd advise you to be very careful around that girl."

"Duly noted, and I will."

"In the meantime I think I will hang on to this." He puts the gun back in the drawer. I'm actually rather touched by his concerns, in spite of myself.

There's a knock on the door and the cardinal calls out. "Enter."

The door swings open without a sound, revealing a group of heavily armed guards in the crimson cloaks of the Red Guard. In their midst are Suki and Wagner. Suki looks very vulnerable next to the soldiers and the Goliath. There's a bruise on the side of her face and her lip is split, but apart from that she appears to be fine. Her spiky hairdo has not survived though, and her sweaty red hair hangs down over her forehead. She looks great.

When she sees me, hope brightens her eyes, and I feel warm somewhere deep inside, in a place seldom reached by light. The fact that I can still feel that means I am still me to some degree, and I am relieved.

Wagner looks like shit, though. His neck, face, shoulders and right leg are wrapped in bandages, and there's a black patch where his left eye used to be. I wonder if he will have the eye regrown. The patch is actually pretty cool. He's also very pale, but there's a transfusion unit strapped to his leg. He's had worse and he'll be back in fighting shape in no time. There's a look of apprehension on his face.

"Leave us." The cardinal waves the guards away and invites Wagner and Suki into the room with a generous sweep of his arm. "Please, enter." They comply but remain standing just inside the door.

Wagner is eyeing the cardinal, who nods. "Yes, Thorfinn. I told him everything."

"Everything?"

The cardinal nods again and Wagner's shoulders slump.

"Don't worry about it, big guy," I tell him. "I would have done the same had the tables been turned."

I'm not sure I would have, but I can't tell him that. To get out of this mess alive I need Thorfinn Wagner at the top of his game, not distracted by guilt and remorse.

The cardinal turns to Suki. "And you, my child, are here at Perez' request. You have him to thank for your life. Be grateful."

"Thanks, I guess." She gives me a strange look and silently mouths '*why?*' I shrug.

"A drink?" The cardinal motions to the drinks table.

Suki turns to the cardinal. "Got any beer?"

"Unfortunately, no. I have wine." He reaches out towards another crystal pitcher containing what is presumably wine but might as well be bull's blood, judging by the colour.

"Wine will be fine." She grabs the glass the cardinal offers her and takes a deep swallow, closing her eyes and savouring the drink. Wagner takes the offered cup from the cardinal's hand and downs it in a single gulp, then holds it out for a refill. The cardinal complies without fuss, to all appearances the graceful host.

"And here we are, like four old friends, sharing a drink while the world moves on around us." The cardinal smiles and reaches out his arms as if to embrace us all.

The door opens again, without a knock this time, and massive Borgia enters, stooping low to get through the opening. He's still wearing his heavy scarlet leather cloak, and with the wizard's hat on his head he looks like a giant scarecrow. He could be Wagner's dark brother.

At the sight of the giant inquisitor, Wagner seems to swell a couple of sizes. He's half a head taller than the Sumerian, but Borgia is broader. The testosterone levels in the room just shot through the roof, and I fear the death of one of the giants is imminent. Never put more than one alpha male in a room if you care about either of them.

"Wagner, heel," I command in a voice I hope does not allow disobedience. He ignores me and just stares at the giant intruder. Violence commencing in three... two...

Suki breaks the tension by stabbing an accusing finger into the giant witch-hunter's chest with her wine glass still in hand, blood-red wine splashing all over the man.

"*You.* You killed Strauss, you motherfucker." Everybody looks at her. Borgia sighs and looks at the cardinal, who replies in his stead. "Yes, that was also unfortunate, but in the great scheme of things, that old man was inconsequential." He waves it away like a delicate but irritating butterfly from his face. "Borgia will accompany you tonight. He will be an asset to you."

He will also be a pain in the ass to have around if I decide to double-cross the cardinal, which is probably the whole point.

The cardinal goes on. "Asher, why don't you fill your friends in on the way? Remember, this city might only have a few hours left and you need to get going. The Terrans come straight for Elysium from the direction of the suns, and the ramstrikes will begin at dawn."

Nice. All our major cities will die as the sun rises and the planet rotates them into view of the ramstrikes. Destroyed by the rising sun, like vampires. How poetic.

"They probably won't dare strike Masada itself, but I wouldn't bet my life on it. Just go find Morgenstern and bring him to me at the Convent of the Mount. You can take my car." He throws me a set of car keys. I catch them, sitting down. "Meanwhile, I have a planet to defend."

I get up from the armchair while Borgia and Wagner stare each other down over Suki's head.

By now they are all but growling at each other.

"Cardinal." I nod my head at the old man.

"Asher." He returns my nod. As I turn my back on the cardinal and walk from the room he calls out after me. "Go with God."

I stop in the doorway and reply over my shoulder. "No thanks." I clap Finn on the shoulder. "I've got Wagner."

"Please, try not to blow up my car."

At the White Bridges of Lacuna Gap

Somewhere high above, a military chopper follows our matte black car through the neon-and-glass canyons of the high-end northern Masada residential districts. It's that magical hour before dawn when the city takes a breath and everything feels unreal. Dark clouds are once again rolling in, pregnant with rain. Muted radio chatter from the pilot crackles occasionally through the coms-unit on the dashboard in front of Borgia, who is riding shotgun. The car the cardinal has provided us with is a hi-tech marvel of modern engineering. The subsonic rumble of the immensely powerful Tesla coils below the low-pitched digital whisper of the electric engine makes the hairs on the back of my arms stand up with pleasure. This is a damn fine car, and I tap the smooth leather steering wheel in appreciation.

It doesn't have the muscle or sleekly dangerous looks of the Gray Industries car we blew up in the park, but what it lacks in power it more than makes up for in style. It runs fine on manual override too. I'm in too much of a bad mood to let the automatics drive right now.

The interior has been especially customised to provide space for a man of Borgia's size up front. The back seat has not.

In the rear view mirror Wagner's beard takes up most of the view. There's a mop of red hair somewhere off to the side where Suki's head is pressed against the window by his shoulder. She hasn't said much since we left the cathedral and spends most of her time staring out the window at the bright lights and empty streets flashing by. The rest of the time her eyes are boring holes in the back of Borgia's thick skull.

In a couple of hours this whole city could be gone, and I'm surprised at the sting of sadness in my guts. Who would have thought I'd miss this dump? I know on some level that the Terrans didn't have a choice in launching their fleet, but that doesn't make it any easier for the people who have to die.

How the hell am I going to get out of this crap? If I catch Morgenstern and hand him over to Gray, the cardinal will kill me. If I give Morgenstern to the cardinal, Gray will no doubt send me off into space again. I'm caught between the proverbial rock and the hard place.

But then, it might not come to that. Morgenstern might kill me when I catch up with him. Hell, I might not even find him before it's too late. I'll just play along for now and see what happens. Something usually turns up.

Usually.

The only people out and about at this early hour are the ones with official permits to ignore the curfew. They are all late-night commuters, on their way to or from their nocturnal shifts. Like the walking dead, they shuffle down the silent, well-lit sidewalks without fear. Measured by random murder and robbery, Masada is the safest city on the settled planets.

Include church-sponsored abductions and executions in those statistics and it's not even in the top ten. As long as you stay on the narrow path, you should be safe in Masada, unless you are really unlucky like that poor kid on the torturer's table. I can't get what remained of his face out of my mind. That image is going to stay with me for a while. Hell, I might even be thinking about him tomorrow morning.

"The strike team is ready to deploy once we confirm Morgenstern has entered the building," Borgia reports as the rain starts to fall. Big drops splatter against the windshield and the automatic wipers start doing their stuff.

"Sounds like you have everything under control, inquisitor. Why don't we just let the strike team handle this and go have a beer somewhere?"

"Sounds like a plan," Wagner says from the back seat, his voice hardly distinguishable from the rumble of the engine.

"The strike team is only there to handle auxiliaries. We handle Morgenstern." Borgia feeds bullet after bullet into the magazine of the huge pistol in his lap.

I nod at the big gun. "You look like a capable fellow, inquisitor. You should be able to handle a skinny guy like Morgenstern. You don't need me and Wagner for that."

"Hey," Suki pipes up from the back.

"Or Suki," I add quickly. I glance into the rearview mirror and see a quick smile flash over her face before she gets it under control and her usual sullen mien returns.

"I hear you are supposed to be some kind of hotshot," Borgia says without looking up from his chore.

"And I hear you are supposed to be some kind of asshole."

He looks up. I'm not smiling.

Suki leans forward between the seats.

"When you guys are done clashing dicks, perhaps you could do something about the car following us."

What? How did that happen?

I glance casually in the outside rear-view mirror, and true enough, there it is. It's just coming around the corner of a building, about two hundred metres behind us in the rain, and I realise it's been there for quite some time. I just hadn't flagged it as suspicious. Suki has got some mean instincts.

"How long have they been following us?" I ask her over my shoulder while flashing through the maps in the car's navigation system, looking for a place to lose them.

"Since the cathedral. They waited for us outside."

"Friends of yours?" I ask Borgia. The giant shakes his head and calls the chopper on the handset.

"Stalker One, Borgia. There's a car following us. Check it."

The sensors on the bird are powerful enough to pick up the license tags on a car from a kilometre away, and, before we have passed another block, the answer crackles back.

"Current owner unregistered. Vehicle last recorded being shipped to a mid-level corporation in the southern quadrant, Minara Holdings. Looks clean."

Impressive. No wonder the cardinal's secret police are held in such awe by the Masada gun crowd. Minara is an anonymous subsidiary of Gray Industries. No one steals a car from Gray and gets away with it, which puts the guys in that car in Gray's employ. Now, why has he scrambled Team Bravo? Is he starting to doubt my resolve? There's no trust between people these days.

Borgia is looking strangely at me. Then he turns to the back seat. "Minara Holdings ring any bells, Wagner?" he asks, his massive frame amplifying the words in a way I've only heard from my Goliath friend before. I bet the girls love his voice.

The inquisitor's eyes never leave my profile.

"No." Wagner's reply is late and not very convincing. Borgia is clever.

"How about you, Perez? Ever heard of them?" If Wagner is a monster, Borgia is an abomination. Where Wagner is the result of centuries of selective inbreeding and some very careful gene therapy, Borgia is the result of a lifetime of drug-enhanced body-building. The guy looks like an over-the-top caricature of the most muscular man you could ever imagine. His upper arm is as thick as my thigh. Hell, even his face looks muscular. He's a regular poster boy for bad steroids. In a fair fight between Wagner and Borgia, I'm not sure who would win, but on top of all the muscle, Borgia has a keen intellect shining behind the deep-set eyes boring holes in the side of my skull as he waits for my reply.

"Nope, never heard of them either," I reply, shrugging my shoulders as best as I can in the deep seat. No need to worry the inquisitor or his master. If they learn who the guys in that car are, Borgia will probably have the chopper take them out, alerting Gray to the fact that I'm on to him. No need to give the old bastard that much of a warning. When I come for him, I want to do it quietly. Something tells me that's not how it's going to go down, but that's the plan.

The inquisitor ponders the situation. Then apparently decides to let it rest. For now.

"Lose them at the bridges," he suggests as he returns to refilling his magazine. The White Bridges is the classic place to lose a tail and the place I was going to suggest myself. Their interweaving ramps and crossroads form a three-dimensional maze of one-way streets, providing the inventive driver ample opportunity to lose someone. "Take the next exit," Borgia suggests in a tone suggesting it's not a suggestion.

"Way ahead of you, buddy." I twist the wheel sharply, tires scream, and we fishtail onto a smaller street, parallel to the main road. Try to get a car on automatic to do that, if you please.

The skyscraper homes of the city's finest rise like a crystal forest above us. Their glass and hypercarbon fronts reflect the night sky far above. I think I catch a glimpse of the chopper against the brighter band of the ring, but I could be mistaken.

Behind us our pursuers have also left the main road, easing back further to keep from alerting us. These guys are good. Probably because I trained them myself. Or Perez did. Or whatever.

Fuck it, *I am Perez.* This double-personalities crap is driving me crazy.

"Who the hell are they?" Suki asks of no one in particular, looking out the back window at the pursuing car. They are still keeping back, biding their time. "And why are they following us?"

"I have absolutely no idea," I lie as we enter a long, brightly lit tunnel, walls painted glaring white. Borgia still doesn't believe me, I can tell, but he keeps his peace. A scowl from Suki tells me she's not sold either.

At that moment my communicator chimes. Another text message from Gray.

I have people on your tail, Perez. Call in, or I will come for you.

So, he's tipped his hand, and there's no need for subtlety any more.

I close the message and tear the communicator from my wrist with my teeth. Then I roll down the window and throw the bracelet out. I don't think I will be calling in again, and his messages are starting to piss me off. Who the hell does the guy think he is? My boss?

"Who was that?" Suki asks, looking after the communicator as it bounces across the tunnel roadway, shattering into pieces behind us.

"My mother," I reply and step on the accelerator, pushing the car up past a hundred as we exit the tunnel and arrive at the White Bridges of Lacuna Gap.

We come flying out onto one of the hundred bridges that criss-cross the void between the twin spires of Masada like the withering neurons in a mad-cow-diseased brain. Suki looks like she's about to ask me something, but the breath-taking view puts her off. The vista truly is spectacular.

The bridges span the five-hundred-metre gap – commonly known as the Cleavage – between the two rocky pillars of Masada. Supported by wires and cables anchored deep inside the living rock on either side, the White Bridges are a wonder of modern engineering. Someone actually put them on the list of the Seven Wonders of the World, and people come here from all over the planet just to drive on these things. Right now, though, I can count the vehicles moving over the bridges on the fingers of one hand. That's a very good thing, considering I'm going at about twice the legal speed limit. Our pursuers have also sped up, no longer trying to hide.

I've always enjoyed the dizzying feeling as the rock drops away to the jungle floor far below, but this time the void makes me irrationally ill at ease. Must be the general acting up again. Being cooped up in a life-support pod for forty years would make anyone slightly agoraphobic.

The view is still amazing, though.

Suki can't suppress a gasp, and when I glance over at Borgia he's looking straight ahead, knuckles white over the gun in his lap. Wagner is stone-faced as ever. I laugh under my breath and return my focus to the narrow roadway as it drops down at a steep angle. Our speed carries us over a little too quickly, making our stomachs rise into our throats. This is as close to flying as you can come without wings.

"So, why do they call you the Sumerian, anyway?" I turn to Borgia for some friendly in-chase chit-chat.

"It's a bad joke. Watch the road."

I smile to myself and return my attention to the road.

We are approaching an intersection where the bridge splits in two, one road going up, the other going down. I head for the one going up, and we're pressed into our seats as the G-forces do their damnedest to do us in. Our pursuers are closing in and I throw the car into a hard left turn down another ramp. Then we hurtle down yet another, leaving us almost in freefall, going all out to shake them off. They will still be able to track us through the detonator in my pocket, but I want to throw them off for a while. I have a feeling they would otherwise come bumbling in and alert our prey as we make our move on the bible school.

Those thugs might come in handy later, though. Having Nero Praetorius Gray hot on my heels could turn out to be very useful when we inevitably end up in a tight spot. I'm playing with the big boys now, and having the biggest bully on the block show up in the nick of time could save my sorry ass.

My antics seem to be effective because our pursuers end up on a parallel bridge fifty metres to our left. A few quick turns later and we're entering Southern Masada through one of the many tunnels drilled into the rock. We come shooting out into the familiar artificial caverns of the Bottoms where dark windows glare down at us from bare concrete walls under the Ceiling. The occasional hooker on a street corner scurries out of the way to keep from getting sprayed as we speed through deep puddles in the pocked asphalt.

"Nice driving." Suki acknowledges from the back seat where she has strapped herself in since last I looked. I throw a quick look at the navigation system and realise we are just a few blocks from our destination. Smooth.

We exit the underground slum and come back out into the rain on the crumbling ledge of the Rim. All around us are empty streets filled with rubbish, languidly blowing on the night-breeze. Low concrete buildings, rusted chain link fences and flickering sodium streetlights surround us. We're not too far from the bar where this whole mess started.

No one in their right minds would want to live out here, this close to the edge. Which makes it the perfect place to run an extremist Bible school.

This is my Identification

"Bible school coming up on our right," I call as I slow down and take us coasting past the place. It's a dreary-looking two-storey facility just a few blocks from the Rim. From the top-floor windows hang banners with the stylish supernova cross of the Church of Christ the Redeemer. Fancy that. Those guys seem to be everywhere these days.

The main entrance is guarded by two dangerous-looking men in classic Bottoms street attire – all long leather cloaks and wide brimmed hats to protect from the constant rain – no doubt local thugs hired for protection. In a neighbourhood like this, the bad guys wouldn't think twice about stealing from a church, so I can see the reason to put them there. But two men at the door seems a little excessive, even for an area like this. They are definitely up to something in that place. The guards could mean trouble, but hopefully Borgia can flash some credentials at them to persuade them to let us by unmolested.

I drive on past the building and reverse down a narrow alley where I park the car next to a pockmarked concrete wall covered in religious graffiti. Our pursuers are nowhere to be seen.

I get out into the night, and I'm almost overwhelmed by the powerful smells of the night, enhanced a thousandfold by the heavy moisture in the air from the last rain. The reek of garbage and human life mixes with the sweet, dangerous smells from the jungle far below, creating the perfect perfume for a night of violence. *Charnel No.5*, anyone?

Borgia and Wagner get out, chests puffed and ready to rumble. I am starting to understand Suki's problems with the macho bullshit.

Wagner's show of strength is hampered by the fact that he's gotten a cramp in his thigh from sitting bunched up for too long. He has to support himself on the wall while he stretches his aching muscles. I clap my big friend on the back and he swears at me under his breath. I smile as I open the trunk and start hauling out the big guns. This time we're not taking any chances.

I throw Wagner a heavy assault rifle and pick an Aitchenkai for myself before stuffing an automatic pistol under my belt, at the small of my back. I hold another automatic out to Suki, stock first. "Do you know how to use one of these?"

She just stares at it. "Fuck you. Give me a real weapon."

"Whoa. I didn't realize you were a *militant* feminist." I hand her another Aitchenkai instead.

"I'm not." She takes the weapon and checks the magazine with a professional ease I did not expect. "But since the fucking cardinal took my gun, I need something with a lot of stopping power if we go up against Morgenstern."

"Whenever you children are done, we need to move." Borgia is standing at the mouth to the alley, already equipped and ready, looking towards the entrance to the bible school. I grab a couple of extra magazines for the Aitchenkai and join him at the corner. I can hear the low noise from the dampened blades of the chopper, hovering high above us in the early morning sky. If you didn't know it was there you wouldn't notice it. Stealth is the main advantage of using a chopper over a turbine flier for these kinds of missions. Besides, I've always liked choppers. There's something rugged and old-fashioned about them that appeals to me.

"OK, now what?" Suki whispers as she peers around the corner. She's so close to my ear I can feel her warm breath on my skin and I inhale deeply, savouring her scent. Despite myself, I realise I really like how she smells. Then it strikes me that the general's body has not known a woman in forty years. It must be his doing that I'm feeling like a love-struck schoolboy. She's a bloody pain in the ass.

With some serious effort I tear my eyes away from the way the streetlights illuminate the soft curve of her neck and do a quick scan of the street in front of the school. There's only one way for Morgenstern to approach when he finally gets here.

"We can't get to him in the street," I think out loud. "It's too open and there are civilians living in those buildings. We can't risk a firefight." I think for a moment, scratching my chin, weighing my options. "I'd say our best bet is to get inside and wait for him there. What do you say, Borgia?"

"I concur. The street is not the place."

"No, it is not good," Wagner confirms, unwilling to be left out of the command decisions. "I say we go in and kill everyone inside, then take out Morgenstern when he gets here." He still has some kills to go before his great reward. We all pointedly ignore him.

"*What?* It is good plan." He's preaching to deaf ears, but I can't help smiling at his stubbornness. I can't understand why he wants to be a breeder anyway. Like most Goliaths he's not interested in women. I know honour means the world to them, but to spend the rest of his life in bed making little Goliaths when he'd rather be out killing people for money? People are strange.

Suki turns to me. "OK, and how do we get inside without killing anyone and leaving blood-splatter all over the front wall to warn him off?" She seems to have a very low regard for my skills of subterfuge.

"We walk in there, through that thing on the front called a door." I draw the outline of a door in the air to explain the concept to her.

"And why would they let us do that? Those guards look like they mean business, and I bet they have been put there for a reason. To keep people like us out, perhaps?"

"Borgia." I turn to the inquisitor. "Don't you have access to all church buildings in the city?"

"Aye. I do." The giant nods.

"Well, there you go," I turn back to Suki. "We go up there, Borgia flashes his dick at them, and we go in. Easy."

"If you say so." She does not seem convinced, but she shrugs. "I'm staying way back, though."

"Keep your idolater of a watchdog on a tight leash." Borgia nods at Wagner who glares back under heavy brows. "And I will go."

I stab a finger in Wagner's chest. "Wagner, stay." He sighs and I bow to the inquisitor. "Do your stuff." He moves out while we wait around the corner.

As Borgia approaches the door, the two guards spring to action. They puff out their chests, pull up their jackets to reveal automatic pistols tucked into their pants, and look all mean and street nasty. When they notice the size of the approaching stranger they start to fidget. When they see who it is, they get seriously nervous. I would too, had I been a member of that ancient brotherhood called Scum of the Earth and was being approached by his Excellency, the high inquisitor Borgia. Save for Wagner, he's the most dangerous man on the planet, and the thugs know it.

"Get the fuck out of here," one of the men calls to the giant. He's waving his arm in what's supposed to look like a commanding gesture but fails miserably because his heart is clearly not in it. He's obviously the less intelligent of the two. His slightly less stupid partner hisses something at him, and the first guy lowers his arm.

It's the middle of the night. They're on a deserted street. They are only two against one.

"I'm here on the cardinal's business. Let me in." Borgia's voice leaves no room for argument, but the stupid guard is too stupid to realise that.

"I need to see some identification," he pipes up. He flinches when Borgia, quick as a snake, thrusts his hand into a deep pocket in his crimson coat and pulls out the heavy, skull-emblazoned badge of his office. The short, heavy chain dangles between his fingers.

"This is my identification, unbeliever." Borgia smacks the badge straight in the guard's face, cracking the back of the man's head against the wall, tearing down an avalanche of crumbling plaster. "Satisfactory?"

"*Fuck, man,* you broke my *nose*," the guard whines, a hand around his bleeding sniffer and another cupping the back of his skull. Blood drips through his fingers.

"Give thanks to the Lord I did not break your spineless back." Borgia waves us forward.

"Who the fuck are they?" the other guard enquires, voice quivering on the edge of just giving up and running off into the night when he sees the hardware we're carrying.

"They are with me." This time Borgia's reply really is final. This is not a debate, and the thug knows it. They step aside to let us in.

Suki makes a face at the stupid one as we walk past them and into the school. He makes a face back at her, blood running down his crooked teeth, and she punches him in the broken nose. Hard. He drops like a sack of bricks.

* * *

Inside, the place actually looks pretty nice. The walls are covered in a reasonably fresh layer of white paint, the carpets are clean, and there are flowers in a vase on the reception desk. Even the holographic cross floating against the back wall is only flickering slightly. Out here on the Rim, this is as high as standards come.

There's an old woman behind the counter who bristles at our early visit and heavy armament. "What is your business here?" she demands in her most intimidating schoolteacher's voice as she stares down her nose at Borgia, trying to put the fear of God in him. Have you ever seen an old woman trying to look down her nose at someone over two metres tall? It looks pretty funny, I can tell you.

When she recognises the inquisitor, her expression changes to one of polite fear as if realising she's in the presence of a celebrity. Which, in a way, she is. There's not a person on the planet who doesn't know who the high inquisitor is.

"My lord. I didn't recognise you."

"Bring the abbot. Tell him it's a matter of state security." Borgia is not one for idle banter.

The old woman looks about to object to Borgia's request when Wagner steps out from behind the inquisitor's back. I can see the exact moment her brain decides that two heavily armed giants are too much even for her mother superior skills of intimidation.

"Of course, my lord. At once." The old woman pushes a three-button sequence on an ancient intercom-unit and waits for an answer. There is none. She eyes our weaponry with a disapproving eye.

"He's probably asleep, but I will go get him for you. If you'd care to sit down, he'll be right with you." Like flipping a switch, she's suddenly politeness personified and looks like everyone's favourite grandmother.

"Thanks, I'll stand." Borgia folds his arms and turns his back on the old woman as she shuffles from the room and starts ascending the stairs.

"I'll stand too," Wagner echoes, folds his arms and turns his back on Borgia. At any other time it would have been cute, but right now, this close to our target, it pisses me off. A little professionalism from either of them wouldn't hurt. However, I don't want them to join forces against me so I let it go. For the time being.

Leaving the giants to their mercifully silent and non deadly battle, Suki and I sit down on a threadbare but rather comfortable sofa. I grab one of the old-fashioned feed readers from the table, scanning the news section. Nothing about the approaching fleet yet, and the police are still searching for the alleged terrorists who shot up a residential block down in the Bottoms last night. Funny. I've never been called a terrorist before. The first casualty of the war on terror is sense of perspective.

My first reaction on seeing the article is to show it to Suki, but then I remember her family was in that fire fight with us and is now dead because of me. I don't think she would appreciate it.

The old woman returns. "The abbot replies that he's in a meeting, but he will be with you shortly. Coffee anyone?" She waves at a scuffed but shining coffee dispenser from last century, standing in a corner.

A meeting? At three o'clock in the morning? I look at Borgia, Borgia looks at me, Wagner looks confused and it's Suki who states the obvious.

"He's already here."

"Fuck." I slide a bullet into the breach of my gun and turn to the old receptionist, a cautionary finger to my lips. "Where's the abbot's office?"

"Up the stairs, first door on the left." She points it out. "You can't miss it."

"Thanks. You'd better get the children out of here. Now."

She nods and shuffles away in her slippers. The children are not safe here anymore.

Hell, if Morgenstern is already here, no one is safe.

He Chose it Very Carefully

We move slowly up the stairs towards the door pointed out to us by the receptionist. Our guns are raised even though firearms are not likely to stop Morgenstern. It feels good though, like we know what we're doing.

Stopping outside the door, I put my ear against it to get an idea about what's going on inside. I hear nothing.

Borgia shifts on the landing, and the floorboards creak beneath him.

The old building was not constructed for people of his or Wagner's size, and the wooden floors are ancient and brittle. As he puts his weight on one foot, the board beneath him creaks and then cracks with a loud snap. Fuck.

"Go," I hiss to Borgia and he puts all his weight behind a kick that sends the door crashing off its hinges. The broom cupboard behind it is small and empty.

Someone starts shouting behind a door across the corridor behind us and we hear running footsteps. Damn it. The old hag tricked us.

Wagner shoulders down the door and I storm into a sparsely furnished study with a desk taking up most of the floor space. Behind the desk is an old priest in a black cassock. I see his hand going for a drawer, presumably reaching for some kind of weapon. Wagner pins the old man to the wall by kicking the heavy desk into his chest, and I hear a sickening crunch as the priest's ribcage cracks. Not a very nice thing to do to a man of God, but it probably earned Wagner a couple of points with his own gods.

There's only one other exit from the room, and that's a door in the wall behind the desk. It's slammed in my face as I lunge for it, and I hear a lock being turned, followed by the pounding of running steps on wooden boards behind it.

"Borgia, the corridor. Wagner, watch the priest." I charge the door, shouldering it open. The room on the other side looks like it's the abbot's personal bedroom. There's a Spartan bed under a small crucifix, a rickety old chair, and a narrow window. An open door back into the corridor shows me which way Morgenstern went, and I rush after him. Only when I skid into the hallway do I realise my mistake. He's nowhere to be seen, and Borgia calls from down the hall. "He didn't come out this way."

From the bedroom comes the breaking of glass as something is hurled through the window. Shit. He opened the door to the corridor and hid under the bed. The oldest trick in the book and I fell for it. *Damn it.*

I dash back into the bedroom with Borgia close behind me, just in time to see Morgenstern drop from view through the broken window. I vault over the bed and boldly poke my head out, drawing a volley of deadly accurate SMG fire from Morgenstern in the alley down below.

The bullets punch holes in the outside wall and I snatch my head back as fast as I can. I still feel a bullet tear a gash in my cheek and moments later I feel the trickle of warm blood down my neck. I risk another quick peek and see him at the corner, splendid in a pitch-black outfit. He's surrounded by five heavily armed men. I drop flat on the floor as they open fire again. Their heavy ammunition punches holes through the plaster, tearing ragged tufts of insulation from the walls and showering me with debris.

"*Go.* They're getting away." I shout to Borgia and Wagner over the noise of the gunfire. Borgia retreats from the room and bounds down the hallway after Wagner. When the gunfire momentarily stops, I get to my feet and run crouching from the room. From outside I hear the roar of a powerful engine. Damn it. They're getting away.

I take the stairs five steps at a time and come stumbling out into the street hot on the heels of Wagner and Borgia.

To my great relief, it's our own car that comes skidding into view around the corner with Suki behind the wheel, charging straight for Morgenstern and his gang of armed thugs. They fire at the car, but their bullets ricochet harmlessly off its reinforced windshield and armoured body.

"*Alpha team is go,*" Borgia shouts into his communicator. Even as he speaks I hear the thumping of a powerful rotor somewhere overhead in the darkness. The air fills with whirling debris as the chopper comes in to hover only metres above the rooftops, pounding us with wind and noise.

"*Fire*," I shout to Borgia. "*Order them to fire*."

"What about Morgenstern? I want him alive."

"He'll live. Trust me."

Borgia shouts something into his microphone and the bird opens fire with its swivel-mounted machine guns. Morgenstern and his men disappear in a cloud of dust, flying asphalt and blood. Simultaneously, four ropes are dropped from the open sides of the chopper and a dozen men in dark city camouflage rappel down. They pull heavy assault rifles from their backs as they drop the last two metres to the ground and open fire on what's left of Morgenstern's crew. I add my own bullets to the chaos, firing blindly into the smoke, just hoping to hit something, anyone. Anything.

Movement off to the side catches my eye and I see Morgenstern running from the destruction, heading back into the alley. It seems he has miraculously survived the metal storm, even though I can see blood splashing from torn and flapping flesh. How the hell are we supposed to stop this thing?

"*He's going for the alley*," I call to Borgia as Suki stamps on the brakes and broadsides the car through the remains of Morgenstern's men.

"The target is going for the alley. Light him up," Borgia shouts into the communicator, and the chopper rises into the night sky, its searchlight playing across the rooftops, hunting for the elusive Prophet.

Borgia turns to his men. "Hold this position." They spread out behind whatever cover they can find and take up defensive positions around the entrance to the alley.

I take off down the alley after Morgenstern. "Take the car around the block and stop him on the other side," I shout. Wagner dives into the back of the car and Borgia steps up on the sideboard and grabs the door frame as Suki floors it.

Morgenstern is fifty metres down the alley, sprinting hard for the back wall of the cul-de-sac. What the hell is he thinking? There's nowhere for him to go. With the dark and the dust, my rifle is useless and I drop it. It will only slow me down. Instead I increase my pace and try to catch up.

Morgenstern reaches the back wall, and then he does something incredible. He jumps up against the crumbling concrete in the corner, pushes off against the wall, kicks off against a windowsill, practically running up the wall. He manages to grab the iron railing of an old balcony a good five metres above the ground. I can't believe my eyes. Even under the weak gravity of Elysium, that jump is impossible.

He swings over the railing and kicks in the balcony door in one smooth move and then disappears inside. I hear the falsetto screams of an old woman or a very scared man inside the room.

I reach the wall and there's nothing else I can do but to follow in Morgenstern's footsteps. I jump and kick and scramble like I saw him do, and I'm amazed at the ease with which I traverse the vertical wall. I don't land as gracefully as the Prophet, but I manage to smash into the balcony and hook an arm over the rusty balustrade. Panting heavily I heave myself over the iron railing and onto the balcony. Through the broken doorway I see a terrified and very naked man screaming wordlessly at me from the middle of a very wide bed draped in cheap silk sheets. I get to my feet and pull my gun at him.

"Shut up." He closes his mouth on the scream like he was strangled. "Where did he go?" He points silently at a doorway opening onto what looks like the kitchen.

I lower my gun and sprint across the dingy bedroom. Before reaching the doorway I drop down into a sliding tackle along the polished concrete floor and come in low through the door. That saves my life when a huge meat cleaver comes sailing through the air and buries itself a hands-breadth into the concrete wall where my head should have been. I catch a quick glimpse of the Prophet's silhouette in a doorway and then he's gone. The naked man starts screaming again.

Before coming to a stop, I throw myself into a roll through the door and out into a hallway just in time to catch Morgenstern disappearing out the main door. He slams it in my face and I lose precious seconds kicking it out of its frame.

Outside on the landing, I hear pounding footsteps above me. The bastard is going for the roof. He knows we have a chopper, so what the hell is he playing at?

I follow him and come barging out onto the flat roof of the building. Clotheslines and hot-wired electrical cables strung between mortared walls and chimney stacks criss-cross the open space, and I can see Morgenstern running for the edge of the roof. If I hadn't seen the ease with which he scaled the two storeys below I would think he was crazy. He reaches the edge and takes the leap, sails effortlessly through the air, and lands light as a feather on the other side, hardly breaking his stride.

Above us the chopper pilot has spotted Morgenstern and trains the searchlights on him. The Prophet is caught in a circle of white, like a ballerina at the circus. He's dodging and weaving among the chimney stacks, impossibly fast. Even above the sound of the rotors I can hear the stuttering as the automatic targeting systems on the chopper struggle to keep up with him. Finally, the aiming AI decides it has his speed and vector calculated and opens fire at the spot where it estimates he will be in the next few milliseconds. Of course he's not, and the bullets reduce a concrete wall to dust and gravel.

As I follow in Morgenstern's footsteps and leap across the abyss I see him changing direction again, inhumanly fast. This time the short controlled burst of deadly tungsten rounds from the helicopter cut a long ragged gash in the cheap concrete roof. I can only hope there are no people living down there.

The landing comes up to meet me and I go for a roll as I touch down, bleeding off some of my momentum. I still don't trust this new body of mine, but it executes the move flawlessly. I roll to my feet and keep sprinting without losing speed. I've never felt more powerful in my life.

Morgenstern is twenty metres ahead and approaching another gap between rooftops when another sound pierces the thunder of the chopper circling above. I cast a quick glance skyward and what I see makes me start. Behind our chopper there is another one. It's a military vehicle, painted in jungle camouflage, and not the standard dark grey of the church forces. The pilot of our chopper sees the newcomer at the last second and pulls his vehicle into a steep, pitched turn, angling away from us. The other chopper follows him, manoeuvring to lock weapons. Morgenstern obviously has friends in some incredibly high places. The two choppers pass just metres overhead and I can hear the distinct sound of the second chopper's Gatling guns whining up to firing speed.

All of a sudden going for the roof does not seem like such a bad idea for Morgenstern. He's hoping for a pick-up. Damn, this is looking worse by the second.

As the two choppers thunder past overhead, the Prophet jumps to the next roof and rolls right through a thin wooden door and into what must be another stairwell leading down.

What is he up to now?

I take the leap, and this time I trust my body knows what to do. It's almost like another mind is driving my flesh. As I land, I feel myself roll without conscious thought and it's so natural, as if I was born for this. Before I realise what's going on, I'm running down the stairs after the fleeing Morgenstern.

We have entered what looks like a low-end, social-housing residential block. There is peeling red paint on the walls and a threadbare carpet on the floor. The only light in the corridor comes from a few badly flickering light panels hung randomly from the ceiling. There's a faint scent of lavender barely disguising the mildew underneath.

Ahead of me Morgenstern kicks down a door and disappears inside.

I reach the broken door and realise he did not choose this building at random, but with great deliberation.

He chose it very carefully indeed.

Inside is a single big room shrouded in near darkness by heavy drapes pulled over the windows. The drapes are covered with cheerful images of unicorns, castles and princesses.

Lining the walls of the room are a dozen cribs, each housing a small, gently rising and falling pile of blankets.

This is an orphanage.

Suffer the Little Children

"Hello."

His voice is deep and musical, as you would expect. The bad audio on the video did not do it justice, and in real life it holds a sweet promise of green pastures and a land of milk and honey. How many men, women, and children have succumbed to it over the years? Countless, no doubt.

He speaks from the shadow between the windows where the dim light from the city renders his dark form near invisible in contrast.

I raise my gun and aim it straight between where I judge his eyes to be.

"I wouldn't do that if I were you," he cautions softly. "Guns and small children are a very bad combination. Put your gun away and we'll talk."

"I could drop you right there and your brain wouldn't even notice."

"Are you willing to bet on that?"

He steps from the shadows, holding a sleeping baby in his arms. He shows it off like a proud father, but no father in his right mind would hold a large calibre handgun to his child's forehead.

"The trigger on this gun is feather light," he continues. "The slightest twitch would put a bullet through the head of this child. Do you think you could live with that?"

The small chest of the baby is rising and falling calmly, safe in the warmth and great strength of the man who is not a man.

"OK, I'll put it away." I hold out my left hand, palm towards Morgenstern, as I slide the gun back under my belt, at the small of my back where I can easily reach it.

"There. It's gone. Now, put the child down and we'll talk."

He just shakes his head. "I don't think so." He rocks the baby gently. "Did the cardinal send you?"

Now it's my turn to ignore him. "Like I said; put the child down and we'll talk."

" 'Suffer the little children, and forbid them not, to come unto me: for of such is the kingdom of heaven.' " He quotes scripture without the slightest hint of irony. "This child stays with me. Move into the light, hands out where I can see them." I do as he asks.

As I step into the pool of light cast by a gap between the curtains, there's a pause, and then he laughs softly. It's a friendly laugh, as shared between old friends, and it scares me.

"Ah." His teeth glitter in the shadows as he smiles. "I should have known it would be one of you. I thought you did keep up rather well."

"So you recognise me."

"Of course I do. I see that face in the mirror every day. You are one of us, brother, but which one? Not that it matters. You are all children, compared to me."

"I'm Meridian."

There is an almost imperceptible hesitation; the slight tremor before an earthquake, ignored by humans, sensed by animals.

"So, I might have some sport after all. I'm so very happy to meet you again, little brother. We heard you were dead."

"Well, I'm back. And so, apparently, are you. I saw the video."

"Yes, rather inspiring, don't you think?" He seems very pleased with himself. The dim light falls across his neck, glittering on a thin layer of perspiration. There is not even a scar where his throat was cut.

"What the hell was that about anyway?" I ask. "Why did you let them catch you?"

I hope he is too full of himself to keep his plans to himself.

"Catch me? I offered myself to them."

This is too easy.

"Why?"

"They had something I wanted."

"The Archangel."

"Indeed."

"Who told you about that?"

"That doesn't matter. Let's just say it was someone with plans for the human race."

"Someone has plans to wipe out the human race and it doesn't matter?"

"No, it does not. What do you care anyway, little brother?"

I don't want to spook him yet, so I decide to change tack.

"I don't. So, why the theatrics?"

"Don't you think the return of God deserves some drama? The people of this planet need to know their saviour has returned, and they need to see it with their own eyes."

"Oh, come on. Why *now*?"

"Some very unsettling news has forced my hand. We were not ready, and so I had to tip the scales in our favour."

"What the hell are you talking about?"

"For years I have been gathering an army, readying for the day when we will overthrow the corrupt church and bring about the true kingdom of God. Today, our army is great, but not great enough to beat the dark forces of Earth."

"You know about that, huh?" The pieces slither together in my mind. "So you staged your little execution to steal the Archangel from the Redeemers and reveal yourself to the people of Elysium at the same time. Inventive. But if you intend to use that thing on the battlefield you are crazier than I thought. You will kill every human being on the planet. Hell, you might even wipe out the entire human race if an infected ship gets back to Earth."

"Then so be it." He shrugs. "The faithful will be spared. 'And when he seeth the blood upon the lintel, the Lord will pass over the door, and will not suffer the destroyer to come in unto your houses to smite you.' " He holds out a magnetic field generator. Of course. Anyone inside the field will be safe from the slaughter.

I sigh. "You know I can't allow you to do this, Morgenstern."

"Why not? What do you care what happens to the human race? We are the angels of heaven and the kingdom of God belongs to us."

"I do care what happens to the human race. I am one of them."

"No, you are not. You were born in a tube, Caspar. You were grown in a fucking vat, just like me."

"I am not like you, Morgenstern, and I never will be. You see, I am not really the World Burner. I just wear his body. My name is Asher Perez and I am here to stop you."

That gives him pause.

"*What?*" I sense uncertainty creep into his voice and he starts circling along the row of cribs towards the door, the gun still pressed to the sleeping baby's forehead.

"Gray betrayed the World Burner and sent him into space, chained inside an escape pod. He drifted for forty years, his mind wore down but his body refused to die. If it were not for you, he would still be out there, drifting deeper and deeper into the void. And I would still be alive."

"What the fuck are you talking about?" He has now reached the door and backs through it. I follow him out into the corridor.

"Gray has been searching for you all these years, Oddgrim, and when he saw your little charade in that video, he knew he had found you. He also knew there was only one man in the universe who could stop you, so he sent a salvage team into space and brought his old friend back. The only problem was that the general's mind was long gone, and Gray needed someone he could trust to pilot that deadliest of weapons. Enter yours truly."

"But that's impossible." Morgenstern slowly shakes his head, the gun never for an instant leaving the face of the sleeping child.

"My thoughts exactly, yet here I am. Asher Perez, chief of security for Gray Industries, who woke up one night in this body."

By now he has reached the stairs to the roof and starts to back up them slowly.

"Then that is why you will fail, Asher Perez." All friendliness is now gone from his voice. In its place is steel as cold as the void between the stars. "Meridian would perhaps have stood a chance against me, but you are a mere human. You are a child at an adults' party. You lack the ferocity of the true angels."

"I wouldn't be so sure of that. Do you know anything at all about human history?"

"You think you are a tough guy, Perez, I can see that, but believe me when I tell you that you are no match for the son of God."

"And here we go again. You are not the son of God. You are a homicidal maniac about to destroy the human race and make yourself king of the left-overs. When did that get fun?" He backs out onto the flat concrete roof, and the sounds of the city envelop us like a comforting blanket of normalcy on this night of madness.

"Do you believe Gray will let you live, Perez?" Morgenstern cocks his head. "Hmm? He's just using you, like he uses everyone."

Speaking of Gray. "Why the message to Gray on the wall, Oddgrim?"

He laughs softly. "I intend to kill him and take over his corrupt corporation. With Gray's resources, my army will be unstoppable."

"Take over Gray Industries?"

"The key is in the blood, Perez."

I realise he's right. Morgenstern is a clone of Gray, and so his DNA will grant him access to the entire might of Gray Industries. He's a clever son of a bitch. But then, if he can do it, so could I. Now *there's* a thought. I shake my head. No way. That is not me.

He sees my hesitation and mistakes it for sympathy. "Join me, and we will rule this world together." He has reached the edge of the roof and there is nowhere left for him to go. This is the last house on the Rim. Below us is the jungle.

"No, Oddgrim. That is not how it's going to be. I'm going to kill you." It's not a promise. It's a statement of fact.

"Big words, but you have to catch me first." He casts a quick glance behind him, balancing on the edge. "Well, I have been enjoying our little chat immensely, but it is time for me to go. We will no doubt meet again, and next time I fear we will not have as nice a conversation. This is all very fitting, you know. You are the one who fell from grace, I am the son of God, and ours is the eternal conflict. I look forward to gutting you."

"We'll see about that."

The noise of the city is drowned out by powerful rotors as the dark shape of a helicopter gunship rises behind Morgenstern, bristling with weapons.

"Good bye, Asher Perez. Until next time."

He raises his arms in a farewell salute and drops the sleeping baby to certain death on the asphalt far below.

I have one chance to pull my gun and put a bullet through Morgenstern's brain.

Fuck it.

I dive for the baby. My fingers close around its chubby little foot just as it disappears below the edge of the roof. The little one wakes up and starts screaming its lungs out, the ungrateful bastard.

I roll over on my back just in time to see Morgenstern close steely fingers around a black rope dangling from the chopper. He looks at me and the baby, a sneer of contempt disfiguring his handsome face. "Humans." Then he is yanked skywards.

I pull my gun and empty the clip into the dark sky after his receding silhouette. Bullet after bullet finds it mark, but he holds on to the rope and within seconds he's swallowed by the low clouds above the city. My scream of impotent rage echoes above the rooftops just as the rain begins to fall again.

I can't believe it. The bastard got away, and now this world will die because I failed. If I had sacrificed this one insignificant little life, I could have stopped him. I know I could.

I also know that I could never have let the little one fall. Faced by the choice, I reacted instinctively and went for the short-term good of saving an innocent life over saving humanity. Maybe not the smart choice, but it was the human choice.

No matter what they say, I am still me.

I look out over the rooftops to the east where dawn is already beginning to paint the sky a rosy red. The baby in my arms stops crying, and for a while we just lie there in the rain, content with the way things are and how they are going to end.

There's a blinding flash somewhere over the brightening horizon, like lightning in the clouds. The ramstrikes have begun, and the two million people of the once proud city of Kandahar are no more. They are wiped out in the blink of an eye by a few tonnes of random metal junk, released hours earlier from an approaching starship at a fraction of the speed of light. The drop is timed to a zeptosecond by a cold and calculating AI to strike the city as the planet revolves it into view.

The junk explodes in the atmosphere over the city in the equivalent of a gigatonne nuclear explosion, and the superheated remains hit the ground with the force of an atomic bomb. The trailing shock wave destroys any structures left standing and flattens every tree within a hundred kilometres of the strike. Dawn is half an hour away, and we don't want to be here when the sun rises.

I'm roused from my musings by the roar of another helicopter rising over the rooftops. This time it's our chopper and Borgia is hanging out of the open hatch, waving for me.

Since I have nothing better to do and I assume he's heading out of the city, I make a run for it and jump, the baby held under one arm. Borgia grabs my wrist in a legionnaire's grip and pulls me unceremoniously into the hold. He's wearing a headset and a murderous expression on his face. It seems I'm not the only one upset over Morgenstern's untimely getaway.

Wagner is there, and so is Suki, as well as a full team of Borgia's heavily armed Red Guards. Suki is strapped into a jump seat against the rear bulkhead next to Wagner. She's shouting something to me, trying to make herself heard over the roar of the engines.

"*What?*" I shout, leaning forward and cupping a hand behind my ear.

"*We've got sat-eye on him.* Borgia pulled some strings and got us access to a spy satellite." She holds up a com-pad displaying a real-time sat-map scrolling furiously as we tear through the rainy morning skies in a wide arc across the city. Below us, the low sprawl of the shanty town rushes by in a blur as we approach the Rim.

"Buckle up," Borgia shouts in my ear. "This ride is about to get bumpy."

Oh, dear. During the Corporate Wars me and Wagner inserted by switch-copter many times. As long as they fly by rotor, the ride is smooth as the pillow talk of a geisha. When the pilot turns on the jets and cranks up the power, the chopper turns into a bone-jarring rocket ship in the blink of an eye.

I drop into a seat between Suki and one of the soldiers and buckle up before giving Borgia the thumbs-up. He cups a hand over the microphone of his headset and gives the pilot the go-ahead.

The noise of the rotors stops and we start falling through the air, arcing over the edge of the cliff. All we can hear is the rush of air and heavy mechanical whirring as the rotor blades are folded down and angled backwards to prepare for what is to come. Through the open side of the helicopter I see the city dwindling above us and the emerald jungle far below rushing up to meet us.

We fall and we fall, and when I think we're going to hit the trees and die the immensely powerful jet turbines kick in. I'm thrown against the seat as the chopper goes ballistic.

It's For You

For a while I just sit there, squeezed between Wagner and Suki, the noise from the engines effectively ruling out any chance of small talk. I don't like that because it leaves me not much else to do but to ponder the implications of today's events.

I am not me.

Instead of charming Asher Perez, incorrigible drinker and stalwart charmer of women, this body belongs to General Caspar Batista Meridian, the most hated man in the universe.

Apart from the personal implications, this whole business raises some serious existential issues. Does this mean there is actually such a thing as a soul that can be transferred between bodies by implanting a recorded mind state into a catatonic body? I hope not. It sounds so very mechanical and boring. But if there is no soul, then what am I? Did the real Asher Perez die and I am nothing but a simple copy with all his memories, believing I am him? If the original Perez had lived, would we both have claimed to be him? Thoughts like that will drive a man crazy.

Luckily, I'm woken from my reveries by Borgia waving a ham-sized fist in my face from across the narrow passenger compartment. I bet he wants something.

"What?" I shout, trying to make myself heard over the engines.

Borgia just shakes his head and taps the headphones he's got on, then points to the wall behind me. I turn around, and sure enough, there hangs a matching pair. I can't help a sigh of relief at the sudden drop in ambient noise as I put them on.

"We're gaining on them fast," Borgia informs me, leaving me no time to enjoy the blissful silence.

"Good. Do they have an E.T.A. on my foot up Morgenstern's ass?"

"They say ten minutes, give or take."

To hide the smile creeping across my face, I look out the open side of the chopper at the green blur of jungle rushing past a mere hundred metres below. We're travelling at a speed usually reserved for corporate jets, but I can still make out the deep gullies that make the Elysian jungle such a pain in the ass to traverse on foot.

The warm little bundle in my lap is moving, about to wake up, and I shrug out of my jacket and wrap the kid in it. My view of the infant is eclipsed by Suki's darling face, staring at me with the strangest look in her eyes. She's slowly shaking her head as if in disbelief at the amazing drawing skills of an idiot savant. There are tears of frustration in her eyes. This kid is seriously disturbed.

"What the hell are you looking at, Suki?" I pull the headphones down around my neck.

"What the fuck is that?" She points to the bundle on my lap. "Is that a fucking baby?"

"Language, girl, language." I cover the ears of the little one with my hands. "Yes, it's a baby."

"Did you just steal a fucking baby?"

"I didn't steal it. I rescued it."

"What? From its mother?"

"No, from Morgenstern. He was using it as a hostage."

"Why did you bring it?"

"I couldn't bloody well leave it to die in the ramstrike, could I?"

"And now what? Are you going to keep it?"

"What the hell would I need a baby for?"

"I don't know."

"I'm the World Burner. Hardly father material, would you say? Here, you take it." I hand her the sleeping bundle.

"Hell no, I don't want it." She hands the bundle back. The bundle starts screaming its lungs out.

"I'll take it." A gravelly voice next to Suki.

"What?"

"I'll take it." It's the huge soldier next to Suki. "I've got kids at home. Love the little buggers."

I hand him the baby across Suki.

"Careful," he admonishes as I place the screaming midget in his arms. It stops crying at once and just looks at the big man. He smiles at the little one. The little one smiles back. Maybe there is hope for the human race after all.

When I look at Suki there's a smile on her face, too. When she sees me looking at her, the smile fades and is replaced by a scowl.

"What?" I ask.

"I really don't get you, Perez. I thought I knew you, but I realise I really don't. You truly believe you are Asher Perez." It's both a question and a statement. She leans in closer, like a lover cruising for a snog. "But you're not. Really." She's dead serious.

"What do you know about that crap?" I ask, surprised.

"More than you think," she replies.

"Well, I feel like me. I think like me. Who's to say I'm not me?" I try to shrug, which is not easy squeezed in next to Wagner. At the same time, I can't help noticing my thigh is pressed firmly against Suki's warm leg. We're both securely strapped in and there is nowhere for her to go, but it's still nice.

Her mind is on other things, though. "Why did you save me at the cathedral, Perez? They were going to kill me and you could just have left me there, problem taken care of. You don't need me, so why did you get me out?"

"I don't consider you a problem, Suki. I got you into this mess; I'd better get you out. Besides, I like having you around."

"Fuck you. Fuck your medieval chivalry, and fuck your perverted fantasies." I can tell her heart's not really in it. "I got into this mess of my own free will, and it got my family killed." She makes a face and turns away. I think I see a solitary tear trickle down her cheek. "You really have no clue why I'm here, do you?" she asks as she looks out at the jungle.

"Nope, but your being here is no coincidence, I know that much. I really want to understand how you and your family fit into all this. I know about Gray's Project. The Cardinal told me everything."

"Now, did he?" She turns back to me. "Somehow I doubt that."

"Oh, yeah? And you would know this because...?"

I dimly hear Borgia's phone ring through the noise.

"I'm not going to tell you that." She turns away again.

I open my mouth to ask her why, but once again I'm interrupted by Borgia. He holds the phone out to me with an incredulous look on his face.

"It's for you."

I reach out for the phone.

"Perez." There's a flash outside that lights up the sky. Another ramstrike, another city wiped out, and not a damn thing we can do about it. This one was close.

"Hello, Asher." I would know that voice anywhere.

"Hey, boss. What's up?" Both Suki and Borgia look at me. Even Wagner gives me a quizzical look. I hold up a finger to keep them on hold. "How did you find me?"

"I have my methods Asher, you know that. This has all been terribly exciting, but I'm afraid I can't let this charade continue. I thought I could trust you, but it seems I cannot. I'm taking you out."

I wonder if he means 'out' as in out of the mission, or out out? Gray goes on. "I'm sorry, Asher, but this is goodbye."

So, it's out out then.

"Hang on. Before you do anything stupid I want you to know we are hot on Oddgrim Morgenstern's ass, ETA less than five minutes." I look to Borgia for confirmation. He nods and holds up four fingers. "Four minutes and counting. If you abort now, you will never get your hands on him."

That gets his attention. A short pause and then:

"OK, one last chance, Asher." I hear the shift in his voice. "Bring me Morgenstern and we will talk. I will be back planet-side soon. Keep him alive." The connection clicks off.

"Gray?" Suki shouts in my ear.

"The one and only. He must really want Morgenstern awful bad. He's on his way. In the flesh. We've got to get our hands on the Prophet before Gray gets here. If we do, we might still have a chance to get out of this mess alive. All of us."

Borgia shows me three fingers and I give him two thumbs-up. Three minutes to rendezvous.

I put on the headphones again and call the pilot.

"Perez here. Does this thing go any faster?"

"Yes, sir." He looks back at me over his shoulder. "We always keep a secret rocket engine in reserve for situations like these." I flip him the bird and he just laughs from behind his huge mirrored goggles. "Relax, pal, we've got this. Just sit back and enjoy the ride, polish your gun or whatever it is you do for a living, and we will have you and your people delivered in no time. We should have a visual on the target as soon as we get out of this canyon. And there it is."

As we exit the canyon I see Morgenstern's helicopter flying low over the treetops about a kilometre ahead of us and finally I feel pretty good about myself. For the first time in days it seems this crap might not actually end in tears and bloodshed. That's always a bad sign.

And true enough...

"What the hell is that?" One of the soldiers points out the open side of the chopper at the middle distance.

I follow his gaze, and I see it too, but my brain won't translate what my eyes are seeing into anything I can understand.

"Yes, what the hell is that?" I echo his question, not sure who I expect to answer.

Suki leans across me and looks out too. "That, you idiot, is the shockwave of a ramstrike."

Even I'm smart enough to know that that means capital B Bad. So is Wagner. He looks me straight in the eye from below his bushy eyebrows. "I'm sorry I killed you, Perez."

"Don't worry about it, Finn. I would have done the same thing."

"Is that supposed to make me feel better?"

"Not really." I turn to Suki. "How long have we got?"

"We ain't got shit," she yells over the noise and barely has time to grab the straps securing her in place. The shockwave hits us like a runaway train and everything turns into screams and pain.

Like the man once said: We're on an express elevator to hell. Going down.

* * *

When I come to my senses, the first thing to penetrate my consciousness is the stifling heat and moisture of the jungle. I open my eyes and find myself staring down at the ground, some five or six metres below the thick vines from which I'm hanging. Above me rise nearly vertical walls of rock, intertwined by the vines and massive roots that broke my fall and saved my life. Leaves, twigs, and debris the size of small pebbles fall from the sky, torn from the forest by the shockwave of the ramstrike. All is dead quiet as if the jungle is holding its breath after being slapped. Something tickles my cheek. I reach up to wipe it off and my hand comes away covered in blood. My ears are bleeding, burst by the sudden change in air-pressure.

That explains the silence.

I must have been thrown from the tumbling chopper before it hit the ground. A quick once-over tells me I'm pretty banged up but I'll live. A dislocated shoulder, something wrong about the angle of my neck, and a million gashes of varying depths seem to be the sum total of the damage. I untangle from the vines and drop to the ground. Blood splatters the earth when I land, but there is not much pain.

The soreness in my shoulder is already fading and I flex it to get a feel for how badly dislocated it is. With a very satisfying crunch it pops back into its socket, and I crack my neck back into shape and feel like a human being again. Which I'm clearly not.

For lack of something better to do, I start walking down the ravine towards the pillar of boiling black smoke no doubt emanating from our crashed helicopter.

The first casualty I find is the big soldier who sat next to me. The one with the baby. He's been impaled through the back by a viciously sharp log now sticking out of his chest, covered in gore. From the feeble scratch marks on the bark and the amount of splinters under his fingernails I can tell he lived at least a little while. I bet he didn't count on this when he woke up this morning.

The baby is lying on the ground, placed carefully at his feet, still wrapped in my jacket. It's sleeping. The soldier must have shielded it with his body when we crashed because it looks mostly unhurt.

Shit.

For the merest of instants I consider leaving it there. Things would be so much simpler if you hadn't survived, little one.

But I may have doomed this whole world because of you, and I can't just leave you to die out here in the jungle.

"You are one tough little bastard, aren't you?" I whisper to the sleeping bundle.

What the hell am I going to do with it?

I can't leave the dead soldier like this either. He deserves better. I put a hand over his eyelids to close them, hoping someone will have the decency to do the same for me when that day comes. If it ever comes.

I feel a strange tingling, as of a weak electric current running up my arm, and I jerk my hand away. After what the cardinal told me, what I see shouldn't come as a surprise, but it still shocks me to the core.

The skin has been eaten from the soldier's skull. The flesh beneath leaks blood down what remains of his face and the naked eyeballs stare at the morning sky.

Did I do that?

There's only one way to make sure. I reach out a trembling hand toward the man's face again and place it on the still undamaged part of his forehead, hoping against hope that nothing will happen.

The electrical tingle is there again, but this time I don't pull my hand away. I leave it there, and I can feel it sinking as the dead flesh is sucked into my own body by the machines in my flesh. I can already feel tingling all over my body as the cuts and bruises are repaired, patched over with the dead man's flesh. I raise my free hand and watch a deep gouge in my palm seal itself, leaving not even a trace of scar tissue behind. A sickening shiver of pleasure runs down my spine.

Not wanting to look at the man who just unwittingly donated his flesh to me, I drape the large handkerchief from my first aid kit over his upper body. The horrible profile of his caved-in face is not quite hidden by the white silk.

Careful not to touch his exposed skin again, I grab the assault rifle still slung around his neck and the gun from his leg holster. He won't be needing them any time soon, but I might. Then I pull the sturdy gloves from his pocket and put them on. I wouldn't want to antagonize anyone by accidentally cannibalizing their flesh.

Then I pick up the sleeping baby and set off down the ravine, looking for survivors.

On the Shoulders of a Giant

There are no apparent fires in the wreck, but the smell of jet fuel is so heavy on the air I fear it's only a matter of time before the whole thing goes up in a fireball. The helicopter is wedged between a huge tree and the wall of the cliff a couple of metres off the ground.

"Hello? Anybody alive?" I call to the jungle and the sheer rock walls, not expecting a reply.

"Over here." The voice comes from below the wreckage and it sounds like Borgia. That bastard really is one tough son of a bitch. I find him next to the tree, trapped beneath a broken beam torn from the busted airframe. His leg is pinned to the ground at what must be a very painful angle and he's bleeding badly from a dozen cuts but seems to be in good spirits otherwise.

"You OK?" I ask as I kneel beside him. From somewhere in the twisted heap of scrap metal of the main wreck above, the ozone smell of busted electronics reaches my nostrils. Not a good sign.

"Felt better," he replies, "but I'm still alive, God be praised." He makes the sign of the cross and it's only then that I realize his leg is broken. The bone pokes through the flesh and fabric of his trousers in a ragged point covered in gristle and flies.

"That looks painful," I observe with a nod at his leg.

He shrugs his huge shoulders in that way that only really big people do. Which reminds me.

"Have you seen Wagner?"

"The infidel is up there, helping the others." He waves in the direction of the main wreck above us.

"He didn't stay to help you?" Finn could easily have lifted the wreckage and freed the inquisitor.

"I told him not to."

"Oh, for fuck's sake. When are you two going to grow up?"

"I will when he does."

Bloody hell. Those two are going to give me a hernia.

From the wreckage I hear the fizzle of electricity and I think I even see a flicker of light from the crumpled cockpit. I'd better do this fast. I put the sleeping baby down on the ground, hoping it will be far enough from the chopper if it explodes.

"This might hurt a bit," I warn as I grab the beam and brace against the moss-covered rocks.

"On my count of three," I tell Borgia and he nods, teeth clenched in anticipation of pain.

"One… Two… Three." I heave and the whole pile of twisted wreckage lifts off the ground. Not by much, but enough for Borgia to roll out of harm's way.

I grab his wrist and haul him to his feet. The guy must weigh at least two hundred kilos. I shouldn't be able to do that.

"Thanks," he nods.

"Need something for that arm?"

"I'll take what you have." He manages a weak smile through the pain.

"What? The good Lord doesn't provide painkillers for his faithful?" I throw the hypo spray from my first aid kit to him. He catches it awkwardly.

"Sometimes the Lord sees fit to visit trials upon his children," he manages through gritted teeth.

"Your Big Boss is not a very nice guy," I observe as I poke my head into the broken-off piece of fuselage, looking for other survivors.

"At least my Big Boss does not have his servants killed and then resurrected for some arcane reason," Borgia replies. I hear him breathe a sigh of relief as he applies the anesthetic to his leg.

I pop back out. "Well, actually he did."

That shuts him up and he closes his fleshy mouth. His jaw works furiously, and bulging muscles chase each other across his face like wildfire.

"Do you dare compare yourself to our Lord, Jesus Christ? Is that how you see yourself, abomination?"

And here I was, thinking we were bonding.

"That's your interpretation, not mine."

The witch hunter closes his eyes and takes a deep breath before continuing.

"Cardinal Santoro warned me of your infidel ways, and he told me to ignore them, but I cannot take an insult like that again. Next time I'm sending you straight to hell, church champion or not."

"There won't be a next time, I promise you that, my big friend."

Church champion? What the hell?

"Now, get your ass up there and help us get them out before this whole thing blows sky high."

* * *

The cockpit is completely caved in against the wall of the ravine and there's something dark and viscous dripping from the mess of crumpled metal. Whether it's blood or oil I can't tell, but there is no way the pilot or the co-pilot could have survived the crash. At least one of the soldiers in the back seems to have survived, and is shouting from the wreckage. He's pinned in place by the crushed fuselage.

"We'll get you out of there," I call to him. Fuck, he's just a kid. "Borgia. Wagner. Help me with this." I slap my palm on the back of the row of seats pinning the man in place. The giants glower at each other, neither of them wanting to cooperate, yet both dying to impress the other with their strength. Sometimes life can be so simple.

Wagner pulls, Borgia pushes, and between them they easily tear the mangled seat away, freeing the soldier. Wagner drops the wrecked seat and it falls to the ground far below. I smile at the two giants.

"There, that wasn't so bad, was it?" I ask them.

They both look away.

That's when I see the soldier's predicament.

His thigh is run through by a broken steering rod. It nails him to the seat like a roast on a spit, and there is no way we're going to get him out of there without some serious power tools.

The soldier sees what's happened to his leg and starts to hyperventilate.

"Oh fuck. Oh fuck."

"Not to rush you, but I see fire," Borgia calls from outside. Damn it.

"We have to get him out of here," I call to them. There is no way Wagner and Borgia will fit in the cramped confines, and they can't reach him from the outside.

"The fire's spreading," Borgia announces.

I look around for something to use as a lever but find nothing. I can hear the crackling of flames and we're talking seconds before the fire reaches the spilled fuel and the tree is turned into a giant torch.

There's nothing I can do for the young man and I scramble for the opening when I feel a weak grip around my wrist.

"Help me," he pleads, his terrified eyes locked on mine.

"You're going to be alright. Just relax and we'll have you out of here." I turn to Borgia, hoping he has a solution. He just shakes his head. Damn it. We can't just leave him here.

"Get me something to use as a lever. We need to pry him loose," I call to the giant.

"Get out of there." Borgia says, his voice unexpectedly gentle as he reaches out his great hand towards me. I look at it and then back at the trapped soldier. He's about twenty years old. In his eyes I see the moment when he realizes what's going to happen and something dies inside me along with his hopes.

"No. Don't leave me here. Please, don't leave me."

I just shake my head as I reach for Borgia's hand and let him pull me from the wreckage. I never for a second let go of the soldier's gaze, trying to calm him. "We're going to get you out, kid. Trust me." But I can see in his eyes that he knows he is doomed.

"Please." Tears start rolling down his cheek. "Not like this. Not like this." He's shaking his head in denial as the flames grow in the cockpit around him. When Borgia pulls me upright, there's a gun in his free hand, stock towards me. I nod and take it.

"Go," I shout, and as Wagner and Borgia start to clamber down from the tree I turn back to the trapped soldier and put a single bullet in the centre of his forehead. The look of absolute betrayal in his eyes will haunt me to the day I die.

Then I jump to safety and everything around me slides into slow motion. I land hard, and as I scoop up the sleeping baby there's a hollow whoosh above me. I dive for the safety of a nearby boulder but I don't quite reach it before the fireball catches me. It sears the hair from my scalp and scorches my skin as

I sail through the air. Then I crash into the hollow behind the rock and I hear pieces of shrapnel ricocheting off my cover.

The smell of burning fuel fills the air, and for a moment I just lie there on my back in the damp moss. I look up at the black mushroom cloud rising from the tree and remember the look in the young man's eyes as he died.

The baby starts crying and it begins to rain. How ironic.

Had the rain come a minute earlier, we could have saved that boy. The universe is a cold and hard place.

There was nothing I could do for the man, but I could at least have tried. I thought I would, but something made me grab Borgia's hand to save myself. Something that is not me. Something that is totally selfish and uncaring about human life, and I realise that the general will never let me die.

The question is, can I live with that?

* * *

We find Suki fifty metres down the gorge. She hangs crumpled and broken against the trunk of a giant tree, her smooth thigh pierced by one of the thin, metre-long spikes protecting the tree against hungry herbivores. Shit.

I put the baby down on the ground, sling the assault rifle on my back and kneel in the moss next to her. Not her. Not Suki.

The heavy rain is now pouring in rivulets from the cliffs on either side of us and the high canopy, drowning out all other sounds. The giants stand behind me, seemingly oblivious to the deluge.

I lean down and put an ear to Suki's face to feel if there's any breath.

"Don't you fucking grope my corpse after I'm gone," she croaks, blood bubbling at the corner of her sweet lips. It's washed away by the rain. Humour is a good sign. Blood foaming at the mouth is not.

"What, not even a little? I never got a chance to show you my stuff."

"Keep your stuff to yourself, thank you very much. Now get me off this thing." She gestures weakly at the grey spear-like point protruding from her leg.

I refrain from any penetration jokes as I doubt she'd find them funny at the moment.

"OK, but this is going to hurt." I shake my head. She is in really bad shape.

"Don't worry, I won't cry." She grits her teeth as I carefully work my arms under her. She's so light. I know it's Meridian's enhanced body playing tricks on me, but it feels like she weighs no more than a kitten.

She puts an arm around my neck and I feel the warmth of her body against mine.

I look at her, the surprise evidently visible on my face.

"Don't flatter yourself." She nods at the impaling thorn. A long trail of viscous blood falls from the tip and spatters on the ground in the rain. "Just get me off, OK?"

"OK, on a count of three?"

She nods.

"One… Two…" I yank her off the spike and she screams. A flock of avian reptiles start shrieking from their shelter in the top of the tree, startled out of their morning sleep.

"Perez, you fuck." She screams again when I lay her down on the mossy rocks, resting her head on my lap. "Damn you to hell."

"Got you off, didn't I?" That sounded better in my head before I said it.

"That's a close as you'll ever come to getting me off." She bites down on the pain and gives me a half-crazy grin. There's blood coating her teeth and flecking her lips. "How bad is it?"

"You've probably got some broken ribs, and there's a hole the size of my John Thomas through your leg."

"So I'm not going to die then."

"Haha, very funny."

She pulls a face that turns into another grimace of pain.

"Godfuck, that hurts."

I grin back at her, hoping Borgia didn't hear her.

He did.

"Whenever you infidels are done blaspheming, we have a fix on Morgenstern." The wreckage burns fiercely in the tree behind him despite the heavy rain. He's holding a scanner in his big hand and a blackened set of headphones to his ear. His leg is now set in a splint.

"Great. How far?"

"Looks like he crashed about a click north of here," Borgia replies and slings a huge Lensfield sniper rifle salvaged from the wreckage over his shoulder. He throws me a pile of scavenged anesthetic pads, sodden but still functional. "We will catch them if we hurry. Are you coming or what?" He looks at me and Wagner through the curtains of water.

Wagner looks at me, I nod and the Goliath answers the witch hunter. "We're coming."

I turn back to Suki. "How would you fancy a ride on the shoulders of a giant?"

I Want to Hear You Say 'Please'

Branches whip my face as we run.

They tear shallow stinging gashes in my flesh that instantly seal themselves but still hurt like hell. Behind me Wagner is carrying Suki on his shoulders. Her weight does not seem to bother him even though he's limping badly from all the beating he's taken. He lost the transfusion pack in the crash, but it seems to have done its job and he can move pretty well. Borgia keeps ups as good as he can with his broken leg. Modern painkillers are great.

It's no longer raining, and we're out of the gorges and into the jungle proper. Our twin suns are starting to break through the morning clouds and cast spears of golden light through the canopy high above.

We jump over roots thicker than I can reach around, we duck under immense vines, and we run along the trunks of fallen forest giants that form wide bridges across the deep gullies crisscrossing the jungle floor. With the massive trees of the jungle disappearing into the misty haze above, it feels like being inside a giant cathedral. The illusion is only broken by the noise of the reawakened jungle.

All around us the forest is buzzing with iridescent life, no doubt intent on eating us or laying eggs in our flesh, but we don't have time for that. We're on a clock and that clock is ticking fast.

Morgenstern has surely seen the smoke from our burning helicopter, but he can't know if we survived or not. I want to keep him guessing, so we slow to a walk as we near his crash site and let the dense jungle and its noisy inhabitants camouflage our approach. We reach a stand of moss-covered trees growing out of a pile of giant boulders that might once have been a building, and I hold up my hand.

"Borgia," I whisper to the witch-hunter, "you stay here with Suki while Wagner and I go for a quick look-see." It doesn't feel good to leave Suki behind, but it can't be helped. It's not that I like her or anything, but she's badly wounded and she's got some questions to answer. I can't risk her life.

I just hope we make it back before she croaks.

The inquisitor nods and droplets of sweat and rain fall from his chin. Then he does something unexpected. He holds out the Lensfield to Wagner.

Finn just looks at it like a baby would look at a fusion reactor as if he wonders what to make of it.

"Take it," Borgia urges.

Wagner shrugs and yanks it out of his hands.

Huh.

The world just got a little brighter.

"If we're not back in five minutes, get the hell out of here," I whisper to Borgia and Suki. Borgia nods and we move out.

We reach the edge of a large clearing and get down on the ground and wriggle the last few metres on our bellies. The gargantuan trees thin out before the ruins of a great Centaur pyramid, rising dark and forbidding above the trees. The massive structure is steep, and the steps are too high and oddly placed to be made for human feet. On top of the flattened pyramid is the great sacrificial table where, according to the prevailing theories, the centaurs slayed their prisoners of war to appease some bloodthirsty god or other. The similarities to the Aztecs of ancient Earth is uncanny. Maybe there is something universally appealing about pyramids and blood sacrifice. Then again, we might be fools to try and judge an alien culture by our own.

What remains of Morgenstern's chopper lies crumpled at the edge of the clearing at the end of a wide path of broken trees. Some distance beyond it, Morgenstern and a small group of injured soldiers are heading for the distant tree-line. They are following what looks like a well-trodden path, which is odd this deep in the jungle. There are no authorised settlements out here, and we are far from any highways or railways, which means we must be close to an illegal camp of some kind. Could this be where Morgenstern has his army holed up?

Spread around the pyramid are the crumbling ruins of smaller structures. I have no idea about their original purposes and intents, but they will provide Morgenstern with plenty of opportunities for cover if we attack him now.

"Shit, he's getting away."

Wagner grunts in agreement.

If we call for Borgia and wait for him to catch up, we might lose Morgenstern. We've only got one shot at this, and we'd better get it right.

With quick gestures I indicate two soldiers supporting a wounded third man as Wagner's targets. He nods, flicks away the scope protector on the Lensfield and takes aim with a terrifying smile. He's getting ready to claim another kill for Odin.

I put my eye to the sights on my own rifle and select the bulkier of the two guys flanking Morgenstern for myself. A deep breath to steady my aim and the rich smells of damp earth and vegetation fill my lungs.

The group is not moving very fast, which is a bit puzzling. I look up from the scope, surveying the clearing. It almost looks like they are waiting for something, but waiting for what?

I lower my eye to the sights again, about to give the kill order when I see what they are waiting for. On the other side of the clearing a sudden movement and a glint of sunlight on armoured glass catches my attention. I raise my head again to get a better look and almost wish I hadn't. The thing coming out of the jungle is a heavy walker tank.

A fucking walker.

How the hell did they get their hands on one of those? This is going to hell with bells and whistles.

"Fire," I mouth to Wagner.

He calmly squeezes his trigger and the head of his target explodes in a pink mist of blood, gristle and hair. The body takes a second to realise it's dead, and during that second my target takes a bullet in the back of the head. As we silently re-target, Morgenstern drops to one knee along with his remaining men and they swing their weapons 'round in our direction.

Wagner's second shot takes out the chest cavity of the man on the other side of the wounded soldier and they both collapse to the ground in a tangle of limbs.

Before the soldier on Morgenstern's other side can bring his rifle to bear on us I put a bullet in his throat, sending him to meet his ancestors. By now Morgenstern is shouting orders to the tank crew, giving fire directions.

"Wagner, we need to move."

"Right behind you." Wagner picks up his heavy rifle like a balsa-wood broomstick in one hand. We keep our heads down and run off into the foliage.

The jungle behind us explodes into chaos as the walker tank opens fire with its twin Gatling guns and pumps twice a thousand rounds a minute into the position we just evacuated. After a couple of very long seconds a new path is gaping through the jungle, straight as an arrow, pointing back to the tank.

We reach the ruins where the others are holed up. "By the luck of Loki, that was close," Wagner exhales as he slams his back against a crumbling wall and checks his magazine. It's empty.

He hands the big weapon back to Borgia who promptly reloads it without as much as a thank you.

"What the hell was that?" Suki asks from where she's cowering with the baby behind the pile of rocks.

"They have a walker tank. How the hell did they find a walker tank?"

"By following the noise?"

"Funny. We need to get rid of that thing if we're going to reach Morgenstern."

I punch Wagner and Borgia on the shoulders.

"Come on, big guys. Work to do." I move off into the underbrush again without stopping to catch my breath or to see if they follow me.

"And what am I supposed to do?" Suki hisses after me.

"Stay down and keep quiet until I call you," I hiss back over my shoulder. "And keep the baby quiet." She gives me the finger.

Out in the clearing, the tank is racing towards Morgenstern, and I can see its tall legs sinking deep into the soft ground with every step.

Shaped like a giant mosquito on four legs, three metres tall and seven metres long, the walker tank is a terrifying piece of military engineering. On top is an imposing array of sensors covering all wavelengths of the spectrum, and under the low snout are the two Gatling guns we've had the dubious pleasure of being previously introduced to. It's probably using infrared scanners to hunt for our heat signatures through the foliage, but by now the jungle should be warm enough for human body temperatures not to stand out against the background.

There is only one flaw in my reasoning.

A normal human body would not be visible against the ambient radiation, but too late I remember that mine is not a normal human body. My body's enhanced metabolism produces a lot a waste heat, and that heat stands out like a clown at a funeral against the jungle backdrop in IR, and the tank opens fire again.

This time we haven't got time to find proper shelter and I dive for the inadequate cover of a hollow formed by the lichen-covered ribcage of some huge, long dead animal. A fraction of a second after I crash into the moss the bullet storm shaves the vegetation from the land around us. Trees as thick as my thigh are sliced clean off and come crashing down through the greenery. Borgia and Wagner are nowhere to be seen, and I can only keep my fingers crossed and hope they have found shelter of their own.

The tank holds its fire long enough for the debris to settle and the gunner to check his targets. I crawl down the valley between the ribs, taking care to keep my head below the line of sight of the tank.

I spit out foul-tasting wet dirt and whisper for my companions. "Wagner?" I hold my breath and wait for a reply.

"Here," comes the whispered reply from behind a thick tree, somehow still standing after the bullet storm.

"Borgia?"

"Over here."

I risk a quick glance and spot his red coat through the undergrowth.

"Don't you think it's time to ditch that Rim-pimp overcoat?"

"I believe you might have a point." Is that a stab at humour from the big guy?

He wriggles out of the coat. Then he grabs a blade of thick grass, wide as my hand, and bends it down towards him before hanging the coat on it. I have no idea what he's up to, but I hope he knows what he's doing.

"What are you doing?"

"Diversion. Ready to run, idolater?" It's a challenge, but not for me.

It's for Wagner, and I'm surprised at a sudden stab of jealousy as I realize I'm not included in the competition for silverback of the tribe. That can be very hurtful for a guy.

"Are you?" is Wagner's whispered reply as he readies to run. He never was very good with the snappy one-liners.

As Borgia comes crawling through the sun-gilded moss, his plan becomes clear. The blade of grass slowly rights itself, lifting Borgia's heavy coat with it.

"Go," Borgia shouts, and once again we're off through the undergrowth like meth-rats down a crack pipe. The blade of grass brings the coat into the line of sight of the tank, and the jungle explodes into yet another shrieking inferno. It's no coincidence they call those guns Banshees.

Borgia's coat is torn into a cloud of leather strips and it buys us precious seconds in which to get away. We keep our heads down and run as fast as we can along the edge of the clearing, looking for an angle of attack on the tank.

There is none.

There's no way we're going to be able to get past the tank without being spotted and shot to shit. At that very moment the tank reaches Morgenstern and he takes cover between its legs.

"Damn it." I clench my jaws in frustration. So close, yet so very far away. We might as well have been on the other side of the damn planet.

Borgia taps me on the shoulder. "Look." He points to the opening in the jungle where the tank appeared just minutes before. If I was hoping for a lucky break of some kind, I might as well not have bothered. Coming out of the jungle is a full platoon of heavily armed soldiers. Unfortunately, this is where he keeps his army. Morgenstern has been recruiting some serious players.

"Shit."

That's the last thing we need. The tank was bad, but, coupled with a platoon of enemy infantry, we can just kiss Morgenstern's ass goodbye.

If the Terran infantry hasn't already landed, they will soon, and the planet will be thrown into the chaos of war. That will give Morgenstern all the cover he needs to slip quietly away and put whatever sick plan he's nursing into action. A plan that no doubt involves the Archangel and genocide on a biblical scale.

And we were so close. So damn close.

Morgenstern moves out towards his troops, leaving the tank behind to cover his retreat.

I turn around, about to abort the mission when I see Borgia reach into a leg pocket and haul out his phone again, a puzzled look on his face as he checks the number. He answers and a great frown sails up on his forehead, thunder-heads on an already dark sky.

"It's for you." He hands me the phone. "Again."

What now? Did I forget a dentist's appointment? That's about the only thing that could make things any worse right now.

"Perez," I answer.

"Hello, Asher. I believe you are experiencing a spot of tank trouble." It's Gray. Big surprise.

"Where the hell are you Gray?"

"On my way. Just give the word and I will rid you of your problem."

"What word?"

"I want to hear you say 'please'."

The bastard.

"Quit fucking around, Gray."

"Just do it, Asher."

I look at my two companions. They look back at me.

"Alright." I sigh. "Could you do something about that tank? Please?"

"See, that wasn't so hard. Thy will be done."

There's a sudden flash of light and a golden lance of light from the clouds stabs the tank through the fuselage. For an instant it's pinned to the ground like a fish on the end of a giant's spear. Then it's torn into a ball of fire and flying shrapnel.

Hot on the heels of the plasma-beam comes the dangerously sleek, dark shape of a dropship falling through the air. Its ablation shields glow red-hot from the friction of atmospheric re-entry, and I've never been so happy in my life to see the cavalry show up. I told you it was a good idea to bring Gray.

As a wave of warm air brings the smell of burning fuel and scorched metal from the explosion of the tank, the enemy soldiers start running across the open field toward their commander. Their weapons swing around, covering every angle of approach.

The dropship fires its engines to halt its descent and steers for the top of the pyramid. Smart move by Gray. That way he can cover the whole clearing with the weapons on the ship while staying out of the enemy's reach.

Morgenstern must have realised he will never reach the safety of either the jungle or his soldiers before he is blown to bits by the ship, and he veers off towards the safety of the closest ruin instead.

The ship touches down on top of the pyramid on a plume of fire, crushing the ancient sacrificial table under its massive weight. Gray never was one for superstition.

As soon as the ship is down, a rear loading ramp falls down and black-clad operatives pour out, weapons at the ready. They start to make their way down the steep pyramid, heading for Morgenstern. Things are looking up for the good guys, and I turn to Borgia and Wagner and smile.

"Let's go get the bastard."

A Blood Mist

We reach the wall of the closest ruin and slam our backs against it. It shakes under Borgia's and Wagner's combined weight and for a second I fear it's going to collapse, but it remains standing. Say what you will about the centaurs, but they knew their masonry.

I peer quickly around the corner and see Morgenstern fifty metres away, sticking his head out of the doorway of the ruin he's hiding in. I snatch my head back and hope he didn't see me.

"Got him. Borgia, I'll cover you." Borgia nods and I clap him on the shoulder. "Go."

The inquisitor ducks through the doorway and runs along the low wall outside, crouching low. I peer around the corner again, my assault rifle shouldered and ready to lay down suppressive fire if anyone should poke their heads up. Borgia makes it halfway along the wall before someone opens fire and he drops into cover. Damn it. Morgenstern's soldiers must be closer than I thought. "Wagner, go." I send a short burst in the direction of the attack and then follow close behind the giant. As I run, I cast a quick glance towards the pyramid. There's no trace of Gray's operatives, meaning they are down on the ground and in play somewhere in the maze of the ruins.

This place is getting crowded.

We reach Borgia where he crouches behind the wall.

"Here they come," he whispers and I look through a hole in the wall to see where he's pointing. At least ten heavily armed soldiers are moving in on our position. They are still forty metres away down what could be the main street of the Centaur village, if that's what it is. They're closing in quickly, expertly using the ruins for cover.

"Distract them." I hand my pistol to Wagner and crawl down to the corner of the next building. On my signal, Wagner opens fire over the wall. He's not likely to hit anyone at this distance, but his fire will force them to go to ground, giving me time to take aim around the corner. The clip spent, Wagner drops back down to reload and the soldiers start advancing on our position again, right into my line of fire. They are wearing light body-armour and I'm not sure my assault rifle will have the force to penetrate it. I take careful aim and drop two of them with perfect headshots.

Five of the remaining soldiers lay down an excessive amount of suppressive fire on Wagner's and Borgia's position while the rest pull their dead into cover. Between the buildings to my right I get a quick glimpse of Gray's men homing in on the sound of the gunfire. We have to do this quick if we're going to get to Morgenstern before the whole damn planet shows up.

I wave for the giants to join me and they get down on their bellies and crawl over to me as the wall disintegrates above them. Our best hope is to get to Morgenstern before his mercenaries realise we've left our cover. We run out of wall and there is no way for us to continue without being spotted and killed.

"Borgia," I shout over the noise, "call Gray and tell him to get those bastards off our backs for a minute."

"Will do," he calls back as he pulls the phone from his leg pocket. He needs to cup his hand over the microphone and shout to make himself heard over the din.

I stick the barrel of my rifle around the corner again and send a short burst in the general direction of the enemy. It's mostly to have something to do while Borgia's on the phone.

The inquisitor cuts the call and gives me a thumbs-up. "Supportive fire incoming."

Synchronised with his words come three heavy crumps from the top of the pyramid. The fire-and-forget shells come curving over us from the dropship, leaving grey smoke trails against the morning sky. They lock onto their target and pound into the ground in the midst of the enemy soldiers. In a single, very satisfying explosion, the rockets detonate, throwing rocks, dirt, and torn remains of human beings ricocheting around the ruins.

We get up and run towards Morgenstern's hideaway, using the smoke and confusion for cover. All around us debris rains from the sky, and random bullets tear swirling paths through the dust. The smell of cordite and death sear my nostrils. There's nothing to do but keep running. If we get hit, we get hit.

I get hit.

A stray bullet catches me in the side of my neck, tearing a hole from side to side through my windpipe, right below the chin. Pain flickers through my brain, barely registering before it's gone. I realize I can still breathe as we reach the entrance to Morgenstern's hideaway and slam into the wall to one side of the door.

"May Odin receive you in Valhalla." Wagner looks horrified when he sees me. It must look worse than it is.

"I'm fine," I assure him.

"Your witch-god can't help him, infidel," Borgia whispers to Wagner and makes the sign of the cross.

"And White Christ can?" Wagner makes his sign against Christians.

My dad is stronger than your dad. They're still at it.

"Focus, big guys," I whisper. "On my count of three, I go in and you cover me, OK?"

"Cover you with what?" Borgia asks. "I'm out." He drops the useless rifle to the ground. Wagner has only got my gun.

"Just cover me, OK?"

They shrug and I start counting.

"One... Two... Three," and I dive through the opening. I execute a perfect roll and come up on one knee, rifle shouldered and sweeping the room. Morgenstern is not there. Damn it, where did he go?

"Clear," I call and I hear the big men move in behind me.

"Where is he?" Wagner's rumbling voice in the close confines sounds like it will shake the dust from the rafters above our heads.

"I'm not sure, but I have an idea." I point to the back of the dark room where a darker shadow suggests a recessed doorway or an alcove of some sort.

The assault rifle is too big for cramped confines, and I motion for Wagner's gun. I hand him my rifle in return. The weight of the gun tells me it's fully reloaded. Small things like that keep the professionals alive while the amateurs die.

I gesture for Borgia to move around to the other side of the opening as me and Wagner inch closer on our side.

Coming closer, I realise it's a doorway opening on a stairway down into darkness. A cold wind blows from the hole, bringing the smell of decaying leaves and dead animals. I have no idea if Morgenstern is armed, but I'm certain he could do some serious damage with only a knife or his bare hands. If only I had a grenade.

I risk a quick glance down the stairwell and from out of the darkness explodes Oddgrim Morgenstern, howling like a lost soul escaping from hell.

In one hand he wields an ancient metal rod, rusted and sharp. In his other hand is a vicious-looking combat knife. I feel my senses go into overdrive and everything slips into slow motion.

As he runs past us he swings at me with the pole and only my superhuman reflexes prevent it from caving my head in. I manage to twist away from the strike and the rusty pole lands on my left thigh. With a sharp crack it breaks the hypercarbon-reinforced bone of my leg. The pain is brief, there only to report the damage, then gone.

Borgia, despite his decades of military experience, has nowhere near my reflexes and he takes Morgenstern's knife straight in the chest. Luckily he listened to his mother this morning and wore his kinetic body armour. The vest hardens in the blink of an eye and the knife gets stuck in the reactive material. I've never seen that happen with a knife before.

The kinetic armour is designed to go from soft to rigid in an instant when hit with sufficient force. It gives the wearer both the mobility of an un-armoured man and the protection of a medieval knight in a single package. High-velocity bullets have been known to get stuck in the material when it hasn't hardened quick enough, but I never knew it could happen with a knife.

Ignoring my broken and useless leg, I lunge for the Prophet and close my fingers around his throat as he runs past us. I pull him off his feet and slam him skull first into the tiled floor as I fall, cracking the back of his augmented cranium against the ancient flagstones. In the split second before his brain recovers from the impact I raise the gun and use the stock to punch him in the face, feeling the bones of his face crumble.

Knowing I only have a fraction of a second before he recovers, I pound him again and again and again until I cave his face in. I know it won't do him any permanent harm, but I hope to hurt him enough to allow us to subdue him before his body has time to repair itself.

"Grab him," I shout to Wagner and Borgia. "And don't touch his skin."

The giants grab Morgenstern's arms and haul him to his feet. My leg is still useless but I can already feel the bones fusing. I put the gun to Morgenstern's forehead.

"Well, hello, Oddgrim. We meet again." I quickly search him and remove all his weapons. There's a canvas shoulder bag slung over his shoulder and I cast a quick peek inside.

"I think I'll hang on to this." I pull it over his head and sling it over my shoulder.

He turns a ruptured eye towards me, and I can tell he's not seeing me clearly. The shape of his face is all wrong. He tries to tear himself free, but the combined strength of Wagner and Borgia is too much even for him.

"In a hurry?" I caress his oozing eye with the gun.

"Do you really think a gun scares me?" His mouth is not working properly either. There is blood running down his ruined face, and pieces of cracked teeth crunch between his lips as he speaks. He starts laughing. Not the reaction I was hoping for.

"My soldiers will be here any second, Caspar. Let me go, and we can talk about this."

"That's not very likely to happen, Oddgrim. Gray is here."

"Nero Gray?" He spits pieces of teeth on the floor.

"He's waiting for you at the top of that pyramid."

"Still working for him, huh? What can he offer that you could possibly want? He can't give you your old body back."

"Who says I want it back?"

"Don't grow too fond of this one. When you deliver me to Gray, he will kill you. You do realise that?"

"The thought has occurred to me." I nod. "Maybe I should hand you over to this gentleman instead," I nod towards Borgia, "and you'll find out what the cardinal has in store for you. It's pretty grand, actually. I think it might be right up your alley."

"The cardinal will kill you too, Caspar, and you know that." He sees the flicker of hesitation in my eyes and smiles a bloody smile. "My, my. How are you going to get out of this one, little brother? You know there is only one way out. Join me, and we will rule this world together. It's what you were born to do."

"Screw that. I was born to drink, fight and consort with women of disrepute."

"If that is what you want, why not do it as a king? Everything is more fun with a crown on your head."

"You can't talk your way out of this, Oddgrim."

"Then how are we going to do this?"

"I don't know yet, but I'll think of something. First of all, you need to call off your mercenaries."

"There's no way you can intimidate me, Caspar. We both know your gun can't hurt me."

"You and I know that, but they don't."

It's risky to gamble everything on the assumption that Morgenstern hasn't told his mercenaries about his regenerative powers, but it's all we've got.

"Move."

I pick up the rusted metal pole from the floor and use it for a cane as Wagner and Borgia haul Morgenstern out into the sunshine. Outside, what remains of Morgenstern's commandos have set up a welcoming committee for us, arrayed in a semicircle around the building. They do not look happy as I press the gun to Morgenstern's jaw. "Drop your weapons, or I will kill your prophet."

Some of the less hardened-looking soldiers cast wary glances at each other, but they keep their weapons trained on us.

"I said, drop them or he dies right here, right now."

"Don't listen to him," Morgenstern calls to them. There's a disconcerting clicking sound from his jaw as he speaks, but he doesn't seem to mind. "I am the son of God. Their violence and hate cannot hurt me. Their bullets will pass through my flesh without injury. I will stand unharmed."

"Oh, yeah?" I turn to Wagner, like a stage magician turns to his assistant before the piece de resistance. "Wagner, give me a hand here, if you please."

The giant raises Morgenstern's right hand and I put the muzzle of my gun against the back of it. "Drop your weapons gentlemen, or I will kill him, one piece at a time. Starting now."

I pull the trigger and they all jump in surprise. They thought I was bluffing.

So was I.

The bullet tears a ragged hole through Morgenstern's hand. Blood and bits fly off along with two of his fingers, and a blood mist spatters the closest soldiers.

I hope they will not stay around long enough to see the fingers grow back.

I'm surprised that I pulled the trigger. I didn't think I was the kind of person who could do that to an unarmed man. It must be Meridian's doing.

It must be.

"Now. What's it going to be?" I put the gun back at the Prophet's jaw.

Morgenstern starts laughing as the blood pumps from his hand and runs down his wrist.

"Behold. The son of God is unharmed."

They can clearly see he's not, and the looks on their faces tell me exactly the story I was hoping for. They just started to doubt if Morgenstern really is who he claims to be. Instead they wonder if maybe he has just been an insane charlatan all along. It's right there in their eyes.

A short pause, then a sergeant raises the barrel of his assault rifle and calls to his men. "Stand down. Stand down. Move out."

"No," Morgenstern howls with rage. "You fuckers. Damn you. Damn you all to hell."

Perhaps not words they ever expected from their Saviour. There is actual hurt in their eyes as they back away between the ruins. As they leave, Gray's men close in around us from all directions, their weapons trained on the retreating mercenaries.

The leader of the newly arrived troop steps up to me. They have Suki and the baby already in custody. Impressive.

"General Meridian, I presume?"

There's not a hint of humour in his eyes. It would have been pretty funny if he'd said it as a joke. Who else would I be? Then again, there's no actual proof Stanley ever spoke those words to Livingstone.

I nod and he salutes me. "I am Colonel Naja."

I know who the colonel is. I've worked with him for years, but of course he doesn't recognise me in this body. He lowers his hand. "Mr Gray is waiting for you, General. If you would care to step this way, sir?" He's polite as an English gentleman at a tea party, but under the thin veneer of civilisation I know there is a very dangerous man. They all are. I should know. I trained them.

"Alright, Colonel. Lead the way."

Morgenstern howls at the heavens in impotent rage as Wagner and Borgia start hauling him towards the pyramid where Gray is waiting.

We Always Get Them in the End

The pyramid is steep, and over the centuries the stonework has crumbled as generations of huge trees have lived and died on its slopes. The structure is a shadow of its former self, but it has still outlived the people who built it. Perhaps there is an enclave of living Centaurs somewhere deep in the jungle, struggling to survive, who knows? Rest assured though, that if their own people didn't get them, we will. We always get them in the end.

It's a beautiful day for war, and as we climb above the treetops, the extent of the devastation becomes chillingly clear. Far off to the east a slowly roiling mushroom cloud is filtering out the early morning sunlight where the city of Kandahar stood not an hour ago. Further off to the east I can see more Stratosphere-grazing pillars of smoke where other cities have been wiped out by the dawn ramstrikes. Behind us to the west I can just about make out the twin spires of Masada, still standing. I'm surprised at the small leap of joy in my chest at seeing that old pile of refuse has been spared. Who would have thought?

A sudden glare in the sky catches my attention. As I shade my eyes I see the fires of the first of the Terran troop-carriers braking from atmospheric entry. It's followed by another and then another until the sky is glowing with them, falling like meteors.

The Terrans will have toys we've never heard of to bring to the playground, but so will we, and we have them at a disadvantage. Their weapons are twenty years old, while ours are brand new. To pull this off, they have to make sure they have the numbers on their side. Judging by the armada in the sky, they do.

The falling dropships are met by orange tracer fire from ground artillery and hundreds of fighter jets piloted by Elysium's finest.

And so it begins.

Returning my focus to more pressing matters, I can't make up my mind if the soldiers escorting us up the pyramid are an honour guard or a prison detail, but I think we are soon about to find out.

For the briefest of instances, I miss my old position at Gray Industries, when these men were my friends. Life was so simple then. I woke up, went to work, beat some people up, went to the pub, and got wasted. More often than not in the company of these men. If push comes to shove, will I have the guts to kill them?

Will the general even hesitate?

* * *

When we reach the top of the pyramid, a familiar figure steps up to greet us. The storm from the idling jets flaps his long coat around him like the wings of a manta ray. An image of a man in the rain on a corner under a streetlight outside a Masada pub flashes through my brain.

Same coat. Same man.

"My dear, dear Asher. Welcome." He spreads his arms as if to embrace the world. "As always, you deliver the goods on time."

When I ignore him he lowers his arms and nods in greeting to Wagner.

"Wagner."

"Boss." The giant inclines his head.

"I am so glad to see you both again."

"Skip the bullshit, Gray," I say. "We know."

"Bullshit? You have brought back the prodigal son, Asher. You have no idea how long I've been waiting for this moment."

"Oh, but I do. I know exactly how long you've been waiting for this moment. Some seventy years or thereabout."

He laughs. "Oddgrim may be a few years your senior, but he's not that old." Like a stand-up comedian playing to his audience he looks to his soldiers for support. They laugh dutifully.

"Now, I believe I haven't had the pleasure of meeting your new friends. Introduce me, Asher."

I decide to humour him.

"Gray, meet Jasper Constantine Borgia. The one they call the Sumerian. Borgia, meet Gray."

"Ah, the witch hunter." Gray actually sounds impressed. That's not like him.

He nods to Borgia, who nods back.

"And who is this pretty little thing?" Gray turns to Suki, who looks like she is barely restraining herself from clawing his eyes out.

"Gray, Suki. Suki, Gray," I say as means of introduction.

"Do I know you, girl?"

"I know you, Methuselah."

That melts the smile from his face. The soldiers sense the change in atmosphere and I see fingers going for triggers.

What did you do now, Suki my girl?

"Ah. I see. I thought I knew you from somewhere."

What the hell? Do they have a history?

For a long moment Gray just stares at the girl. Then he looks at me, the question clear on his withered face. I shrug. I have no idea what she is on about.

He seems to weigh his options and come to a decision.

"Well, never mind an old man. Now, bring him to me."

Fuck, this is not going the way I hoped. With all those soldiers around, there's no way I'm going to get to Gray without Wagner getting killed. Or Borgia. Or Suki. The thought surprises me. I hadn't thought about it before, but I really don't want any of them to die. Over the past few days I've grown to like them. More than that. I would even go so far as to call them friends, and getting each other killed is not what friends do. Fuck.

I walk over to the kneeling Morgenstern and pull him to his feet.

"Come on, brother. Let's do this."

He leans close. His teeth are still broken and he slurs his words. "There is still time to do the right thing, Caspar."

"We're doing this my way. Come on." I push him towards the others.

Gray stands on one side. Borgia on the other. They both look certain that I'm going to hand over the Prophet to them. How I hate making people disappointed.

I stop between them.

Gray nods to my prisoner. "Hello, Oddgrim."

"Hello Father."

Gray reaches out a hand to me. "Asher, give him to me," he demands, in his most reasonable voice.

Borgia reaches out his hand too. "Perez, we have a deal."

I look between them. Things are coming to a head.

"Asher." Gray is starting to sound impatient.

"Perez," Borgia commands in his best thunder voice.

Wagner and Suki just stand there, looking between Gray and Borgia like a very odd couple at a tennis match.

At a sign from Gray, the soldiers shoulder their rifles and take aim at my chest.

"Asher, my dear boy. Stop messing around. He is mine. He always was."

"The church demands that you hand him over." For the first time since I met him, Borgia sounds like he's losing his temper.

Time to do something.

In a single move I pull the knife from my pocket, flick it open and pull my elbow around Morgenstern's throat, holding him as a living shield before me. The momo-blade tickles the soft skin above his carotid artery, drawing blood. Gray motions for the soldiers to hold their fire.

Morgenstern laughs. "Is this a dagger I see before me? I really want to see you getting out of this mess, little brother."

"Come now, Asher." Gray is trying to be reasonable. "This is leading nowhere. If it's money you want, just name a figure and I'll pay."

"It's not about the money, Gray. This is much bigger, and you know that."

"I don't know what lies your new friends have been telling you about me, but I can assure you they are lies. You know me, Asher. We've known each other for a long time. Have I ever given you reason not to trust me?" He smiles in his most fatherly way. "Have I?"

"The old Asher Perez never had reason to distrust you. But secrets have been told and things are no longer what they were. I know what I am. And that changes things."

"Ah." His smile fades. "No more need for the Asher Perez charade then."

"No."

I flex my elbow, putting pressure on Morgenstern's windpipe. He chokes and starts coughing. "Come on, brother. What's it going to be? The suspense is killing me." he gasps, his face growing red with the increased blood pressure.

"Don't hurt him," Borgia commands. "We need him alive."

"Caspar. Don't hurt him," Gray echoes calmly. "He's your brother, for fuck's sake."

I've never heard Gray swear before. That is not a good sign.

Morgenstern starts laughing. With the pressure of my arm around his throat, it's not a pretty sound. "Yes, I'm your brother, for fuck's sake." He can barely get the words out, and spittle flies from his lips with the effort of breathing at the same time as speaking. "Come on Caspar, let me go and let's kill these fuckers."

I'm damned if I do, and I'm damned if I don't, and there is only one thing left to do.

I look to Gray and Borgia. "I guess you've heard the story of King Solomon and the baby?"

They all look at me. At first uncomprehendingly, but then, as the message sinks in, their eyes widen in disbelief.

"Caspar, no." Gray shakes his head.

"Perez, don't," Borgia pleads with me.

"Solomon never killed the baby," Morgenstern sputters.

"Well, you know what? Solomon was a pussy."

The blade slides easily between the vertebrae at the base of his skull. With a few quick twists, the mono-molecular edge severs his immortal spine and his headless body falls twitching to the ground. Just another blood sacrifice on the shining steps of progress.

A scream of denial comes from Gray as I kick the limp corpse over the rim of the platform. Blood splashes over the blackened steps as it starts a horrifying descent to the clearing far below. If the old gods of the centaurs are ever going to be reawakened, this is their chance.

I'm a little disappointed when nothing happens.

I throw the severed head down the other side of the pyramid and turn to face Gray, my knife dripping Morgenstern's immortal blood onto the stonework. It's done, and what happens now is beyond my control.

"Caspar, what have you done?" Gray screams at me. Borgia stands looking after the tumbling body, an unreadable expression on his face.

Suki is leaning heavily on the edge of the broken stone table, keeping the weight off her injured leg. Her eyes are locked on mine and there's a thin smile at the corner of her lips. Wagner has moved closer to the soldiers. They are too focused on the major events playing out before them to notice.

Gray pulls a gun from his pocket and aims it at my face.

"Do you know what this is, Caspar?"

It looks just like the one Suki had. The one that kills my kind.

"This is the end for you."

He pulls the trigger and I brace for the final impact.

It never comes.

Instead I see Suki, sweet Suki, throw herself between us a split second before the gun fires. She takes the bullet straight in the chest and drops like a rock.

Gray looks in disbelief at the weapon in his hand, at me, then at Suki's crumpled body. Apparently the gun is a one-shot deal. He blinks in silence, staring at me. Then the spell is broken and he turns to his soldiers and screams in a panic. "Kill them. Kill them all."

Time slows to a crawl and death lowers her dark wings over the top of the pyramid.

I drop to the stone paving a split second before the soldiers open fire. Their bullets whistle mere centimetres above me as I hit the ground and roll. Wagner punches the nearest soldier in the kidney and jerks the rifle out of his hands. Borgia backhands another man in the face, and his meaty fist sends the poor man flailing to his death at the end of a very long drop.

Before the soldiers have time to realise what's happening, Wagner opens fire from point-blank range and I bury my trusty blade just below the Adam's apple of the first soldier I reach. It's the colonel. He drops in a spray of arterial blood.

The fight turns into a bloody melee, and Borgia goes down under the combined forces of four big soldiers, a fifth climbing over his wrestling comrades. There's a big combat knife in his raised hand, and he's about to plunge it into the exposed throat of the High Inquisitor when Wagner steps in.

He picks the climber up by the scruff of the neck and smashes him against the floor. Borgia shrugs off his attackers and together the giants tear their enemies apart.

Through the chaos I see Gray running for the ship, screaming for the pilot to lift off.

We can't have that.

I scrabble around for something to throw and find the rusty iron rod on the ground. I hurl it after Gray like a javelin. The old man reaches the side of the ship just as the metal spear hits him in the shoulder. It pierces his frail old body and nails him to the hull. With the old man stuck to the side of the ship, the pilot can't lift off, which leaves us plenty of time to mop up.

* * *

The fight is neither short nor clean, but when it's over, the good guys remain standing. Except for Suki. She's barely breathing, and there's a lot of blood on the stones around her. It's pooling between the stones, and insects have already begun to feast on it. I drop to my knees beside her and take her cold hand in mine.

Wagner and Borgia step up, covered in blood, for once not about to kill each other. Bleeding together has a curiously bonding effect on people.

"We're done here," Borgia states in a flat voice.

"And where does that leave us?" I ask, looking up at the giant. Behind him the battle in heaven still rages and burning wreckage falls everywhere. The sky is full of fire and dark vapour trails.

"We're done too." There's a chime from his communicator and he casts a quick glance at it. "The cardinal sends his regards."

Fuck. It may not have gone strictly to plan, but I still gave the old bastard part of what he wanted.

"Well." I shrug. "I'll see you around."

"Not if I see you first." The old jokes are always the best. I give him a lopsided smile. His fleshy lips draw back into an unaccustomed grin. Then he turns to Wagner.

So this is it.

I'm about to see the two greatest warriors on the planet battle to the death.

For a long time nothing happens.

Then Borgia raises his huge hand and holds it out to Wagner. "Wagner."

For a long time, Finn just looks at it. Then he reaches out and takes it in his equally big one. "Borgia."

They shake. Hard.

The muscles of their arms bulge, their eyes locked on each other. Neither face betrays with even a flinch the titanic struggle going on and I can almost feel the ground quake beneath them.

Aw, they are so cute.

As far as I can tell it's a draw, but Borgia lets go first.

Suki coughs in my lap. "Didn't see that coming," she croaks. There is so much blood.

Borgia turns and walks away, limping on his splinted leg. On his way across the platform, he picks up a discarded assault rifle, checks the magazine and moves on. If he's planning on walking home he's going to need it. If there is anyone who could survive the walk, it's the witch hunter.

He limps down the stairs and is gone without so much as a backward glance.

Another cough from Suki brings me back to the messy present.

"Don't worry, Suki. Everything is going to be all right."

It's not, and she knows it.

Sit With me

"Don't bother, Perez. I know I'm done for. No need to waste your breath lying to me." I'm impressed with her composure.

In the periphery, Gray and the baby fight for the prize for most pitiable screaming.

"Before I go, Perez, there are some things you need to know."

She's breathing in shallow gasps.

"I bet there are. Have you got the time?"

"Stop asking stupid questions and I might."

She coughs blood all over my hands as I try to wipe the gore from her face.

The screams of the wounded are starting to get to me.

"Wagner," I shout, "make them shut up." Then I turn back to Suki. "Go on."

She seems to ponder how best to proceed when instead she bends her head backwards as her body locks up in cramps. "Fuck me, it hurts." Then she takes a deep, shuddering breath and looks back at me with a sad smile. "Meeting you cost me my family and my life, and now it's up to you to end this. If I wasn't already dying, the irony of it would kill me."

I give her a sad smile, and she looks at me for a long time.

"You're not the World Burner, are you?"

I look off into the distance and sigh.

"Yes, I am."

"No, you're not. Not really. What happened to you? The real you, I mean. Asher Perez."

"Wagner killed me."

"What?"

"It's a long story."

"Try me. I want to understand." She starts coughing again and I humour her.

"Well, according to the cardinal, Gray created Morgenstern because he was lonely. Morgenstern had no intention of being a pet and ran away. When the war came, Gray created Meridian and the Cherubim to fight the Terrans. We all know how that went. As punishment for burning the world, Gray plascreted Meridian into a life-support pod and sent him into space where he drifted for forty years. Then Morgenstern showed up again and Gray realised General Meridian was the only one who could stop him. Meridian's mind was all gone by then, so Gray killed his favourite footman, a.k.a. me, and implanted his – my – mind in the general's body."

"Fuck. I didn't know..." She looks away for a long moment. When she looks back there are tears in her eyes and she seems about to say something, but instead she starts coughing again. She hasn't got long.

In the background I see Wagner punch Gray's lights out, cutting off his screams like flipping a switch. The old man slumps against the ship like a discarded cloak. Watching Wagner deal with the baby will be very interesting.

"And where do you and your family come into all this?" I ask her.

She takes a deep breath. "OK. Here goes. Do you really think Gray Industries discovered the secret of immortality in a lab and decided to just give it to you?"

I shrug. "I don't know. They didn't?"

"No." She shakes her head. "They didn't. Nero Praetorius Gray owned the key to eternal life long before that project started."

"And where did he find it, and why do you know so much about this crap?"

"This is something my family has been interested in for a very long time. You see, with me dies a bloodline that can trace its roots back to the dawn of history and beyond. Our single purpose down the ages has been to find them and kill them, wherever they show up."

"And who, pray tell, are 'they'?"

"The Immortals."

"Immortals? What, like vampires?"

"Damn you, Perez, you're not taking this seriously. You hide behind your cynicisms and jokes to keep from having to face up to reality."

"On the contrary. Cynicism is what keeps me real. I believe that if people stopped asking *what's in it for me?* and started asking *what's in it for them?* before buying into anything, the world would be a better place. But that's perhaps just me being a cynic."

"This is not a joke, Perez. This is happening right here, right now. But to answer your question: no, they are not vampires in the literally blood-sucking kind of way, but in effect, yes, they are."

"But if they don't suck the blood of virgins, how come they're immortal?"

"We don't know. It's a fluke of nature. Every now and then, when the stars are right and the genes collide in just the right way, a child grows up an immortal. Lucky for us the bastards are sterile, or they would have bred us out by now."

"Really? And Gray is one of them? Fancy that. What are the odds that the richest asshole in the system turns out to be an immortal?"

After the events of the last couple of days, I'm ready to believe anything.

"You have it backwards, Perez. It's no coincidence the difference between immortal and immoral is only one letter. When you live as long as they do, you lose your humanity. In the end, all that remains is your own success. They use the battles of man to fight their own, bigger wars. Always have, always will, unless someone stops them. That someone used to be us.

"Back when humans started painting caves, the immortals tried to enslave humanity, but the tribes rose up and killed them, writing them off as warlocks and witches –"

"Or the son of God?"

"– we've had a few of those too – and so they learned to keep a low profile. They started wandering between the tribes, moving on before arousing suspicion. For a while they lived among us, hiding in plain sight, until one man realized the threat they posed to the emerging human civilisation. He vowed that he would not rest until they had been wiped from the face of the Earth. He was my great, great-to-the-power-of-a-thousand grandfather, and we of the Family still uphold his legacy. We hunted the immortals down the aeons, and we followed them to the stars."

"Then why don't we know about them?"

"They are totally ruthless, and they kill everyone who even comes close to finding out about them. Besides, the world wants to be deceived. We're always grateful when someone higher up takes the hard calls, and they are the ones at the very top. Follow any hierarchy high enough and you will find them. And they hide behind layers of secrecy. The best place to hide a dark truth is beneath an even darker lie. Defend the lie ruthlessly enough and no one will care to look for the real truth. They gave us the Bilderbergs, Area 51, the Illuminati, and other such crap and no one thought to look any deeper. Yet still, every human civilization has its myths about immortals. Some call them the Anunnaki. Some call them the Nephilim. We just call them the Bastards."

"And Morgenstern?"

"Yes, Oddgrim Morgenstern." She sighs. "When he got himself executed on worldwide television we knew he was one of them. Then a routine analysis of your blood from a down town clinic turned out to match that of the immortal General Meridian and we knew something big was on the move. So we decided we had to infiltrate your little crew. Enter yours truly."

"Well, I did think you were a bit too perfect for it to be a coincidence."

"Thanks. I think." She swallows hard and goes on. "When you showed me that video in my apartment and it turned out that you, the World Burner, was hunting Oddgrim Morgenstern, things went seriously, fuck-all, ass-over-tits unreal. We decided to take you out while we still had the chance in my apartment. But you got away. And then I started to suspect you were not entirely who we thought you were."

We're running out of time and I press on. "You said the immortals are fighting a war. Why? What are they fighting over?"

"Everything. They have been competing with each other since the dawn of time, moving the human race before them like playing pieces. They made us into what we are today, for better or worse. To them it's all a game. They call it the Great Race."

I know that phrase from somewhere.

"As in Master Race?"

"As in Competition."

"Ah. So there are more immortals on Elysium."

"Yes."

"Who?"

"Can't you guess? Have you met any old men in high places with a short attention span lately?"

"The cardinal?"

"Give the man a prize." She claps her hands.

I cast a quick glance at Gray, still impaled against the hull. Still unconscious. He's not going anywhere.

Suki goes on, knowing she hasn't got much time.

"And there you have it. Gray created you. He used you, betrayed you, and tried to kill you. He buried you alive in space for forty years, killed you a second time and brought you back to life only to use you all over again. That's what they do, Perez, all the time, to all of us. Can you guess who will be on those Terran battleships when they land?"

"More immortals?" I venture.

"More bloody immortals. I don't care if this is a religious backwater full of poisonous bugs; this is our home. They don't care about us. To them our resources are just a chance to pay another ante in their fucking game. Someone has to stop them, and that someone has to be you."

"Why not let them take care of each other? Sounds like we just have to wait and they will destroy each other."

She manages a weak smile. Even with blood bubbling at the corner of her lips she's still cute as a button.

"When immortals go to war, it's with the patience of colliding continents. Relentless. All destroying. Unless you kill every…"

She pokes a weak finger into my chest, underlining her words. "fucking… last… one of them, and keep killing them whenever they show up, the human race will never be free. Don't you see? This is a way for you to atone for what you did. What Meridian did. Do it, Perez. If not for us, then… at least do it for yourself. For vengeance. Whatever. But, please, just do this for me. Please?"

She sees she has me hooked. There are tears of gratitude in her eyes.

"By my death I pledge you to our cause, Perez. And by 'ours' I don't mean my family's, but Ours, humanity's cause. Protect us."

She looks deep into my eyes. "Come on. It's only forever."

There's a sad smile on her lips.

What can I say? I need something to do. I look off into the distance where the clouds from the ramstrikes are coloured blood red by the raging fires of war below. Far above the clouds the sky is still blue. It's beautiful.

I turn back to her.

"I'll do it."

"Thank you." She draws a sigh of relief, closes her eyes and swallows before her body is racked once more by bubbling coughs. When she relaxes there is more blood on her lips.

"Where will you go now?" she asks.

"I don't know. Maybe I'll go see Winger. Hole up with her and wait for the war to end."

"Who's Winger?"

"A girl I know."

"Have you been seeing other women?" She smiles weakly.

"You caught me there."

She sighs and I can almost see the life running out of her. "Not much of a plan."

"I'll think of something."

We sit in silence for a while.

"One more thing," she whispers. Her voice is no more than a leaf rustling in the wind and I lean closer to catch her words. She puts a weak hand on the back of my head and pulls me down even further. Tears start to stream down her face.

"What?"

"I'm scared."

She kisses me on the cheek and falls back down into my lap.

"Sit with me, Asher. It won't be long."

I sit with her until she is just a husk.

* * *

I bend over her and kiss her still warm forehead.

Good-bye, Suki. Had things been different, I think we could have been friends.

I tap a finger to my forehead in a salute, sending her off into the afterlife. Then I grab a discarded rifle and turn to Nero Praetorius Gray. He has woken up and wriggles helpless like a beetle on a pin. Finally I have a purpose. It may not be a noble one, but still, it's a purpose to my life, and that's more than most will ever have. If I have to become someone else to fulfil it, then so be it.

I dig deep beneath the implanted memories I once mistook for reality, and there he is.

A dark shape rolls over beneath the cracking ice of my ersatz personality, rapidly rising from the depths. The Dread General. The Enemy of Man. The World Burner.

And he is fucking furious.

Whoever we Choose to be

I grab the end of the iron rod and tear Gray off the hull. The old man howls in pain as I hold him like a fish on a spit. His arms flail uselessly as he tries to reach me.

"Hello, Gray."

His eyes scan the scene in panic until they land on Finn.

"Wagner. Kill him."

Wagner just shakes his shaggy head as he uses his huge knife to carve a final gouge in his arm. "No." He has his one hundred scars and he will be a breeder.

"That's an order," Gray screams. "I order you to fucking kill him."

"Already did that." Wagner shrugs. I smile.

Gray howls in impotent rage. He can hardly breathe through the pain, but still he manages to play the tough guy. "Then I guess there is nothing left to say. Kill me and be done with it."

"Oh, I'm not going to kill you, Gray."

He closes his eyes in gratitude as I call to Wagner over my shoulder. "Wagner, clear that dropship."

"Aye. What about the crew?"

"Let them go. They might survive the jungle, they might survive the war." I shrug. "I don't care. It's their problem." I pull the rod out of Gray's withered flesh and he screams like a little girl. Wagner nods and enters the ship.

"What are you doing?" Gray looks at me through his pain, blood pouring out of the wound and discolouring his linen jacket. "Let's get out of here. A starship is waiting for us in orbit."

"Relax, Gray. You will soon be in space. We just have some things to discuss first."

I adjust his rumpled collar, and as I do so, I slip the detonator into his breast pocket. "You did try to shoot me, you know."

"That was not serious, Caspar. I was angry. You killed Oddgrim."

I sigh. The pilot and copilot come running screaming from the ship and disappear down the stone stairs. Wagner can have that effect on people.

"Come on, Caspar, let's leave the past behind and plan for our future. And what a future we will have, you and I."

"Yes, what a future we will have. Too bad we won't be spending it together." I raise the stumpy assault rifle and aim it at his eye.

"What do you mean?" He looks at me as I motion with the weapon for him to enter the ship. "Of course we are." He raises his hands and starts walking.

"The cardinal sends his regards."

"Ah. So he's behind all this? I should have known." He begins to laugh as we enter the cargo hold. "He told you a good story, no doubt. He's very good at telling stories, the cardinal. Did he tell you the story of the World Burner and what happened to him?"

I nod. "He did." We have reached the door to the cockpit and I press the button that opens the heavy door. Gray laughs again as I wave him inside with the gun.

"Oh, Caspar." He actually looks disappointed. "With some clever lies and well-placed half-truths he has convinced you that I am the devil, when in fact it is he who is Lucifer to my Michael. The church has been after me for decades, you know that. You were always there to protect me from them." I motion for him to sit in the pilot's chair and he does. "Who better to turn against me than my own friend? Don't you see it, Caspar? He's brainwashed you. Oh, he's a clever man, the cardinal. So very, very clever. But didn't his stories strike you as somewhat contrived? A bit far-fetched, even?"

I give him a reluctant nod as I start strapping him into the seat. "Perhaps a bit."

"Occam's razor, Caspar. Go with the solution with the fewest assumptions. Do you want me to tell you what really happened?"

I shrug as I pull the straps tight around his thin old body.

"It's very simple. After you got shot outside your door by that robber, I took the liberty to have the doctors effect some… improvements to your body. We've been doing some very successful research into body modification over the years at Gray Industries. I knew you would like what we did to you, so I didn't tell you about it. I figured it would be like Christmas come early as you discovered your new abilities. Unfortunately your brain had taken some serious damage from oxygen deprivation. After all, you were clinically dead for several minutes before they got your heart started again. Naturally, there were mental side effects, and the cardinal used that confusion to seed your mind with lies to bring you into his fold. Like men of the cloth of all religions have always done."

I start punching buttons on the control panel, preparing the life support system.

"I know this hasn't been easy for you, Caspar, but I forgive you. Now, go get Wagner and let's leave this planet behind and wait for this silly war to end." His enthusiasm is infectious. I lower the gun. "And let's forget all this nonsense about immortals."

The smile on his face is warm and fatherly.

"Immortals? What immortals?"

I never mentioned any immortals to Gray.

The smile on his face freezes slowly, like frost covering a midwinter corpse. In slow motion I see the realization that he has given himself away creep over his features. The deceiver has outsmarted himself.

I raise my eyebrows. "Oops."

Then I push the button that slides the thick tubes of the life support system into his back and he screams. Usually, the subject has been drugged by the system before that happens.

I look at the old man, strapped like a piece of meat into the pilot's chair. "Suki and her family had a job to do, Gray. I'm going to finish it for them."

Too late I notice he's managed to sneak a tattered hand into his jacket pocket.

"Well, we can't have that." He smiles through the pain and my sensitive ears pick up the soft click of a trigger the instant before the detonator explodes and everything goes super-nova bright.

* * *

When I come to, there's blood dripping from every surface of the cockpit, and I can't hear a thing for the ringing in my ears. When my vision clears and my hearing returns, it brings Gray's bubbling laughter.

He's almost been cut in half. "You got me there, Caspar." He shakes a gory finger at me and dark blood flows from his lips with every word. His chest is a gaping hole and his intestines are tangled around the armrests, but he's still alive. I can see a few of the tubes of the life support poking through the mess.

I had counted on the fact he'd given himself a dose of the nanites to thwart any attempts on his life. It would have been something of an anti-climax if he died now.

"I know you think of yourself as some kind of hero, Caspar, but there is no good or evil. There is just us. The world is not black or white…"

"… Its Gray, yeah I get it. Cute."

"And how do you plan to spend your eternity?"

I shrug.

"Let me tell you what it's like, eternity; after a few decades it gets fucking boring. Fifty years from now and you will be thinking of suicide. A century and you will have tried and failed. Do you know what it feels like to blow your brains out? I do. After the last call girl leaves, there's nothing left but you and your darkness."

Diagnostics light up all over the console as the life support comes online and starts to pump recycled nutrients and drugs into his torn bloodstream. Under ideal conditions a system like this can keep a man alive indefinitely. Besides, the nanites in his bloodstream will patch him up in no time.

"I'm not you, Gray." I look through the windshield at the sky where the forces of Earth are winning the battle of Heaven.

"And you are not one of them either, Caspar. You never will be. You were born to rule the human race along with the rest of our kind."

"Funny. Morgenstern said something very similar a while ago and look what happened to him." I start punching target coordinates into the navigation system.

"Exactly my point. You were not born a man. You were born to be a killer of men."

"A wise girl once told me that we are not who we are, but whoever we choose to be."

"An idealist, from the sound of it."

"Yes, I believe she was."

"Admirable, I'm sure. What happened to her? She grew up?"

"You shot her."

"Ah." A sad smile. "Those are fine words, Caspar, but the humans will kill you when they learn what you are."

"I think I can handle them." I straighten my back. "Well, it was nice talking to you, but you have a flight to catch." I punch the last commands into the console, priming the ship for launch.

I can sense his desperation growing. "Is it Gray Industries you want? You have my DNA. The systems will respond to your touch. You can have it. You can have it all."

I look up from the console, for a moment tempted. I could be the richest man in the world.

I could be just as bad as him.

I shake my head. "Thanks but no thanks." I'd better not.

"Come on, Caspar. Think this through."

"I have, and my answer is still no."

"And what are you planning to do now?"

"Tell them the truth."

"The truth?" His voice takes on a falsetto of outrage as he struggles to move his shredded body against the restraints of the chair.

"That's the plan. Let the maggots hatch out. Bring the filth out into the open. Some shit like that. And then I'm going to hunt your kind down."

"No, Caspar. You can't do that. Why destroy something that has worked so well since the dawn of time?"

"It's time for humanity to start making its own fuck-ups."

"But it has always been like this."

I tap the execute button on the command console and initiate the lift-off sequence. Then I cock my head and make a point of listening to the shuttle's generic female voice begin the countdown to zero. "Do you hear that, Gray?" I point to the speakers. "That's the sound of progress." I reach under the console and tear out the control-core and hold it up to him. "I'll hang on to this, if you don't mind."

Just to be on the safe side, I empty the magazine of my assault rifle into the controls, destroying any chance of overriding the autopilot. The burst echoes across the jungle and through the cockpit windscreen I see a thousand creatures rise into the air in fear. "Bon voyage, Gray. Give my regards to the Andromeda galaxy."

It takes a second or two to sink into his pain-dulled mind.

"No. No… Not that. Please, not that."

"You did it to me once, remember? I've always been one for poetic justice."

"Caspar, please." He looks at me with tears rolling down his wrinkled cheeks. "You don't have to do this."

"No, I don't have to do this." I realise he's right. "I don't have to do this. But I want to."

It's almost time and I reach for the button to close the cockpit door when I remember something.

"Oh, I almost forgot. I brought you something for the trip." I reach into Morgenstern's shoulder bag and pull out a small heavy object wrapped in an oily cloth and place it on his gory lap.

"What's this, Caspar?" He looks up at me, unable to open the package with his torn arms strapped in place, so I remove the greasy covering for him.

"That," I point at the gunmetal egg shape, "is a gift from Oddgrim. Something to keep you occupied on the trip. And the name's Perez, by the way."

"What?"

"My name is Asher Perez. You killed Caspar Meridian, remember?" I pull the safety pin on the Archangel and step out of the cockpit. "Goodbye, Gray."

He screams after me. "Asher!"

I punch the button for the airlock and quickly get out of the way as the door slides closed on the old man. The hermetic locks engage with a well-oiled heavy click, and Nero Praetorius Gray is forever cut off from the world, sealed in his own personal life-supporting hell. I watch him through the small observation window in the door as the grenade clicks open, releasing its deadly cloud of all-consuming nanites. As the swarm spreads through the cockpit, hunting for something to eat, he stares at me, imploring me to save him from the horror. Then the darkness descends on his exposed face and hands and he screams.

In seconds the skin is eaten from his head, revealing the tendons, cartilage, bone and muscles beneath. His mouth turns into a slowly widening hole of soundless pain. Just as quickly as the flesh is eaten from his bones it's being regenerated, the rot moving on to other parts of his body like an ever changing Game of Life in reverse. The dark cloud swirls around the cramped confines of the cockpit as it feeds on Gray's body, and I close my eyes and leave.

I hurry out of the cargo hold just as the bay doors close.

One down.

The ignition has started, and I walk across the platform to Wagner. The scalding heat from the engine exhaust burns on the back of my neck and I feel the rumble of the engines in my bones.

Wagner is holding the baby, still wrapped in my jacket. I can see it's screaming, but I can't hear it over the noise. Better not loiter.

"We're done here. Let's go," I shout to my giant friend. Even though he can't hear me, he gets the message.

If Nero Praetorius Gray had been the hero of this story, this is the moment when he would have worked his way out of the elaborate execution prepared for him by the villain. But he's not the hero here.

This is my story.

As we jump over the edge of the platform, the dropship rises on a pillar of all-destroying fire behind us. I hope it's small and slow enough not to be shot down by the Terrans. I want Nero Praetorius Gray to go out with a whimper. Not with a bang.

We watch as the ship rises like a shooting star in reverse into the clouds and comes bursting through into the sunshine above. It grows smaller and smaller, and when it's no longer visible we start down the steep stairs of the pyramid.

Heading for an exciting future.

Epilogue

What happens now, nobody knows. Nothing is certain, everything is possible.

What I do know is that I will be out there, watching, waiting for Them to make their next move. It will come soon, and it will be merciless. They have hidden in the shadows of the stage for so long, pulling the strings of their puppets, and they will stop at nothing to keep it that way. I ask you who read this story to help me spread the word of their existence. They can't silence us all.

Help me shine a torch into the shadows where they hide and flush them out of the dark and into the light. Where I can kill them.

I am The One Who Fell, and I owe the human race for burning a world. If I can make this universe a better place by ridding it of the immortals, consider that my down payment. For as long as I draw breath I will be out there, fighting them in the wings of the theatre, far away from the eyes of you, the good people in the audience. You might not see much of our battles, but never for a second doubt that the Immortals are out there in the darkness, running the puppet show.

And when you go to bed at night, just before you close your eyes and sleep, remember this: Humans are not the top of the food chain any more.

We are.

* * *

Johan M. Dahlgren Biography

'Twas a maelstrom of thunder and death, the day the dark princeling came into the world. The foul trumpets of Kaz'an heralded his arrival with blasts powerful enough to change the winds in the sky and the mindless thralls of the kingdom stood at attention all the way to the crimson horizon to hail their new master. The cries of the newborn echoed around the throne room and the denizens of the land roared in furious joy. The man child already knew where his destiny lay.

* * *

Or that's the way Johan would like it to have been on the day he was born. Instead it was a fine spring morning in 1973 in the pleasant town of Gothenburg in western Sweden.

He didn't have a clue what he wanted to be when he grew up.

And there was not a mindless thrall as far as the eye could see.

Johan and his parents moved into his grandparents' old house by the sea outside Gothenburg, and soon his two younger brothers arrived. Sadly, there were still no trumpets of Kaz'an.

At a young age Johan discovered the joy of books. When he started school at the age of seven, his mother told the teacher that the little boy had just finished Jules Vernes' *Journey to the Center of the Earth*. The teacher thought she was joking. She was not.

Ever since then he's been interested in science fiction and the fantastic. In school he was never happier than when it was time to write essays. He would churn out page after page of action stories instead of the usual "What I did during summer holiday" drivel the teacher had asked for.

Luckily, his teachers never seemed to mind.

Maybe they liked action stories.

When he was ten, he - like so many other young boys at that sensitive age - discovered the forbidden but darkly alluring pleasures of role playing games.

He and his friends would sit for days on on end, rolling their dice, moving their meticulously (but not very well) painted metal orcs and spin tales of dark and dangerous lands.

And the occasional drunken halfling who betrayed his companions to the city guard and had them all arrested.

Who made up all the tales of dark and dangerous lands?

Guess three times.

The friends kept playing their RPGs far longer than the other kids on the block. In fact, on certain nights, when the stars align and the moon shines red with blood, they still gather their worn dice and meet up for more adventures in the dark and dangerous lands. The only difference is the Mountain Dew has been replaced with micro brewed IPA and fine Scotch and they no longer have to wear fake beards to look like grizzled adventurers.

The drunken halfling still makes the occasional appearance, though.

After high school Johan did his military service in the Swedish Royal Marines. That was a bit of a heaven and hell experience for him.

On the one hand, it was great fun (he loves to blow stuff up, shoot big guns and ride in cool boats).

On the other hand, it was a real pain in the behind, because he discovered he is allergic to running mile after mile in full combat gear, crawling through icy mud and making hundreds of push ups. It makes him very tired and nauseous.

And he doesn't like to kill things.

Not even mosquitoes. Unless they've drawn first blood, in which case they will be dealt with swiftly and painlessly.

Still, he got a green beret for his troubles and learned how to blow up bridges. It's always good to have career options when you don't know what you want to be when you grow up.

After surviving the military he went to university to get a degree. Since he still didn't know what he wanted to be, he asked his parents for advice.

His mother suggested teaching (she was a teacher), since Johan likes to explain things to people and can't stop telling people useless bits of trivia they never asked for. By the way, did you know you can fly to Mars in 2-5 days with an acceleration of 1g? Amazing.

His father suggested studying computer science (he worked with computers), since Johan likes to play video games.

It was a close call, but the video games tipped the scales, and four years later he had his Masters degree in computing and went to work in the IT business, where he is still plodding along.

The trumpets of Kaz'an? Silent as the grave.

Johan still doesn't know what he wants to do when he grows up.

Maybe writing is his thing.

Making stuff up for a living sounds like a job for a responsible adult.

Right?

Lightning Source UK Ltd.
Milton Keynes UK
UKHW012019131120
373373UK00001B/126

9 781715 777128